Other novels by Lucian K. Truscott IV:

Dress Gray
Army Blue

RULES OF THE ROAD

BY

LUCIAN K·TRUSCOTT IV

Carroll & Graf Publishers, Inc.
New York

Copyright © 1990 by Lucian K. Truscott IV
All rights reserved

First Carroll & Graf edition 1990

Carroll & Graf Publishers, Inc
260 Fifth Avenue
New York, NY 10001

Library of Congress Cataloging-in-Publication Data
Truscott IV, Lucian K., 1947–
   Rules of the road / Lucian K. Truscott IV. — 1st Carroll & Graf
ed.
      p.   cm.
   ISBN 0-88184-583-3 : $18.95
   I. Title.
PS3570.R86R85   1990
813'.54—dc20   90-1666
                                                      CIP

Text design by Terry McCabe
Manufactured in the United States of America

For those who were there when the phone didn't ring.

Kent Carroll
Bob Gardner
Mimi Irving
John Lombardi
John Prizer
Tim Seldes
Charles Thensted
David Vaught
Dan Wolf

And, of course, Carolyn.

IT WAS NINE A.M. on a bright, cold, late October morning, and the modified was right where he'd put it when he left home—how long ago was it? Could it be? Yeah, it was fifteen years ago on a morning just as cold and bright that he left for his first year of college. He zipped up his field jacket against the early morning chill and headed across the barnyard. It seemed like forever since he'd wrapped his hands around the smooth rubber of the modified's steering wheel, laid his right foot against the firewall, and heard the roar of the big V-8 and the squeal of the tires. The modified was parked in the lean-to shed over on the north side of the chicken coop. As he crossed the barnyard, feet kicking up little puffs of dust in the well-trampled dirt, he could just make out the shape of the car through the slats of the coop. It looked a little dusty, but it was the old modified all right.

Sam Butterfield, Jr., was in between—in between assignments, on his way from Germany to Fort Campbell, Kentucky. In between marriages, his first having dissolved in a sweat-pit of yuppie recriminations when he refused to quit the army to accompany his wife to New York when she graduated from law school and was recruited by a large law firm there. In between ranks—he had just made major, a rank in the army for which there was no command position. As a captain you commanded a company, and as a lieutenant colonel a battalion, but for majors there were only paper-pushing staff jobs and teaching assignments and public relations slots, four or five years behind a desk biding your time until the army figured you were old enough, or bored enough, to go back to the troops. Since Sam Butterfield had left his southern Illinois home those many years ago, he had graduated from ROTC at Southern Illinois University, been through Infantry Officer's Basic, and Airborne, and Ranger schools at Fort Benning, Georgia. Then he spent two years out at Fort Leonard Wood, Missouri, in command of an infantry platoon. He went through the Infantry Advance Course, he did a year on the DMZ in Korea while his wife was in her first year of law school, then he got a company command at Fort Carson, Colorado, where his wife completed law school. When the army told him he was headed next to a battalion at Fort Lewis, Washington, his wife laid down the law. Either he went with her for a job on Wall Street, or she was filing for divorce. Childless, with much pain but few regrets, it was over.

Two years at Fort Lewis were followed by the Command and General Staff College at Fort Leavenworth. From there, he went on to a company command in Germany and a subsequent promotion to major. Now came the dreaded mid-career downtime and its inevitable blues. Everybody suffered as a major. Though the jobs you were assigned gave you much to do, none of them meant a whole lot. How many motor pool efficiency surveys could you get excited about when you knew to begin with that motor pools weren't very efficient and they weren't going to get that way anytime soon? The same was true of the endless studies done by personnel officers (majors all) on the AWOL problem, studies that had begun in Hannibal's day, every one of which had doubtlessly concluded over the centuries that yes, AWOL was a problem, and no, it wasn't going away.

So when Sam returned from Germany and walked in the front door of the family farmhouse, he was wearing the grim visage of a man nearing middle age who was all too well aware of the pitfalls ahead. Women, for one. Where in hell was he going to meet anyone at Fort Campbell, Kentucky, one of those edge-of-the-earth military reservations conveniently located next to a strip of used car lots and fast food joints and little else? It even got down to where he would live. He was too old to camp out in the BOQ, Bachelor Officer Quarters, ineligible for all other on-post housing because of his obvious lack of wife and kids, and he didn't really relish buying a house downtown (wherever the hell that was) and starting the whole lawn-mowing, chatting over the back fence, good-neighbor thing again. In Germany he'd spent most of his time in the field. At Leavenworth, his time had been taken up by studying large unit tactics and strategy, and since he was there only nine months, a furnished apartment sufficed. The truth was, for three years he had successfully put off the idea that it was time to start over, but time-in-grade, a receding hairline, and an increasingly sour outlook on life had caught up with him. Now he was ready to face the fact—that it was indeed time to start over—but he didn't know where to begin. He hadn't been home since he left the States for Germany, so he figured if he was going to start anywhere, it may as well be there.

He had been away from southern Illinois for almost as many years as he had spent growing up there. It was good to be back on the family farm, but it was strange, too. He had watched his younger brother die in an equipment accident when they were just boys. They'd been plowing forty acres, converging on the middle of the field from opposite sides, each on his own tractor dragging a gang-plow at just under ten miles an hour. His brother was plowing along when the plow caught on a buried tree stump. The tractor snapped to a halt, reared straight up in the air and flipped over backwards, crushing him between the engine cover and the top of the plow. Sam stopped his tractor and ran the hundred yards of rich soil that separated them, but by the time he got there his brother's eyes bulged out of their sockets and a soft gurgling came from his mouth, opened wide in a silent scream.

They were three years apart, and though they had split chores on the farm pretty much evenly, Sam never really had the love of farming that came naturally to his younger brother. Tommy was one of those kids who took so naturally to dirt and grass and woods, it was hard to imagine him with anything but a hoe or a shotgun in his hand. While Sam had played Little League baseball and football in junior high, his brother had no interest in organized sports. Every day after school he did his chores and spent whatever time there was before dark hunting in the woods. It wasn't ever spoken of out loud, but by the time Sam was thirteen and his brother ten, it was assumed that Tommy would become his father's partner on the farm when he grew up. The next year his brother was killed, and still the subject of Sam remaining on the farm never came up. He took his savings and bought the frame and engine for the modified and began spending every afternoon in the shed building his race car. His father would pass the shed on his tractor as he came in from the fields in the evening, and inside the shed a dim light glowed and the sounds of grinders and sanders and air-hammers filled the still air. He knew.

His father died of a heart attack in December of Sam's junior year at college. He knew the pain it would cause his mother when he told her that he still intended to make the army his career. When he left the farm for the army he felt triple guilt: he was contributing to the demise of the family business, betraying the memory of his father and brother, and leaving his mother alone with seven hundred acres and no man in the house. Fifteen years had done little to dull the feeling. It bore against his heart like a fist and made him feel more than a little mean. His mother had kept the farm going by employing hired hands, sharecropping the rich lowlands, and leasing the less desirable land as pasture to a few local cattlemen, but farming was a man's business, and the chicken coop and other outbuildings had a forlorn look about them, as if their weatherbeaten clapboards missed the attention they would have gotten if Sam had taken up their care where his father had left off.

He slipped the lock on the ancient shed door and pulled it open. She was covered with a sixteenth of an inch of good reddish-brown Illinois farm dust, but she was coal black and low to the ground and menacing as hell anyway. He stood in the doorway of the shed for a moment, staring at the modified, a low-slung open-wheel race car, the yellow-dog mutt of the dirt track circuit. The car was an amalgam of parts—a 320 small-block Chevy engine, body panels from a wrecked Gremlin, hand-formed sheet metal hood and sides —all lashed to an Olsen tubular steel racing frame and wrapped with four huge dirt-track tires that jutted from the Gremlin body like dark afterthoughts. He'd owned it since he was a kid of fourteen, drove it in races every weekend all the way through high school and college. Now he propped the shed door open with a piece of two-by-four and switched on the lights. In the yellow glow of the overhead spots, through two years of dust and neglect the big numerals "58" could be seen on the hood and doors. He had built the car from the wheels up in this very shed, sprayed the suspension flat black, welded the exhausts, fitted the oil-cooler, tuned the suspension, ground the valves, polished the ports, balanced the cam and the crank. In his late teens, he had practically lived in the shed. An old army cot still set up in the corner attested to that fact.

Now he grabbed a bath towel from a bin against the wall and with long, slow strokes began rubbing away the dust. Through the slats in the side of the coop, he could hear a few dozen hens stirring and clucking. Outside, atop a fence post by the driveway, a big red and black rooster with tail feathers two feet long crowed at the rising sun.

Slowly the depth of the shine in the black lacquer paint began to show. He tried to remember exactly . . . twelve, or was it thirteen coats of paint? Thirteen, hand rubbed between every coat. That was it. He'd decided thirteen was his lucky number, and all the guys down at the body shop teased him. Only a kid would figure thirteen to be lucky.

They laughed at him. He had bit his lower lip and kept rubbing down the modified's paint. He'd show them, he swore under his breath. And show them he had. He'd driven on dirt tracks in three states, all the way from southern Illinois, through Evansville and Terre Haute, Indiana, to the championships in Cincinnati, Ohio, and after six years of racing every summer, he held two regional titles and one state title, in Illinois, his home state. He was known in the region as the good-natured, clean-cut kid who drove that black modified like a rabid rat. He wanted those checkered flags, and by the time he was finished racing, he practically owned the flag in his racing class.

Ah, if the boys down at the body shop could see him now, still rubbing the hand-formed hood of the race car with loving strokes of the cloth, bent over like a crooked question mark to reach the underside of the rocker panels, perched on two stacked milk crates to reach the center of the roof . . . rubbing, rubbing, still rubbing after all these years, and loving every minute of it, every swipe of the cloth, every square inch of the shiny black lacquer. It was as if the steel beneath his hand were alive, and in a way it was, for he'd given birth to it himself. Only people who raced cars or worked on race cars could understand his devotion to the old modified. Anybody else would write him off as crazy. Anybody else like . . . Betsy. What made him think of her right now, with the iron flanks of the modified beneath his hand?

He smiled. He always smiled when he thought of Betsy. They had met his first year at Southern Illinois University and had gone steady thereafter. Everyone—Sam's mother, her parents, all of their friends at school—always assumed that they would marry when they graduated. They talked about it—talked and talked and talked. But no amount of talk got them around the fact that Sam was heading into a career that meant constant reassignments and moving, and Betsy, a small-town girl, didn't relish the notion of never really having a home she could call her own. When the time came to bid farewell to the farm and his hometown, he bid farewell to Betsy, too.

He stopped for a moment to wipe his brow. A vigorous, if hardly youthful, countenance stared up at him from the shiny black hood of the modified—white sidewall sandy-colored rapidly receding hair, clean-shaven cheeks, the beginnings of a leave-time mustache darkening his upper lip, red sunburned skin. What, besides his advancing years, was putting that wrinkle in his brow, even as he stroked his beloved modified? Betsy. He shook his head, amazed. Coming home for a couple of weeks between assignments was having an effect on him he hadn't counted on. The years since his divorce—three years of blind dates, recent divorcées, military nurses over in Germany, a fairly steady thing with a schoolteacher at Leavenworth—hadn't been a social desert, but a string of indifferent relationships to which he paid marginal attention did not make a life.

He unlatched the sheet metal cover over the engine. There, in all its black iron and anodized aluminum splendor, was the heart of the beast: a 302-cubic-inch Chevrolet V-8, bored and stroked to 320 cubic inches, the maximum allowed in the modified class. The engine had an Edelbrock intake manifold and a big oversize Holly 4-barrel carburetor up on top, Hedman headers jutting out the sides and disappearing beneath the side panels in a maze of twisted exhaust manifolding and collector boxes. It ran a Bosch magneto with a gold-tipped wiring harness, and a special plastic fan up front that feathered itself at high speed, thus allowing the engine to use less power to run it. But it was what you couldn't see inside the engine that gave it the six hundred horsepower a dynamometer testing had said it had.

The Chevy ran an Iskenderian cam and roller lifters. The intake and exhaust ports were bored and polished, and the entire engine had been disassembled, polished, balanced, and blue-printed, brought up to exact specifications. It ran a special racing crankshaft and titanium piston connecting rods and racing pistons machined on top to accept oversize valves. The big Chevy was basic American power, huge and heavy and sturdy. At full scream, it was loud and scary as hell. You put your foot on the gas and you stood on it and you held on for dear life because all those horses under that hood could speed you over a guard rail and up on your backside just as sure as they could head you for the checkered flag. Those big Chevy horses didn't care where they went. They were there for only one purpose: to get there first.

His love affair with the modified race car was one of the things that his parents had never really understood about him. As farmers, they couldn't quite get the notion of strapping yourself in a big iron machine and going around and around in a circle until somebody waved a flag and it was over. All they saw was dust and noise and smoke. The acrid smell of burning oil filled his mother's nose at every race, and though she was happy for her son, pleased at his expertise and thrilled when he won, none of it made a damn bit of sense to her.

Sam finished wiping down the modified and climbed in through the driver's window. There was no car interior to speak of. A roll cage enveloped the driver in tubular steel.

He sat in a metal bucket seat facing an aluminum firewall, tachometer, oil pressure and water temperature gauges, accelerator pedal, clutch, brake, steering wheel with an engine kill switch mounted where the horn button should be. A red metal canister containing the Halogen fire extinguisher system sat to his right on the aluminum floor pan. He wondered if she'd start. He grabbed the wheel and hit the starter switch on the dash. The big engine cranked over slowly a couple of times, cranked faster, and caught. Silently he thanked his mother. She must have had the hired hand recharge the battery when Sam called to say he was coming home. The roar of the exhaust pipes shook the shed, and the chickens in the coop next door scrambled from their nests in a flurry of clucking and feathers. The rooster flew from his perch, landing in the barnyard at a dead run, disappearing around the corner of the barn. He let the engine warm up for a moment while he strapped himself into the bucket seat with his seat belt and shoulder harness. He grabbed the Hurst floor shifter, depressed the clutch, and slid her into first. He slipped the clutch and pulled the modified out of the shed into the morning sunlight. It was time for one last drive before he sold her later that day. One last blast down the dirt roads and back lanes that bled through the surrounding hills like grass stains on an old pair of jeans.

Come on baby, talk to me, take me through your paces, drift me through those curves, rock me baby, whisper six hundred horses in my ear, rub me through the floor through the seat with the sweet rumble of your headers, purr for me baby, tell me just one more time what it was truly like. . . .

*   *   *

Three counties away in a sparsely furnished room, sunlight peeked around the frayed edges of a yellow window
shade pulled down to the top edge of an ancient, wheezing
air conditioner. No clutter. Bed, chair, writing desk, rag rug
neatly centered in the middle of the room, pedestal sink
against the far wall. The air conditioner slowed momen-
tarily, as the building's electrical system struggled under its
morning load of lights and shavers and coffee pots. Not a
sound. It was as if the room were unoccupied. Then, from
beneath the undisturbed bed covers, a barely discernible
figure stirred. Coughing, hacking. The covers were thrown
back, revealing an arm so thin it looked like a stain on the
fabric of the bedsheet. A man was lying in the hammocklike
depression of the bed. Two-day stubble. Cheekbones that
wouldn't look out of place on a corpse. Small diagonal scar
under the left eye. Eyebrows permanently cocked.

A hand fumbled on the tiny bedside table, located the last
cigarette in the pack, found lips, fumbled again for a match,
lit up. Smoke exhaled into the dim, bare room. Two or three
puffs. Hacking, coughing, rubbing of red-rimmed eyes. Anx-
ious shiver of bony shoulders. A grunt. A pair of skinny, lily-
white legs emerged from the covers. Feet slid into cheap
rubber flip-flops. Head hung between legs for a moment,
then rising slowly to face the day: Johnny Gee. He shuffled
across the room to a cooler sitting under the desk, removed a
beer, wiped it dry on his drawers, cracked it open, and took
a long swig. This caused his left knee to twitch visibly, so he
swigged again. And again. He shook the can, held it to his
eye, looked into the pop-top. Empty. Squinting, he looked
around the room. He'd lost something. Pulled back the covers on the bed, felt around. Opened a closet containing two
pairs of pants, one pair of shoes, one suit. Ran through pants

pockets, jacket pockets, toes of shoes. Nothing. Into the bathroom. Lifted lid of the toilet tank. There, taped to the underside of the lid, a wallet.

Johnny Gee flipped it open, counted the cash. Twenty, forty, sixty . . . one . . . two . . . three. Sixty-three dollars, two pawn tickets, a driver's license belonging to somebody called Denny Miller.

Relief.

Johnny Gee sat on the toilet seat and took a few deep breaths, then walked back into his room and fumbled in the cooler for another beer. Last one, floating in a pool of tepid water. He cracked it open and sipped it slowly as he shuffled over to the dresser and flipped on a cheap transistor radio. There was an FM station up in St. Louis you could get sometimes, and sometimes you couldn't. He twisted the tuning knob. Yes! There it was! The rasping tones of the Butthole Surfers crackled through the static, filling the room. He danced a little shuffle back into the john, put the beer on the edge of the sink, and looked at himself in the mirror. It hadn't been the best of years for Johnny Gee. His skin had the permanently grayish cast of one who had spent a bit of time under a bare light bulb in a windowless room. Indeed he had: a short stretch in a state medium security prison for possession of gambling paraphernalia, namely, betting slips in his pocket and two slot machines in the trunk of the car he was driving at the time. The fact that the car he was driving wasn't his—"I borrowed it from a friend, Judge, sir" —failed to persuade His Honor of the obvious innocence of the accused, and he was sentenced to three years. He got two off for good behavior. A recently ended term of parole had introduced into the life of Johnny Gee a new concept, an office, and it was to his place of business he was headed after morning ablutions.

He was looking at a two-day growth of beard, but before he shaved, there were decisions to be made. What was on the day's agenda? Any collections overdue? Nah. Couple of guys who needed some gentle prodding about upcoming due dates, but that could be done on the phone. He liked to make collections with a two-three day growth. It made him look perpetually hassled and pissed-off and . . . tough. If anything could be said to make the undernourished, ratlike features of Johnny Gee look purposeful and tough, he figured a couple of days' growth was it. In truth, however, his was the face of one accustomed to taking orders from and doing the bidding of others. Nothing he tried in the bathroom could cast his features in any light other than that which stared back at him in the mirror: a small-time hustler going slowly to seed, who clung to the last vestiges of a punkish hipness that was losing relevance at approximately the same rate he was making money: slowly, but inevitably.

Ahhhhh, fuck it. He splashed some water on his face, and ran a pasteless tooth brush quickly over a set of inordinately pearly white teeth. He squeezed some Brylcreem on one palm, rubbed it against the other, and ran his fingers through his hair. With a fine brush, he swept the front of his hair into a pompadour, smoothing back the sides, admiring the neat trim a barber kept around his ears. There were many things that had escaped the attention of Johnny Gee, but a decent haircut once a week wasn't one of them. He enjoyed getting his haircut so much that he had attended barber school while he was in the joint, taking a job briefly at a bus depot barbershop when he got out. The barber job didn't last a single day past the obligatory six months the

terms of his parole dictated. Johnny Gee moved on, changing cities and parole officers so often no one really ever had
a chance to check up on the status of his employment before
he departed the scene. He never violated parole, exactly,
never missed a single interview with his parole officer, always listed a valid residence, always showed up for obligatory visits to the state employment office. The thing was, he
just never held a job during the long year of his parole, with
the exception of the first six months cutting hair at the bus
depot. It was a source of great pride to Johnny Gee that both
in and out of the joint his greatest skill was keeping most of
the people happy most of the time, something that was best
accomplished by tap-dancing to whichever tune was playing
at the moment. He might have looked like a page out of
some very distant, very beat past, but the fact was, he lived
in the present tense and was almost incapable of planning
any more than a day in advance. While this manner of living
kept the wits in tune, it frequently left the wallet flat.

But this was of little consequence to one who had as few
needs as Johnny Gee. He perused a closet that precisely fit
his life. One suit, two shirts, and a pair of jeans were at the
cleaners. That left the other suit, which he pulled from its
hanger. It was sharkskin, vaguely purplish-black and shiny.
It was also twenty years out of date, with slash pockets and
side vents, ruler-thin lapels, and a black velvet collar, exactly
the off-kilter image he wanted to present to the world. The
pants were peg-legged, tapered to a fourteen-inch bottom,
leaving just enough room through which to force one's foot.
Johnny Gee slipped into the pants and put on his starched
white shirt, carefully turning the cuffs back two folds. He
took a shoe brush from the closet shelf and ran it expertly

over his high-heeled, pointed-toe shoes. Even in the smoky dimness of his room, they gleamed like black chrome.

Suitably attired for the street, he walked to the door of his room, patted his wallet, ran a comb through his hair, buttoned the middle button on his suit jacket, examined the crease in his trousers.

He glanced in the mirror over the writing desk.

Not bad, he said aloud to the empty room. Not bad at all.

The sheet metal flanks of the modified shuddered over the ruts in the drive down the hill to the gate to the Butterfield farm. Sam pulled to a stop at the gate, adjusted his shoulder harness, and snapped a woven nylon net into the driver's window.

Eyes on the gauges, he ran the engine up to five thousand rpm. Everything normal. With a glance in either direction, he pulled onto a shoulderless dirt road. He checked the rear view mirrors. Nothing. He floored it. The modified left the gate in a great spray of gravel and dirt, the scream of its V-8 echoing off nearby rolling hills. Thirty-five, four, forty-five, five, fifty-five, six thousand rpm . . . shift . . . three, thirty-five, four, forty-five, five, fifty-five . . . shift. The modified crested the hill doing eighty miles an hour, coasting in third gear . . . shift . . . down to second, the engine whining, wheel thrown to the left, rear tires loose, tail trying to come around in front, steer into the drift . . . there . . . just so, back off a touch, pull it around, straighten her out, floor it again, fifty-five, six, sixty-five hundred rpm . . . shift.

Speed. Noise. Smoke. Dirt. There was enough in the experience of drifting a race car around a single turn to give one reason to live. This had occurred to Sam Butterfield at the wheel on many occasions, and yet . . . and yet . . .

There was something about being able to do it so goddamn well time after time that was just plain boring. He pointed the modified down a hill at ninety miles an hour. There was absolutely nothing about driving this car at ninety miles an hour on a twisting, hilly road not crafted for the purpose of racing automobiles that disturbed him. He felt as natural at the wheel of the modified as he did in an army uniform. It was a feeling of control and ease, a marvelous sense that all you had to do was pay attention, and nothing could go wrong. It was one of the things that had drawn him to the army in the first place, and it was one of the things that had kept him in. There was something about being in a company—he really couldn't put his finger on what it was. All he could do was feel it.

He was fifteen miles down the road from the Butterfield farm nearing the county line. Without stopping, he threw the modified into a power slide, reversed direction, and headed home. It was time he talked to his mom about a few things. She would have the answers to the questions that were flooding his mind. He knew that she knew what was on his mind already. She wasn't a font of wisdom, but she was the closest thing Sam Butterfield had ever come to one.

He put the hammer down, the modified leapt ahead, and as the squat black car crested the last hill, he could see the farm over to the right, lazy against the denim sky. His mother was in the side yard hanging laundry out to dry. He shifted down into first and took the turn through the gate like a gentleman. Like an officer.

* * *

The stairs were unlit, dark even at midday. Johnny Gee grabbed the worn wooden banister and took his time, picking his way around corners of torn rubber tread sticking up at ankle level on every other step. No sense in scuffing a good shine. No sir. No sense at all. At the bottom, he straightened his shirt collar and stepped outside. The sun was blinding. He squinted up and down the street before proceeding. No sunglasses. Not today. You don't wear sunglasses with your suit. Too much. Catch too many eyes. Attention on the street is the kind of thing you want in controlled doses, and you want to do the controling. Like today. Suit's looking good, shoes looking good. Fresh shirt. Newly mown hair. Looking sharp, and when you're strolling, sharp's enough.

The thing about the street is, you want to respect it. You want to treat the street the way you'd treat the road in a car. You know that thing about driving defensively they're always babbling about on the radio and shit? Same with the street. Drive yourself down the sidewalk like you mean it, and like you know everybody else out there means it, too. The street's the great equalizer. You want to use everything available to get a leg up. The way you look, that's an ankle up. The way you walk stands you a little taller still. See? It's like a thing that adds up, and everything you got counts.

Johnny Gee left the stoop at a leisurely pace, placing his feet precisely in front of one another, as if he were walking a crack. Left arm swinging in an easy, curving arc, from a foot in front of his waist, around to six inches from the middle of his back, the very definition of taking it easy. Right hand almost still at his side, might as well be tucked in his pocket. Sometimes was. He gazed around disinterestedly. A kid played a boom box across the street, somebody's look-out.

Railroad crossing down, ding-ding-dinging away at the end of a side street. Grain elevators gray and foreboding in a permanent haze of brown dust on the other side of the tracks. He glanced over his shoulder. The sidewalk was glaring white like ice cream. The door to one of the bars was open; the bartender was sweeping out. Across the red light, a Trailways bus pulled out of the depot, two blasts of its horn signaling the dispatcher. The sign outside the window of his room blinked faintly, lettered vertically from the fifth story to the first: *Terminal Hotel Wkly Rates.* Its red and blue neon lent a soft, comforting glow to his room at night. But at noon, the sign was faded just like everything else on Third Street.

The thing about streets as down and out as Third Street is that you want to fade right into them. Daylight, see, you can wear a sharkskin suit and nobody notices, the suit's just like the neon sign. Sharkskin's at its best in a bar, in low, yellow light. High white light drops it out, disappears it. So what you do is, you stroll and you mind your own business and you check out all the other business on the street, and you aim for where you're going in no big hurry and you get there whenever you arrive, you know? Daytime, worst thing you can do is look purposeful. Nighttime, you want to look like you're pursuing a higher calling, you're on the way to meet somebody bigger than the street, bigger than the damn town. Daytime, you stroll. Streets you don't tear up, not unless you're a jackhammer, and years have gone by since Third Street has seen a jackhammer.

Johnny Gee had honed his Third Street theory of relativity to a fine edge. Excepting his time in the joint, he'd been on Third Street for years, since the year he'd dropped out of school, anyway. He used to live out past First, in the midst of what they used to call the Shacks. He got out of the Shacks just before something called urban renewal came along and tore them down. Weird thing was, nothing ever came along to replace the Shacks, at once a place to start out for the newcomer and a place of resignation for those who had given up.

He'd moved to town from a crossroads. The first thing he heard when he hit Third Street was someone behind him: "Country come to town," the voice muttered. He didn't look back, he was too scared, but that voice taught him his first lesson. He'd glance over his shoulder from then on. And he'd take to the streets of a town the way he had taken to the woods of the country. He'd fit in. He knew from growing up out there that you either fit in or you died. Johnny Gee had noticed back when he was carrying a slingshot hunting in the woods that the only creatures who stood out were birds, their plumage bright like flowers. Thing was, birds could fly. Barefoot boys couldn't fly. Neither could grown men who walked the street in well-shined shoes. For this reason, Johnny Gee was extremely careful. Despite the fact that he had been arrested numerous times, convicted once, and served his time, he had never had a close call. He had never gotten away by the skin of his teeth, the ways it's said savvy criminals often do. The time they got him, they had him dead to rights, they'd built a case no self-respecting soul would fight. He didn't. He copped. Every other time, and there were many during his years on the street, they never even came close. Johnny Gee fit in so seamlessly, he knew the rules so well, he was beginning to play by them. This was a function of either age or wisdom, he didn't know which. Nor did he particularly care. He was content to spin atop his little corner of the world like a nickel on a bar, and

as long as he kept spinning, that was a big enough piece of
future for him.

Right now the future was through the swinging doors. He
wheeled right, glanced over his shoulder, and shoved himself out of the sun, back into the dimness.

2

BEHIND THE DOOR of the room where he had been a boy
for a long, long time, Sam sat on the edge of his bed and
stared at the wall over his dresser. On the left was a Bob
Marley poster stapled to the wall just over a Rolling Stones
poster. Pinned on the wall next to the posters were two,
maybe three dozen eight-by-ten photos of a grimy-faced
young kid standing next to a grimy Number 58 modified; it
was a modified all right, but in several of the photos taken at
night, you really couldn't tell. All you could see clearly was,
the kid had won. He was holding three-foot-tall gaudy trophies, each one topped by a miniature race coupe. He was
grinning so wide it looked like he would burst. There was
no variation between pictures. In one photo he was grin-

ning, holding his first checkered flag, the same as he grinned in another where he was holding his last. There was no letting-up on the wall. He'd wanted to win, and when he did, he was thrilled. Now the man who'd been that kid in the pictures sat on his bed and marveled. It used to be that he could visit home and look over his trophies and remember every race, hell, every *lap* of every race. But now all that stuff on the wall represented memories that had pretty much faded, and at thirty-three, even he wasn't that faded yet. He looked at the trophies on the shelf next to his dresser. The largest was over five feet tall, some kind of Hercules holding aloft what looked to be a 1940 Ford coupe. . . . If the little gold coupe wasn't so classic, it'd be pathetic. He had read somewhere in college about what confronted him, and though he didn't understand it then, he recognized it now: he was looking at cognitive dissonance, midwest-style. He'd always known college would mean something someday.

He bent to the task at hand: packing his army duffel bag. Fatigues were stacked at the end of the bed, starched and folded, his mother having washed and ironed last night and all morning to produce the neat olive drab pile. With one hand he held the duffel bag open, with the other, he carefully eased the folded uniforms into the duffel, alternating shirts and pants up and down to make things even. It seemed like yesterday, all the stuff on the wall, yet it was a long, long time ago. He was somebody else back then, not in the sense of being a race car driver as opposed to an army officer, but just . . . somebody else. He had less of an idea of who he was now. A divorced American male approaching middle age? Yeah, he was that all right, but . . . All he knew was that everything was different now, for some reason. He didn't recognize his own bedroom's scent. It had been too long since he had visited the room he grew up in. It seemed like if you were away long enough, either you changed, or everything else did.

The door to the room cracked open.

"Are you going to call Betsy before you leave, Sam?" His mother was standing in the hall, wiping her hands on a flower print apron. "You know, she doesn't live far from here, over in Mt. Vernon. Did I tell you? She's got a new job with the state, running one of the governor's local outreach offices. She's in charge of liaison for all state programs in the south twenty counties."

"You told me. Several times."

"Well, are you going to call her? I'm sure she'd be delighted to hear from you. She's not married, you know."

"I know. You told me that, too. Several more times."

"You two made such a cute couple. . . ." Mrs. Butterfield looked up. Also on the wall was an old photograph of Sam and Betsy at the ROTC ball his senior year. He was wearing his dress uniform, she had her hair in one of those French twists, and they were smiling so widely it seemed their cheeks would crack.

"Look, Ma. I don't know how to explain it, but I really don't think I should be calling her. I mean, it doesn't feel right. I'm gone from here for eleven years, I haven't even been back to visit for the last two years, and suddenly I show up, divorced, lonely, and what do I do? I call my old college girlfriend. What am I supposed to say? Long time no see? It's a damn cliché, Ma. Don't you see?"

She walked into his room and sat down on the bed next to him.

"I understand that it might feel awkward, Sam, but I still think she'd like to hear from you."

"What have you been doing? Talking to her on the phone every week?"

"No, Sam. I haven't."

"Then how did you know about her new job?"

"I called the outreach office a few months ago trying to get somebody to listen to me about that bridge near our land over in Hamilton County. You know the one. It's between that eighty we've got on the west side of the Saline River, and the three-twenty on the east side. We've got to cross it with our big combine every fall, and the county let the bridge go to pot, so this year we weren't going to be able to make the crossing. We would have had to go thirty miles out of our way to get from one field to the other to bring in the corn."

"Is that the land Mr. Jones farms for you?"

"Yes, it is."

"Isn't that his worry?"

"Sam, Herman Jones may get three-fifths of the crop on that land, and us two-fifths, but the risks and the problems are shared equally. And I've been so mad about that bridge . . ."

"What's the problem with those people in Hamilton County, anyway?"

"I'll tell you what the problem is, or *who* the problem is. It's that Harlan Greene. He still runs the county like his own personal feudal empire, and he wants to be paid off every time somebody walks across one of his damn county bridges, much less wants one of them repaired. Your father, for one, never paid a cent in Hamilton County, and I'm not about to either."

"That's one of the things I could never understand about Dad, Ma."

"What's that, Sam?"

"I know he worked against guys like Greene all those years, but I just never could understand how he stayed involved in politics for so long. I mean, the kind of unbelievable crudballs you have to associate yourself with. . . ."

"Yes, Sam, but your father knew lots of good men, too. The fact that a man like Harlan Greene is still around makes you kind of forget the men like your father's friends who opposed him."

"Yeah, I guess you're right, Ma. I remember that year he was running for county supervisor, and I had to take him messages out on the tractor. He was plowing that field up and down, back and forth, and I had to sit by the phone taking calls from that buddy of his . . . who was he?"

"Oop Gibson. He ran every one of your father's campaigns."

"How could I have forgotten Oop Gibson? So Oop calls me, and I jump in the truck and run out to the field and tell Dad the message, and he tells me what I should say to Oop, and I run back and call Oop. . . . Christ, it went on forever. I remember one day, I must have driven out to that section we had near Enfield thirty times."

Mrs. Butterfield smiled and propped a pillow up against the wall and leaned against it.

"Yes. Oop was a real character, all right. Your father wouldn't make a move without him. Remember he had that store down in Norris City, with the big potbellied stove in the middle of the floor, and your dad would take you down there on Saturdays and he and Oop would sit around telling stories and you would play pinball all day? You used to love that."

"Yeah, I did love pinball. But politics, Ma, I hated with a

passion. I don't know if I ever told you, but that was one of the big reasons I wanted to be an army officer, to get as far away from politics as I possibly could and still remain a citizen of the United States."

"You told me, Sam. I understood then, and I still understand now. You may have gotten yourself clear of politics, but it still takes some serious arm twisting and vote counting down here in Southern Illinois if you even want the garbage picked up."

"So what happened between you and Betsy?"

"Well, I called the governor's outreach office over in Mt. Vernon, and who came on the phone but Betsy! When I told her who it was, she couldn't believe it, and I must say, neither could I!"

"What'd you say?"

"We talked for a while, you know. She wanted to know where you were, and when I told her Germany, she laughed. She said she always knew you'd get yourself off somewhere no one could get you on the phone. Then I told her we'd been trying to get that damn bridge in Hamilton County repaired for six months, and she told me she'd look into it. The next day, she called to say a state crew would get out there at the end of the week, and a few days after that, the bridge was repaired. I don't know who she talked to, but that was the fastest I'd ever seen a bureaucracy move in all my years on this earth."

"Well, that's great, Ma. But look. I've got to leave tomorrow, and I guess most of all I just don't feel like, ah, making up some reason to call her. It just feels too awkward, that's all."

"Are you still taking the bus, Sam?"

"I don't have much choice. My car won't be in from Germany for another three months."

"You could take my car and return it after yours gets here. I'd still have the truck."

"That's all right, Ma. The truck is a wreck. I wouldn't trust it to get you around for three weeks. The bus is okay. It's only a four-hour trip. Besides, I don't think I've been on a Greyhound since I was in college. It'll be fun."

"Okay, dear. If you need any more laundry done today, you just let me know. I'm going to get supper ready."

"I'll be down in a minute, Ma. And . . . thanks."

She blew him a kiss from the doorway and went downstairs one step at a time. She was getting old, Sam thought. Too old to be running the farm, even if she did have two hired hands and sharecroppers. The loose, wet feeling of guilt washed over him again, and he turned his attention back to his duffel bag, trying to forget.

He packed the duffel, and thought about the modified. In his mind, he was still out there on the road somewhere behind the wheel, twin pipes in his ears, oil smoke up his nose, dust in his eyes. He sat upright and rubbed his face, focusing his eyes on the quilt at the foot of the bed, trying to shake the feeling. The quilt had belonged to his grandmother. Looking at the intricate stitching of the patchwork reminded him of her shoulders when she sewed, stooped and leaning forward over her sewing table, busy in the mornings, rocking back and forth knitting in the afternoons. Was that her, sitting at the end of his bed, wise and gray and short-tempered? He blinked his eyes and she was gone.

He jammed another set of fatigues into the duffel. They were perfect. It was almost a crime to shove them into an already overcrowded duffel bag. The creases in that olive drab cotton, the stiffness of the starch . . . he knew how much his mother had put into laundering and ironing ten sets of fatigues. It wasn't fair. They were going to look like hell by the time he got to Fort Campbell. There should be some kind of ribbon for a mother, he thought, for the only female in one's life who really understood what was at stake, for the only one who never bitched and complained, for the only girl you knew who would be there forever and ever and ever. . . .

Johnny Gee nodded a greeting to the fat man behind the cash register, who was chewing on a donut.

"Hey, Johnny . . ." The man choked on the words. He swallowed. "Top Jimmy's lookin' for ya. He tole me to tell ya. . . ."

"I know all about Top Jimmy," said Johnny Gee with finality, silencing the fat man. Johnny Gee stood with hands on hips surveying the scene. He nodded to The Weasel, the skinny black man with the broom. Two men wearing chincy-brim hats, who were seated on stools against the wall, waved at Johnny. He couldn't see their faces through the smoke, but he waved back.

The room was two pool tables wide and ten pool tables long. Lined along one wall, four coal-burning potbellied stoves awaited winter. Three shaded lamps hung low over each table. There were no other lights in the place. The light from the lamps shone on the green felt tables through the green lamp shades, giving the low-ceilinged room a glow similar to that of a swimming pool that had been left untended for a summer, its sides glowing with algae.

Not that Johnny Gee would have described the pool hall

that way, for he had never swum a stroke in a pool, nor had he ever lain next to one, taking the sun. Johnny Gee never really noticed the light in the pool hall, the greenish cast it gave the faces of its denizens. To him, pool hall light was appropriate coloration. Didn't matter what time it was outside. It was always coming up on midnight in the pool hall down on Third Street.

How many years had he been hanging out in pool halls? First time he shot pool, he must have been eleven, twelve years old. Everybody else in his class was going out for junior-high football way back then, Johnny Gee took a look at his skinny hundred-fifteen-pound frame in the locker room mirror, and put his pegged pants back on. He marched himself down to Third Street, put a nickel on the table, and waited for The Weasel to rack the balls. Other guys could beat their heads together out there in the hot sun on the field behind the school. Johnny Gee would rather click ivory balls together in the pale green glow of the pool room.

Johnny Gee's office was located in the far right corner of the room, on the wall. It was a pay phone, an old black model that still had a black plastic cord. Johnny Gee picked up the phone, dug in his pocket for some change, and started making his calls. First thing he did, he tried to collect a few debts. Fifty here, ten there . . . it added up. Before you knew it you got a hundred dollars, and then you know where you are? You're a hundred ahead, that's where you are. So you made a run at the money they owed you first. Then what you do, you take the payments promised, and you subtract from them all the deadbeats, and all those known to be chronically late . . . guys who say, like, they'll pay today, but you know you ain't gonna see a dime till tomorrow, if then. Then you add up whatever's left, the money you expect that if everything goes well, if your luck holds, well, you'll have it in hand by five, maybe six o'clock. That's the initial take for the day. Something you could just about count on.

Johnny Gee proceeded with the business at hand, and an hour later he had a figure, which he had worked out on his desk, which was the pool table immediately adjacent to his office, which was the pay phone. Okay, so now you know what you're worth at, say, six o'clock, so what you do is, you make some bets. But first, you got to read the sports pages and the racing form, which Johnny Gee did on his desk, under the three green lamps illuminating its wide green felt surface. Having digested the day's sports wisdom, he stood up and made a few more calls, taking the spread on this game, going for a long shot on that horse. Then, having finished the first two orders of business for the day, he turned finally to less pressing business.

His debts.

As if he knew that Johnny Gee was now ready to deal with the less pleasant aspects of the day, the fat man with the donut in his mouth materialized in the office.

"I told you Top Jimmy has been calling you all morning, Johnny," said the fat man with the donut. "I told Top Jimmy you ain't been in."

"That's very good," said Johnny Gee, looking up from the racing form.

"Top Jimmy says he been tryin' to call you all week. You know what he said to you last week, Johnny."

"No, what'd he say last week," sneered Johnny Gee.

"He said if you was late this week, he wouldn't bother with you no more. He said he'll sell you to those guys from up-county."

"Yeah, well, I only owe him a grand, and I paid the vig on Wednesday."

"Top Jimmy said that was last week's vig," mumbled the fat man with the donut in his mouth.

"So? I'll have this week's, I don't know, by nine tonight," said Johnny Gee. "That oughta keep him happy."

"He said you're still three days late, Johnny. You got to remember better."

"What else is new?" asked Johnny Gee with a shrug.

"What you want me to tell Top Jimmy when he calls again, Johnny?"

"Tell him I stepped away from my desk," said Johnny Gee, looking imperious, tugging at his shirt sleeves, positioning them at an appropriate distance between wrist and elbow.

The thing about Johnny Gee, he just never thought anyone would catch up with him. Since he was a kid, he could read people better than he could read situations. People didn't change as you studied them and took them in. But situations did. With people, all you had to do was read them and react. Situations demanded the ability to see past the present into the future, a feel for how things would develop. Dealing with situations demanded too much planning. Like with Top Jimmy. What are you going to do with a guy like Top Jimmy? Johnny Gee would have Top Jimmy's money in hand up to nine o'clock, but he should have had it together three nine o'clocks ago. Sorry 'bout that, Top Jimmy. Catch you later, man.

It was the same way hustling pool. It was time to pick up some loose change from the kids filtering in from the local high school. Truth was, they were the only ones usually available to be hustled, but that was okay. He'd never really been a good pool hustler because he couldn't plan out the hustle long enough, play along and lose a few games so he could set up the opponent and take him for a bundle with a close-out game. High-school kids he could deal with. They were as impatient as he was.

The kid who challenged Johnny Gee to a game was wearing a Motley Crue T-shirt and had his hair in a ponytail. Fifty cents or a buck, Johnny Gee snorted derisively, thinking: Jesus. Heavy metal. What a lack of class.

Two bucks, the kid shot back. Johnny Gee signaled The Weasel to rack the balls. He was stroking the cue on the break when he noticed the kid reach into his shirt pocket and pull out a small brown vial. The kid poked a tiny spoon into the vial and pulled out some white powder.

"Want some?" the kid asked, as he snorted the powder deeply. Johnny Gee shook his head no. The kid dug into the vial and snorted another spoonful.

Johnny Gee broke the balls, sinking two on the break.

"Hey, the dude can shoot," said the kid, sniffling and wiping his nose on his sleeve.

"You better fucking believe," said Johnny Gee. He sank two more balls. He had dealt the occasional baggie of reefer over the years, but it saddened him that it had come to this. You hustled two-dollar games from punks who stood around and snorted coke right out in the open. He sank another ball and chuckled softly to himself. Just then, the phone rang. He put the cue down and answered it.

"Yeah?" he said, lighting a cigarette.

"It's me, Johnny," said a man's deep voice.

"How you doin', my man? Where you callin' from?"

"Out on Route 49. I'm on my way into town. Listen, you gonna be free in a couple of hours?"

"Yeah," said Johnny Gee, turning to the wall so the kid couldn't hear him. "What you got in mind?"

"I want you to meet me at the diner in a couple hours, around six. I got something I want you to do."

"Like what kinda something?"

"I want you to watch my back," said the voice.

"What for?"

"I got to do a thing with some guys, you know."

"What kinda guys?" asked Johnny Gee, his curiosity piqued.

"Local, from over to Hamilton County."

"What kinda thing?"

"I owe some guys some money. I got to pay some guys what I owe them."

"Shouldn't be any trouble. What you need me for?"

"I just want to make sure everything goes right, you know?" said the voice without a note of nervousness. Businesslike. To the point.

"Okay. Six. See you, my man," said Johnny Gee.

Sam Butterfield heard tires on the gravel drive and looked out his bedroom window. It was the hired hand in the pickup. He stepped from the pickup cab, tucked in his shirt, and disappeared into the barn. For a moment there, just a moment, the hired hand had looked like his father, coming home from a day in the fields. God, how his father had loved that land, and how he had hated to see his son planning to leave it.

"What time do you have to catch the bus, Sam?" his mother asked from the bottom of the stairs.

"Three o'clock, Ma. We've got plenty of time."

"Do you really have to be at Fort Campbell tomorrow, Sam? Can't you stay a couple more days at home? I've hardly had a chance to talk to you since you arrived from Germany. Can't you spare your poor old mother another day?"

"I'd really like to stay an extra day, Ma, but that's what they told me. I've got to be there first thing Monday morning."

"Are you still planning to sell your race car today? You know it's fine with me if it stays in the shed. It's been a nice reminder of you around here."

Sam tried not to look at his mother's face as he pushed the front door open and stepped outside. The same thing had happened when he left the last time he visited home. After his brother died, he had become, in effect, an only child, and he felt guilty all over again, going off and leaving her alone on the farm. He threw his duffel bag into the bed of the pickup and tossed the overnight bag through the window. His mother followed him outside and stood on the porch with her arms crossed.

"I know it's a pain," said Sam, "but I've got to get down to Fort Campbell early to take delivery of the shipment of my stuff from Germany. It arrived earlier in the week at Port Elizabeth, New Jersey, and I'm supposed to meet the train tomorrow afternoon at five."

"I'm sure you do, Sam. But what about your car? Don't you want me to keep it for you for old times' sake?"

Sam fixed his mother with the brightest smile he could muster.

"I'm selling the modified at two o'clock to George Biderman. It's time I finally passed it along, and George says he really wants it, and he'll keep racing it. He'll keep it on the track. That's where it belongs. Out on the track. Do you think you could follow me over to George's and give me a lift down to the bus depot?''

His mother nodded her assent, turned wordlessly, and walked back inside. He thought he caught a glimpse of a tear in her eye, but he wasn't sure. Jesus. Throwing out the collected debris of childhood just never got any easier. Parents always say they want you to grow up and go to college and leave home and become a success in your own right, but when it comes down to the details, you're robbing them of everything but their memories, and it hurts, especially the fact that in the process, you become another person instead of a son.

He walked back into the house and found his mother in the kitchen. She was standing by the sink, looking out across the barnyard. The low sun of autumn cast a soft light on her face, but even in its flattering glow she looked tired. He walked across the kitchen and put his arm around her and hugged her to his chest.

"I'm just going down to Fort Campbell, Ma. I won't even be one state away. When my car gets here, I'll be able to drive home on weekends for the first time since I've been in the army. Campbell is the closest to home I've ever been stationed. You know that.''

His mother handed him a glass of iced tea and took his arm. She had that look on her face as if she were going to tell him not to worry, that everything would be fine. But when she turned to him, she said:

"Please don't sell the car, Sam. Please. Every once in awhile, I'll walk out there and open the door and just stand there and look at it, remembering all the work you did building it, remembering how happy it made you, remembering all those Friday and Saturday nights at the race tracks around here. I never really understood all that racing you did, but your father and I, well, we thought anything that made you that happy had to be just wonderful, and we were so proud of you, every time you won. . . ."

Sam put a finger to his mother's lips.

"Okay, Ma. I'll call George and tell him the deal's off. Hell, now that I'm going to be so close, maybe I can enter a couple of races just for old times' sake. Who knows?"

His mother rested her head on his shoulder, and together they stared out the kitchen window.

"You know, you may not remember this, but I became obsessed with racing right after Tommy died, remember?"

His mother nodded.

"It was what I did to keep my mind off Tommy. I missed him so, Ma, you know, having the little guy following me around, getting in my way, standing outside the door of my room when I was talking to girls on the phone . . . all of that little brother stuff. . . . God, how I missed him."

"I know that, Sam. I know. We all did."

"And the modified . . . working on it, driving it around the dirt roads every day, having it sitting out there in the shed waiting for me when I got home from school . . . that car became my substitute for Tommy. When I was day-dreaming at school, instead of thinking about missing Tommy, I could think about what I was going to do to the car that day, you know? And every race I entered, I entered it for Tommy. And every race I won, I won for Tommy. I always figured, if he was still around, I'd give him the car when I left for the army. But . . ."

"I know exactly what you mean, Sam. There were things I did to forget, too. You remember when I started that huge flower garden, and how I started selling cut flowers down at the corner at that little stand? I worked that garden practically day and night, and when I wasn't working it, I was selling at the stand, or delivering flowers to my regular customers. And your father, well, politics was it for him. He was political before Tommy's death, but afterwards, politics took up every waking moment for that man."

"Yeah, I remember. It was the summer after Tommy died that I had to take all those messages to Dad on the tractor, wasn't it?"

"Yes, it was."

"Well, okay, Ma. The modified stays. I'll call George right now."

As he walked into the living room, heading for the phone, his mother called after him:

"I'm going to cry when I put you on that bus today, Sam. I cried the last time, when you went to Germany. I tried not to let you see me, but the tears were there."

He stopped in the doorway and looked back at her. She was busying herself at the sink, stacking the lunch dishes.

When he returned he said: "I couldn't get George on the phone. We'll have to stop off at his place on our way downtown."

They took the pickup over to Biderman's, about four miles down the blacktop toward town. Biderman raced street stock, and the modified would have been a big step up for him. He loved the car, and was disappointed when Sam told him he had decided to hang onto it.

At the depot, Sam loaded the duffel under the bus, put his overnight bag on one of the seats, and went back outside to say goodbye.

His mother hugged him and held him for a long moment. When she let go, Sam stepped back and looked at her. She was tiny, standing alone next to the big truck. He kissed her again and climbed back on the bus.

The pickup was still sitting there when the bus pulled out. He could see his mother's hands on the steering wheel. He couldn't see her face in the shadow of the cab, but he didn't have to.

It was like she said it would be. He knew the tears were there, and she knew, too. But neither mother nor son could see them.

3

BY THE TIME Johnny Gee arrived at the diner on Route 49, it was dusk and cars were starting to turn their headlights on. But in the sky above the roof the sun still shone from beyond the horizon, bathing the stainless steel front of the diner in a light as old and tired as the day itself.

The Camaro pulled up right in front. Johnny Gee could see his friend sitting in a booth by the window. He tossed a dollar bill on the front seat for gas, took the steps of the diner two at a time, pushed through the glass doors, waved hello to the cashier, and sat down across from his friend.

Howie Radian and Johnny Gee had known each other since Johnny started hanging out in the pool hall in junior high. When Johnny Gee was in junior high, Howie had seemed so old and so wise that he couldn't possibly get any older or wiser. Johnny Gee became a sidekick to the man about town. Now Johnny Gee looked at him across the booth, and it seemed more than the years separated them. They'd lived completely different lives, and it showed. Howie had been a state Democratic Party district committee-man, spent two terms as county chairman, and was still in charge of a dozen voting precincts on the south side of town every election day. Johnny Gee had never quite figured out how Howie actually had time to make a living with all the political activity he engaged in. He knew the older man's wife had held a steady job until she'd passed away the year before. Howie lived in modest circumstances in an old farm-house on the edge of a new subdivision not far down the highway from the diner. He drove a five-year-old Cadillac Eldorado. Johnny Gee remembered going over to Howie's for dinner the night he'd finished paying off the car. The old man had bought two bottles of Asti Spumante sparkling wine, and his wife made a cake. The Cadillac, then almost four years old, still looked brand new. God, Howie was proud of that car. He even built a carport next to the house to keep it out of the weather.

"You're late," said the old man, taking a sip of coffee. His face was deeply lined and tanned. Beneath the tan, you could make out burst blood vessels on his cheeks and nose. Johnny Gee knew he'd been drinking more than usual since his wife died, and he looked it. His bulbous nose glowed in the diner's fluorescent light, and his hands shook as he lifted the coffee cup to his lips.

"Fifteen minutes, what's fifteen minutes?" asked Johnny Gee, signaling the waitress. "I had a hard time getting a ride. You could have come down to Third Street and got me."

The old man put the coffee cup down, and rubbed his face with both hands. Johnny Gee noticed that his eyes were bloodshot from lack of sleep.

"Couldn't. Had to drive over from Hardesty County this afternoon. Bad traffic on the interstate. They're still fixing that fucking road out there past Route 30."

A waitress in a red wig and electric blue minidress cocked her head and cracked her gum twice to get their attention.

"Grilled cheese, pickles and onions, fries, coffee," said Johnny Gee. "You want anything else?"

"Nope," said the old man, tapping the rim of his cup with his wedding ring.

"That'll be it." The waitress sashayed off in the direction of the kitchen. Two pencils stuck out of the side of her wig like exotic hair ornaments.

"What you got on tonight?" asked Johnny Gee in a low voice. His friend stared at him across the booth for a moment before he spoke.

"Like I said, I want you to watch my back. You can do it from right here where you're sitting. Just take your time with supper. It ain't happening for another hour."

The waitress brought the fries and the coffee.

"All you got to do is watch the front seat of my car. See where I'm parked, over by the hedge?" The old man pointed out the window. The bright red Eldorado was nosed up against the hedge at an angle. The car still looked almost new under the lights that illuminated the parking lot of the diner.

"Who are these guys? They been giving you a problem? Johnny Gee popped a french fry into his mouth and studied his friend.

"I told you. Just some fellas from over to Hamilton

County. You wouldn't know 'em. I got to know 'em when I was county chairman. They offered me an opportunity, and I took it. Didn't turn out the way I thought. I ended up owing a bundle. This is supposed to be my last payment."

Johnny Gee stirred cream into his coffee and lit a cigarette.

"You got the money, Howie?"

"Not all of it."

"What happens if you don't come across?"

"I got insurance, Johnny. Don't worry. They know I got it. They won't try nothing."

It was dark outside now, and the diner was beginning to fill up. Two long tables against the far wall were reserved for truckers. A cluster of Kenworth and Peterbilt caps along the wall said that business hadn't dropped off among the highway cowboys. A half dozen dusty pickups were parked next to the Eldorado, and their overall-clad drivers sat along the counter, equally dusty from planting winter wheat in nearby fields.

"I got to make a call," said the old man, getting up from the booth. "Back in a minute. Gimme a wave if you see a blue Buick drive up."

"Sure thing." Johnny Gee watched his friend walk slowly toward the phones on the wall at the other end of the diner. He moved in a kind of lopsided shuffle, and he'd put on a pound or two since the last time they'd seen each other. Johnny wondered how he looked to Howie. It was getting so that every time they got together, something had changed with each of them. Johnny Gee put his cigarette out and watched the parking lot.

*   *   *

It had to be one of the nicest sounds in the whole world, a big interstate bus at speed down the road. The low rumble of the diesel engine . . . all those wheels singing the highway song . . . it came right up through your backbone and filled you with the most comfortable sensation of peace and power. You didn't have to worry about a thing. Somebody else was moving that box of aluminum and steel at sixty-plus. All you had to do was tilt the seat back and enjoy.

Sam Butterfield was still hours from Fort Campbell, and already it was getting dark outside. He turned his head and looked out the window. The bus had left the interstate highway, and was headed down a two-lane state road somewhere deep in southern Illinois. Stopping in every little one-red-light town along the way. . . . For some people that was a waste of valuable time, but to him, it was part of the experience. Every time he traveled by bus he saw parts of the country he'd never seen before. He squinted into the gathering darkness. Rolling hills, corn ready for harvest, a stand of oak and ash here and there, roadside farm stands selling broccoli and cabbages and fresh apple cider . . . Daylight would show the burnished reds and oranges of autumn, but just before dark the passing countryside was suffused with hues of the deepest darkest blue. In just a minute it would be dark, and he wouldn't be able to make out a thing unless the bus passed through a town, so it was a challenge, catching the last glimpse of the disappearing landscape, guessing where you were, when you'd get where you were going.

That was part of the magic of buses. They were old-fashioned and romantic and . . . slow. Riding the bus down to Fort Campbell, he was glad in a way that his car was still on the way from Germany. It gave him an excuse to hop a bus

and remember why the big rolling boxes had always capti-
vated him.

And to remember how he'd met Betsy.

They had met on a bus when he was a junior in college.
Well, they didn't exactly meet on the bus. He arranged their
meeting, more or less, after he had seen her in the crowd at
an "away" basketball game at Indiana, but he knew she
hadn't seen him. She was an eye-catching blonde, slender
and giggly, like most freshman girls. She was wearing a
heavy turtleneck sweater and jeans and brown leather boots
and a long wool overcoat, but even buried beneath that pile
of winter cover, she was as shapely as she was cute. She was
talking to a girlfriend at half-time; they were comparing sorority rush stories, complaining about their roommates, grip-
ing about dormitory food. The usual freshman topics. He
could hear every other word or so. He remembered thinking
at the time that such freshman silliness would have turned
him right off if he were in his right mind, but staring at her
at the game that night he was as far from his right mind as
he had ever been in his life.

By judicious inquiry around campus, he found out that
her name was Betsy Kane and she was from Vandalia, Illinois, about three hours north of Carbondale, where Southern Illinois University was located. He could have easily
arranged it, but he didn't want a campus introduction,
which would lead to a series of dull movie-and-a-burger-
and-a-beer dates, and if executed properly would land him
in bed with her in some dingy motel on the outskirts of
town. Every guy on campus had been down that road, and
Sam was tired of the campus life. He wanted excitement,
juice. Something weird and unpredictable had to happen,

because he knew if it did, he'd fall in love, and if it didn't? Hey, what the hell. At least he'd given it a shot.

He got a frat brother to check out where she was going for spring break. He was hoping she was on one of the tours to Florida, so he was more than mildly disappointed when the news came back that she was headed home to Vandalia. He thought quickly. How was she going? By bus, came the news from his spy. When was she leaving? Next Friday night, right after class. The six o'clock northbound Greyhound. Sam worked on his plans for a week. When Friday came, he was ready with his ticket for Grable, one town north of Vandalia. He got on the bus right behind her, followed her down the aisle, and plopped down next to her in a rear seat. She took out a book and started reading before the bus even pulled out of the depot. Sam waited until the bus was at speed out on the interstate, then made his move.

"Where you headed?" he asked.

She turned and looked at him, and Sam held his breath. There was no glimmer of recognition. His discreet spying over the past two weeks had worked. She had no idea he had arranged their seeming chance encounter.

"Vandalia," she said, turning once again to her book.

"You go to S.I.U.?"

"Yes." She was still reading her book.

"Good school," he said. He pulled out a car magazine and flipped through it, then closed the magazine and turned to her.

"Can I say something to you?" he asked.

She looked up, startled.

"I—I guess so."

"I have a confession to make," said Sam. "I set this up. I arranged it."

"What?"

"I arranged to meet you on this bus. I found out where you were going on spring break and that you were taking this bus, and I got a ticket so I could sit next to you and meet you. I had this whole plan . . ."

"I don't believe this," she said. "You're kidding me."

"I'm not. I go to S.I.U., too. I saw you at the Indiana game. I sat two rows behind you. I had this plan, that we'd meet on the bus, I'd tell you this tale, like I'm not a college kid, I'm a stockbroker on my way to St. Louis by bus because my BMW broke down in Carbondale and I don't like to fly. That's why I'm wearing this stupid suit."

"This is ridiculous."

"I know. That's why I'm confessing to you. It *is* ridiculous. I feel ridiculous. I should have gotten that girl, what's her name? Kathy Connor, the vice president of your sorority, to introduce us at a party. But I thought: that is so trite, and she'll just think I'm another college schmuck on the make. I'm so sick of those stupid parties. If I see another plastic cup of beer I'll lose it."

She threw back her head and laughed.

"I know what you mean," she said. "That's why I'm going home. The thought of seven days of baking my body and soaking my brain really turned me off." She turned to face him. "You're not kidding me, are you? You really set this up?"

"Honest to god," he said. He held out his hand. "I'm Sam Butterfield."

"I'm Betsy Kane," she said, taking his hand. "But you already know that." She laughed again. So did he.

"So where are you going?" she asked.

"Grable. Next town past Vandalia."

"What in the world do you plan to do in Grable?"

"Get on the next bus and go back home," he said sheepishly.

"You went to all this trouble, and what exactly did you expect when you met me? Did your plan have a point?"

"Well, I thought I'd sweep you off your feet, and a few weeks from now I'd admit the scam I pulled on you, and it would turn out to be a big joke between us, because by then we'd be in love."

"In love? You're serious, aren't you?"

"I guess the whole thing sounds stupid, but yeah, I'm serious."

Betsy smiled.

"What are you studying?" she asked.

They talked all the way to Vandalia.

Sam spent the night at Betsy's parents' house, introduced as a friend from school. When she took him to the depot on Monday afternoon, she stood on her tiptoes and kissed him full on the lips just before he got on the bus.

"See you on Sunday," she said.

He was in love . . . they were in love, he hoped. And it had happened on a bus.

Now he felt the bus slowing, the road rumble quieting to a hum. He pressed his face to the window. Up ahead he could see a sign: ROUTE 49 DINER and underneath WELCOME TRAVELERS. He checked his watch. Nearly seven. Must be the supper stop. He stood up and grabbed his overnight bag. May as well check over his orders while he ate. He hated to read on the bus. Made him sick. What he liked to do was watch the passing scene and sleep. Best sleep in the world, almost.

The bus pulled off the road and stopped with a great hiss

from its air brakes. He looked out the window. It was a classic diner, long and narrow, rounded corners, stainless steel on blue enamel. They'd have a good hot roast beef sandwich for sure. The door opened, and he followed the other passengers out.

He put his overnight bag in a booth by the window, and headed for the bathroom. He'd only been riding for an hour, but already he had the grubbies. He was wearing traveling clothes—worn-out Levis, a pair of tired, tattered Nikes, a frayed polo shirt and a droopy cotton sweater. He looked at himself in the mirror. Were it not for his white sidewall haircut, he wouldn't be recognizable as an army officer. He liked dressing so he blended in. That way you didn't attract any attention, and if you wanted to meet someone, all you had to do was start a conversation. If not, you just minded your own business, and everybody else minded theirs. That was one of the great things about this country. You could be an Airborne Ranger, a trained killer, and nobody would ever know it. They'd sit down across from you, check you out, and figure you to be a lonely guy catching up on your reading.

Sam washed his face and hands, splashed water on his neck, ran a comb through what was left of his hair, and walked back to the booth, picking up the local paper on the way. A gum-cracking waitress tossed a menu at him, and he ordered a hot roast beef sandwich and a Coke. She cocked her head and asked, "That all?" "Yeah, all for now," he said. He took a look around. The place was full of locals—truckers, farmers, housewives gossiping over coffee and apple pie. Most of the people from the bus sat in a section in the back that had been reserved for bus passengers. In the next booth, two men had their heads together whispering about something. The old man was nervous. Sam could hear his coffee cup rattle against the saucer every time he picked it up. The scrawny man kept touching his arm and telling him to take it easy, everything was going to be all right. Looked like a death in the family, he figured. He flipped through the paper and sipped his Coke.

It was weird. You could sit in a place like this diner for twenty minutes, and if you paid attention you could get a handle on the whole deal. That couple over there are having their fourteenth argument of the day, and he's about to lose for the thirteenth time. Those three truckers are complaining about the price of diesel in this part of the state. The two guys in overalls are arguing about whether the corn is dry enough to harvest yet, and the guy who says he's got one of those new-fangled moisture gauges is going to end up ignoring it and harvesting the same day as the others, who will rely on biting a kernel to tell when it's dry. The waitress who's cracking gum is complaining about her boyfriend, a traveling salesman, who promised he'd be through town today and hasn't shown yet. Seems like everyone behind the counter has heard that complaint before. Somewhere in the back, the short order cook is banging on a bell, trying to get the waitress's attention.

"This damn hot roast beef gonna have icicles on it, time you get your ass back here."

Comfortable diner din, completely undisturbed by the outside world.

The lukewarm hot roast beef arrived with a swish of electric blue nylon minidress, and Sam dug in. The waitress was on her way to the kitchen when the diner's glass door banged open, catching her on the shoulder and knocking her aside, spilling the coffee she was carrying. Four men

who were most definitely not stragglers from the bus swept
in and looked around. The youngest of the four ordered
coffee to go, black, four times. Nobody apologized to the
waitress, who was wiping up the mess. The young guy took
the coffees in a sack, and the four trooped out the way they
came in.

"Nice guys," Sam said to the gum-cracking waitress. She
was standing over his booth, looking out the front window.

"Lovely. Did you see what kind of car they drove up in?"
Two of the men had disappeared, and the other two were
standing under a streetlight, drinking their coffee.

"Nope." Sam glanced out the window. "Have you ever
seen them before?"

"I seen the kid in here late some nights. He comes in
around four, orders breakfast, sits around playing the juke
box till it gets light out. Don't look like he ever did an
honest day's work in his life. He's been takin' lessons from
the other three, you ask me."

A bell sounded in the kitchen. The waitress touched
Sam's arm gently and moved off. He turned back to watch
the two men under the streetlight. In the reflection of the
diner's window he saw the old man in the next booth stand
up to leave. The scrawny man grabbed his shoulder and
whispered something. The old man nodded and headed out
the door. The scrawny man sat down, lit a cigarette, and
looked out the window. Sam could see his reflection for the
first time. He had the narrow, angular face of one whose
family had come up to Illinois from the hill country of Kentucky or Tennessee. Sharp pointed chin, receding hairline,
hawklike nose, piercing blue eyes set back under high
cocked eyebrows. Sam had been around people like him in
the Army long enough to know that more often than not

there was more going on behind those eyes than you'd like to know.

Out in the parking lot, the old man was approaching the two men under the streetlight. They exchanged some words. He shook hands with the big man in the gray suit, who seemed to be in charge. The big man put his arm around the much smaller, older man. They walked toward a Cadillac Eldorado parked near the hedge. The old man took out keys and opened the front door. He touched the door lock button, unlocking the passenger door. He and the big man got into the front seat and closed the doors. The other man stood outside, his back to the car. Sam looked around the parking lot, but he didn't see the other two. He did see a reflection of the character in the next booth doing the same thing he was doing: looking for the other two.

The old man and the big man were still in the front seat of the Eldorado when he caught a glimpse of the others, in the shadows, next to a dumpster near the corner of the diner. Then something happened back at the car. The big man got out and walked around to the driver's side and pulling the old man out by his collar, threw him against the Eldorado's fender. He slammed a fat fist into the old man's kidneys. The scrawny man in the next booth was on his feet and running for the door. He was yelling something as he ran across the parking lot. He didn't get far. One of the men from the dumpster cut him down with a kick. The old man was on his knees next to the Caddy, and two men were beating on him. The other man appeared from behind the dumpster, and the three of them picked up the old man by the arms and dragged him along the hedge toward the corner of the diner.

Sam had seen enough. He threw a ten-dollar bill on the

table, picked up his overnight bag, and ran for the door. He hit the bottom of the stairs full tilt, reached the corner of the diner, and stopped. The alley next to the diner was dark, but he could hear crunches and thumps and whacks. He made out dim figures: somebody was holding the scrawny man by his shoulders, and another was preparing to swing on him with a short length of two-by-four. He was slumped over, blood dripping from his mouth.

The old man lay on his side on the ground. The big man was kicking him in the stomach and back. Sam took a couple of quick steps and drop-kicked the figure closest to him. The two-by-four spun into the air like a baton, and Sam leapt into the air. He landed in a crouch, swinging. He caught somebody in the leg and heard a sickening crunch. The figure crumbled and Sam kept moving, knees bent, swinging the two-by-four. He caught another man on the chin. His jaw cracked. The man went down.

He heard something, and turned just in time to collect a fist in the stomach. He doubled over and kept going down, rolling forward on one shoulder back to his feet. Someone yelled. Sam slapped himself against the wall of the diner, holding the two-by-four across his chest. A body flew out of the darkness. Sam glimpsed the flash of a blade and dropped to his knees. He swung the two-by-four blindly. It felt like he caught the guy in the gut, and he heard a whoosh of exhaled air. A body crumpled at his feet. Sam took another couple of steps into the blackness, swinging the two-by-four like a bat. No one moved. The alley was suddenly silent. Sam's eyes adjusted to the dark and he saw the scrawny man pick himself up from the pavement and crawl over to the old man's body.

The scrawny man shook him hard and turned him over.

Blood flowed from the corner of his mouth. He listened to the old man's chest and looked up at Sam.

"Help me with him," he croaked. "He's still alive."

Sam reached down and helped him to his feet. Together, they lifted the old man from the ground, but he couldn't stand. Sam grabbed the old man under his arm, and they made their way down the alley. One figure struggled to his feet as they passed. Sam swung the two-by-four in a short arc and caught him in the ribs. He went down.

"Motherfuckers!" It was the big man, maybe fifty feet behind them now.

"He's got a gun," said the scrawny man.

"Come on," said Sam. "Keep moving." Two more steps and they were on the other side of the dumpster.

Sam glanced over his shoulder. The big man was still on the ground. He raised the gun with one hand, steadying himself against the wall of the diner with the other.

"You fuckers are dead!" the big man yelled down the alley. Two shots rang out, hitting the dumpster.

Sam stayed low and moved ahead automatically. They reached the Eldorado, and the scrawny man pulled the door open.

"Help me get him in here. C'mon, man. Help me."

"We've got to get an ambulance," said Sam. "This guy's in real trouble. He needs a doctor."

"Fuck the ambulance. We gotta get outta here. Pick him up. Get his legs." Sam picked up his legs and shoved the old man in the back seat and slammed the door. Just then, another shot rang out and a slug hit the car fender. Sam turned in the direction of the fire and saw one of the figures from the alley. He was just around the corner of the dumpster, and he was holding his jaw with one hand and shooting at them with the other. Another slug hit the car. Sam ducked behind the car door.

"Get in!" yelled the scrawny man from behind the wheel. He turned the key and the Eldorado came to life. Sam hesitated. His ears were ringing. What was going on? He felt himself slipping, getting light-headed . . . Jesus! He was getting . . . dizzy . . .

The car jerked backwards.

"Get in, man! That fucker's tryin' to kill us!"

Sam looked across the parking lot at the diner. *Where was the bus?* It was gone. Two dozen faces filled the window of the diner and someone was standing in the door, screaming. Another shot rang out. This one missed the car, going over his head.

He was the target.

With a screech of tires, the scrawny man backed the Eldorado onto the highway in a great sweep. He slammed the car into drive and they were off into the darkness, no headlights, just the scream of the engine and the pounding of Sam's heart.

In the army, they would say you were committed. The white lines of the road whipped by. He squinted into the darkness, instinctively watching for curves. He yelled to the driver, *bend left,* and the Eldorado drifted . . .

Yes indeed he was . . .

Bend right!

Committed.

JOHNNY GEE FLICKED a switch and the Cadillac's headlights illuminated a narrow, tree-lined drive somewhere off
the main road, a couple of miles from the diner. Sam
glanced at the speedometer. The car was doing sixty-five,
and Johnny Gee was having a hard time keeping it on the
road, crowned in the middle, causing the car to drift left and
right toward the shoulders.

"Slow up," said Sam. "You're going to lose it."

"You wanna drive?" asked Johnny Gee, looking quickly at
his passenger. "I ain't even got a license."

That was all Sam needed.

"Pull over."

Johnny Gee slowed the Caddy and turned onto a dirt

path, stopping in a grove of trees about a hundred yards from the road. He jumped out of the car and climbed into the back seat with the old man, who could be heard groaning softly.

Sam moved behind the wheel, grabbed the shoulder harness and buckled up. He found the seat controls and moved it forward. He heard the car's back door slam shut. He put the car in gear, and headed back along the dirt road.

"Which way are we going?" he called over his shoulder.

"Right," said Johnny Gee. "Same way we were going before."

There were no cars coming, so he swung back on the paved road.

It felt weird to be behind the wheel of this big, unwieldy Cadillac, but the V-8 responded when you put your foot to it. It was sluggish in the corners. The floating sensation would take some getting used to.

Jesus! What am I doing thinking about how the Caddy responds? What the hell am I doing in this car to begin with? How did I get here? What the hell happened back there? What happened to the bus? How am I going to get to Fort Campbell? Those bastards were shooting at me back there. Who the hell are these guys? What the hell have I gotten myself into?

First things first.

He took a deep breath and gripped the wheel a little more tightly. Glanced at the speedometer. The car was rocketing down the narrow two-lane at seventy-five. Didn't feel too bad.

"Do you think those guys are still after us?"

"You better fucking believe they are," said Johnny Gee.

"Hey, be careful on those turns, man. You're tossing Howie all over the back seat."

"Where will this road take us?" asked Sam as he rounded another corner, a little slower.

"Just drive. I'll tell you when we get there," said Johnny Gee.

Sam slammed on the brakes, throwing the Caddy into a slide. The car ended up sideways on the two-lane. Both bodies hit the back of the front seat. He turned to face them.

"One: Don't ever talk to me that way again. Ever. Two: What the hell happened back there in that alley? Three: Who the hell are you, and who's the guy you call Howie? The way I see things, I've got some answers coming, mister. Either I get them right here, right now, or I turn this thing around and drive straight back to the diner and turn you over to the guys in the alley."

Johnny Gee was holding Howie's head on his lap. The older man tried to raise his head. He coughed, spraying the front of Johnny Gee's shirt with blood.

"Jesus." Sam stared open-mouthed at the scene in the back seat. "We've got to get this guy to a hospital."

"No . . . hospital," Howie coughed, blood oozing from the corner of his mouth. "Farm . . . farm." He opened his eyes. "I'll . . . be . . . okay," he said, again trying to raise himself from Johnny Gee's lap. He looked pleadingly at his friend.

Johnny Gee stared out the Caddy's side window. He was scared.

"We haven't got much time," he said. "I'm sorry . . . I'll explain everything. We've got to get Howie to his place. Can we get going? We're blocking the road."

"Sure," Sam said. He put the Caddy in drive. "Which way?"

"Same direction as before. Keep going till you hit a four-way stop, then take a right," said Johnny Gee.

"No-o-o-o." The word came out of the old man's mouth in a slow gurgle. "F-f-farm. F-farm."

"Okay. Okay," said Johnny Gee. "Keep going straight at the four-way stop. It's about ten, twelve miles. There's a turn next to an old Sunoco station. It's on the right. I'll show you."

"Listen," barked Sam. "We've got to get him to a hospital. I'm not driving him anyplace but a proper facility, where he can get medical attention." He glanced in the rear view mirror. The old man had his eyes closed again, and he was breathing very softly, coughing every third or fourth breath. The scrawny man wiped blood from his mouth and chin with his shirttail.

"Look, man. The truth is, I don't know what happened back there. I think Howie's in some kind of trouble. If he is, we're in trouble. We didn't know what we were getting into, but those guys didn't exactly have our best interests in mind. I think we better do what he says, till I can get him to tell me why those guys jumped him."

"They didn't jump him. He was sitting in the car with the fat man . . . the one who looked like he was in charge. And they didn't just beat up on you. There were two guys shooting at us when we got out of there."

"I know. I know," said Johnny Gee, searching for a way to keep him driving. He had to placate the driver, keep him from freaking out and heading for the cops. Half an hour, no more. Long enough to get Howie to a safe place, get him fixed up . . . far enough so the sound of those gunshots stopped ringing in his ears.

"Look. Whatever Howie was doing back there, it had to be okay. He was Democratic Party chairman for fifteen years. He used to be the sheriff in this county." The second part was a lie, but it sounded good.

Sam stood on the brakes and pulled to a stop at the side of the road. He turned around so he could get a better look at the back seat. The old man was bleeding profusely from the head. His left arm was hideously twisted out of shape, broken in at least two places. He was coughing blood.

"Your friend looks bad," Sam said. "If he doesn't get medical attention, he could die. I'm not moving this automobile until you tell me where the nearest hospital is."

Johnny Gee didn't know what to say. The driver was probably right. They were in enough trouble as it was. If Howie died in the car, or out at the farm . . .

"Okay," said Johnny Gee. "Keep going down this road like I said, but take a right at the four-way stop. We'll take him to a clinic near here. It's the closest thing we've got to a hospital in these parts."

Sam put the Caddy in gear and pulled back on the road. He could see rolling hills and the outlines of barns against the night sky. They were headed vaguely south and west. It seemed as if it had been an hour ago since he was sleepily headed on the bus for Fort Campbell. Now he'd been in a gunfight, and he had two bleeding men he didn't know in the back seat of a car he didn't own. His head started to swim. What the hell had happened?

"When we get to that clinic, I want some answers," he said, the tone in his voice somewhere between bewildered and angry. "And we've got to make some arrangements to get me on another bus. I'm a major in the Army, and I've got to get to Fort Campbell, Kentucky, or I'll be in even bigger trouble than I'm in now." He glanced in the rear view mirror. "Hey, what's your name, anyway?"

Johnny Gee looked up, startled.

"My name's Johnny. Johnny Gee. This is Howie Radian. What's yours?"

"Sam Butterfield. I'm from Hancock County, north of here. We're headed down towards Marion, aren't we? I mean, if we keep going straight, that is."

"Yeah. We sure are. But I thought you didn't know where we were going. Hey. Don't forget to turn right at the four-way stop."

"That'll take us over towards Annoyance, won't it?"

"Yeah. So how you know your way around here all of a sudden, anyway?"

"I used to race down south of Marion every summer at the dirt track. The best driver around here was a good friend of mine. Dave Spicer. Owned a Shell station and a body shop. He drove an old Mercury that was painted bright purple. Kept it shiny, too."

He peered into the darkness looking for the four-way stop. There it was.

"How much farther?" he asked.

" 'Bout ten miles. You better step on it. Howie's coughing up a lot of blood, and he's not breathing so good."

Sam put the accelerator to the floor. He could hear the labored breathing in the back seat, and it made him nervous, so he flipped on the high beams and concentrated on driving. It amazed him how a car at speed at night becomes a capsule apart in time and space. All you could see of the outside world was a narrow corridor of illuminated blacktop on the other side of the hood in the headlights. Everything else just rushed past in a dark, silent blur. You could hear the engine and a whisper of wind from the windows, closed against the night. Inside, the air was almost stuffy. Outside, it rushed by at sixty, seventy, eighty-five miles an hour, powerful enough to knock you down if you were standing still. But in a car at eighty-five miles an hour, it was the rest of the world that stood still on the other side of the windshield, still and dark and cold on this fall night going places you've never been with people you've never known.

"It's right up ahead," said Johnny Gee, leaning forward for a better look. "See the lights? That's Annoyance. Take the first left, just past the bank, then take the first right. The police station and clinic will be at the end of the block."

Sam made the turns, looking for the clinic. He glanced at his watch. It was just about time for the national news to come on TV, and the little town looked as if it had been asleep for hours. He pulled up in front of a broken backlit plastic sign that read MED CLINIC.

"Gimme a hand," said Johnny Gee. Sam got out and opened the back door. Johnny Gee handed out the limp body of Howie Radian, and Sam grabbed him under the arms and pulled him from the car. When his feet dropped from the car seat to the ground, Howie Radian opened his eyes, turned his head, and saw where he was.

"Get . . . my . . . brother," he whispered.

"Sure thing, Howie," said Johnny Gee, wrapping his arm around the older man's waist, helping to carry him into the clinic. A nurse opened the glass doors, pushing a gurney.

Johnny Gee grabbed Sam by the arm and pulled him into the hall.

"I'm going to call Howie's brother. He's chief of police

here. Why don't you wait here and give them any help they need. It doesn't look like too many medical types are on duty in this burg tonight."

"Okay."

"Listen, if the doctor asks about his injuries, tell him Howie was beat up by some punks. We'll get everything straightened out when his brother gets here." Johnny Gee was tense, shifting from one foot to the other, looking into the emergency room nervously. He kept clenching and unclenching his fists. He was going to have to come up with some answers soon, and he didn't have them.

Johnny Gee strode through the door to the clinic's reception area, his face swollen, shirtfront covered with blood. A nurse at the desk. She was in her fifties, with a face like a bulldog and bleached-blond hair teased into an unkempt beehive.

"Can I use your phone?" asked Johnny Gee.

The nurse had the medic thing down pat: long on attitude, short on emotion. She didn't even take the cigarette out of her mouth when she spoke.

"What for?"

"There's been an accident. I just delivered an injured man into your emergency room. They're working on him now. I've got to use the phone and notify Vincent Radian now, because that's his brother Howie in there, or you're going to find yourself picking up your last paycheck when this is over."

The nurse paused and looked Johnny Gee up and down. She took the cigarette from her mouth, carefully stubbed it out in an ashtray, and picked up the phone.

"I'll make the call. What'd you say your name was?" The nurse's tone was measured and low. She acted as if she knew that the man standing before her spent the better part of his time up to no good, but the mention of the chief's brother caught her up short, and she held her tongue.

"You gonna call the chief?"

"That's the general idea," said the nurse.

"Tell him Johnny Gee's with his brother. Tell him Howie's been injured pretty badly. He'd better get here as quick as he can."

The nurse dialed the phone and got an answer. She asked for the chief of police, then hung up.

"They said he's gone home, and he doesn't want any calls unless it's a genuine emergency."

"Call them back and tell them . . . tell them to call Vincent and tell him that it's an emergency involving his brother. He's hurt pretty bad."

The nurse dialed the phone again and relayed the message.

"He'll be on his way in five, ten minutes," she said.

"How long before he gets here?"

"If he turns his lights and siren on, maybe half an hour, maybe forty minutes. He lives way on the other side of the county."

"Thanks a lot. I'm going to get back, see how Howie's making out." Johnny Gee started for the door.

"Did you fill out an admitting form yet?" The nurse smiled thinly and shoved a sheaf of papers across the desk.

"I'll wait till the chief gets here. It's . . . uh . . . his brother. I think he'll want to handle it."

"Whatever." The nurse swiveled in her chair and picked up a newspaper.

Johnny Gee stepped outside into the chilly autumn night and lit a cigarette. He had to think. Howie's brother on the way . . . the guy getting antsy . . . he had thirty minutes, tops. He needed to talk to Howie. He had to find out what was going on, and he had to do it quick.

The driver was still standing in the doorway of the emergency room. Johnny Gee approached quietly and tapped him lightly on the shoulder. He jumped sideways and landed in a crouch.

"Hey, man, it's just me," said Johnny Gee. "You look pale. Why don't you step outside for a breath. I'll keep an eye on things here."

"What's going on?" Sam was embarrassed at his reaction, but not much.

"The chief of police will be here in thirty minutes. Tell you what. Why don't you walk down the street and see if you can get us some coffee. There's one of those stop-and-shops or shop-and-gos, or whatever, around the corner at the end of the block. Take a little air. It'll do you some good, and I sure could use the coffee."

"Okay," Sam said, pausing. "But when I get back, I want to know what's going on, and I want to know how you're going to get me on a bus to Fort Campbell. You got that?"

"Sure," said Johnny Gee. "Now, don't forget. Coffee, cream and sugar for me. And get some air. I'll be right here waiting for you."

Sam walked out of the clinic and headed down the street. Johnny Gee watched him until he turned the corner. He could hear Howie coughing through the emergency room door. He didn't sound good, but it was better than not hearing anything at all. He pushed through the swinging door. They had moved him from the gurney onto an examination table. He was lying on his back, shirtless. His bruised and bloodied chest had been swabbed with some kind of orange disinfectant and dressed. His face had been bandaged. He was already bleeding through the fresh dressings.

"Howie, can you hear me?" asked Johnny Gee, stepping to his side. The nurse must have been going through the clinic looking for the doctor, because no one was with him.

"That you, Johnny?" Bandages covered both eyes. The old man lifted his right hand weakly.

"Yeah. I'm right here." Johnny Gee took his hand and placed it back on the examining table.

"You're not looking so good," said Howie with a low chuckle.

"This ain't no time for jokes, man," said Johnny Gee. "I want to know what happened back there at the diner, and you better talk fast, 'fore that nurse returns."

The old man turned his head and coughed. Blood mixed with saliva sprayed the curtain separating the examining tables in the emergency room.

"I don't feel so good," he said, wiping his chin with the back of his hand.

"You'll live. Mainly because that guy came out of nowhere."

"Who is he?" Howie reached up and lifted a corner of bandage so he could see Johnny Gee.

"I'll tell you after you explain what you was doin' at the diner. What went wrong back there? Who were those guys? They woulda killed you, you know that, man? They were serious. They were shootin' at us when we pulled you outa there. Two of 'em. They had guns and they were shootin' at us, Howie. We've done a lot of shit together, but I never been shot at before, Howie. You know what I mean? We pulled a scam here, a scam there, but never any guns. Never."

"I'm sorry, Johnny."

"That's not good enough." Johnny Gee grabbed the old man by the shoulder and squeezed. He let out a yelp of pain.

"Okay. Okay. Let go the shoulder." Johnny Gee relaxed his grip.

"You heard of Harlan Greene? Hamilton County?"

"I can't say as I have," said Johnny Gee.

"County leader of Hamilton County, and he runs about five other counties. He's one of the most powerful men in the state."

"So?"

"So I borrowed some money from him a while back."

"How much money?"

"Fifty thousand."

"And that's the debt you were supposed to pay off tonight?"

"Yeah."

"And you didn't have it."

"Not all of it. I already paid twenty. I was supposed to pay the rest tonight. I asked him for another two weeks, and that Lou went crazy."

"Lou?"

"Lou Bosco. He's Harlan's collection agency."

"Who were the other guys?"

"I don't know. A couple of his punks. I think I recognized one of them. I had him arrested one election day."

"What are you doing fifty grand in the hole to that asshole from Hamilton County, Howie?"

The old man coughed and took a deep, wheezing breath before he answered.

"I had a chance to get in on a mineral lease thing. I needed the money. Thought we could turn 'em over in a couple of months. How did I know the bottom was going to drop out of the oil market?"

"I don't feature you in the oil hustle, Howie. That ain't your style."

"I should have talked to you in May, Johnny."

"Guys like us shouldn't lose touch, man. We ain't talked in, what? Two, three months?"

"More like six," said Howie, picking up the corner of his bandage again, so he could see his friend. "Now tell me about the guy who bailed us out."

"Never seen him before. He's in the Army, from over to Hancock County. He was on his way to Kentucky tonight. I've got to be gettin' him back on a bus pretty quick."

The old man grabbed Johnny Gee's hand and pulled himself up on his elbow.

"Hey. Lie down, Howie," said Johnny Gee. "Don't put no strain on that gut of yours. It's looked better."

"You got to get out of the county. Tonight. Harlan don't give a fuck, Johnny. You've got to get out of here, as far away as fast as you can."

"This guy Harlan Greene . . . is he connected?" asked Johnny Gee.

"More ways than one," said Howie. "He's got every sheriff in this part of the state on his payroll. Everybody and his brother is going to be looking for you. You've got to get out of here and go south. Take the guy with you. Take the car. You leave it here, they'll find me for sure."

"Your Cadillac?"

"Hand me my jacket," said Howie, reaching toward the

chair in the corner of the cubicle. Johnny Gee picked up the torn and bloody sports jacket and held it next to his friend. Howie reached into the inside breast pocket. He pulled out a wad and peeled off five bills and handed them to Johnny Gee.

"Here's a hundred. Take it. First thing tomorrow morning, put the Caddy in a pay lot somewhere. You know, in a corner. Slap some mud on the plates, so you can't make out the numbers. You call me and tell me where it's at later. Keep going. Drop that guy off at a bus depot. Don't tell him any more than you have to. For God's sake, don't let him call the cops. He calls the law, Greene will nail you like you were standing still."

"Jesus, Howie, I don't know about this shit. . . ."

"Listen, Johnny. You don't have time to waste. Unless you get your ass out of this state before dawn, he's gonna get you. I know Harlan Greene. He won't stop until he gets me. And if he finds you, he'll use you to find me. He's a bad actor. You don't know how bad."

The old man took a deep breath and grimaced.

"When you get set up out of state, give me a call. I'll send you a couple of grand to get you started."

"Sure, Howie. Sure."

There was a whoosh of air as the swinging doors opened. The nurse returned with a tall, bearded doctor in tow. Johnny Gee quickly stuffed the bills in his pocket.

"Well. How are we getting along, my friend?" said the doctor in tones of mock familiarity. Johnny Gee stepped out of the curtained cubicle and edged toward the door. Howie lifted his bandage and looked at the doctor. Then he dropped the bandage and waved his hand in a get-out-of-here motion.

Johnny Gee turned on his heel, pushed through the emergency room door, and met Sam coming in.

"Thanks for the coffee, man," he said, taking the plastic cup. "Let's go."

OUTSIDE, IT HAD turned from chilly to cold. The town of Annoyance seemed to be lit by the glow of color televisions in living room windows up and down the street. Every driveway contained a car and a pickup truck, and most had a bass boat tucked up against the house. Falling leaves whistled along the gutters on crosswind puffs of night air.

"What time is it?" asked Johnny Gee, lighting a cigarette.

"It's just after eight," Sam said.

"They're watching 'Cheers.' No, that comes on next. Am I right?"

"You're right, but you're not making any sense. What's going? How's your friend?"

"He'll be all right. The doctor's with him now. They

cleaned him up. He's hurt bad, but he'll make it. He's a tough old dude." Johnny Gee pulled his suit lapels up around his neck against the cold.

"You got any clothes in that satchel of yours?" he asked.

"Yeah. Shorts, socks. Couple of shirts. Toilet articles."

"You think I could borrow one of those shirts?" He opened his suit jacket. His shirt was covered with dried blood.

"Sure. It's in the car."

"C'mon then. I'm freezin'," said Johnny Gee. He climbed in on the passenger side and Sam got in behind the wheel.

"Start her up. Let's have some heat," said Johnny Gee as he slipped out of his jacket and shirt. Sam fished in his bag and handed over a sweatshirt.

"This is it?"

"That's it."

"Guess it'll have to do," said Johnny Gee, pulling on the sweatshirt. He wrapped the suit jacket around his shoulders and flipped the visor mirror into view.

"It don't look so bad. Kinda European, know what I mean? Italian-like."

"Now that you're sartorially splendid, do you think you could explain to me what happened back at that diner tonight? I want to know what caused the fight, and I want to make sure the police have been informed, and then I want to get myself on the next bus to Fort Campbell. I was glad to give you guys a hand with those punks, but I'd like to make the proper reports and get back to my own life now."

"I already called the police. Howie's brother is chief of police here, and he's on his way. I've got twenty bucks for your trouble. How's that sound, my friend?" Johnny Gee grinned ear-to-ear. The intent of the grin was to relax the driver. His infectious smile had gotten him out of more than one bad spot over the years, but something told him he was going to need more than charm to get through this night.

"I don't need any twenty dollars. All I need is to get back on the next southbound bus."

"I don't think the bus is such a good idea," Johnny Gee said, the grin evaporating from his face.

"What's the matter with the bus?"

"They'll be watching the buses," said Johnny Gee. "And besides, there's no more tonight." He pushed the window button and flipped out the cigarette. He tried to blow a smoke ring, but a breeze sucked the smoke out the window.

"Watching the bus? Who's watching the bus?"

Johnny Gee turned and looked at Sam. It was right that he come clean, and now was probably the time.

"Who do you think? The assholes who shot at us, that's who. The assholes who beat Howie half to death. You don't think they're gonna be lookin' for us? We didn't exactly exit the scene on the best of terms, man."

"What'd your friend tell you in there?" Sam goosed the accelerator. They were still sitting outside the clinic, head-lights off. It was warm inside the car, and he wasn't going anywhere until this skinny stranger told him what was really going on.

"Okay. My friend, Howie, he owed some money to some guys he shouldn't have been borrowin' money from. He paid back some of it a couple of weeks ago. He owed the rest tonight, and he didn't have it. They got rough with him. That's when you and I came in. I didn't know what was happening. I swear. He's a friend. We're havin' coffee, next thing I know I look out the window and they're using his ass to resurface the parkin' lot."

"How much money?"

"Fifty thousand."

"Fifty thousand dollars? He owed fifty thousand dollars? To whom?"

Johnny Gee burst out laughing.

"Jesus, Jesus, I'm sorry," he said, trying to stop.

"What the hell is so funny?"

" 'To whom.' You said, 'to whom.' S'the funniest thing I ever heard. I don't know why. I guess I'm scared." He looked at Sam, relieved to see the beginnings of a smile on his face. He understood.

"So who were the tough guys? You were laughing so hard you forgot to say."

"Harlan Greene. Howie said he's a real bad actor. He's a big hoopdeedoo from around here, and he's connected. He's nobody to mess with, and neither are his people."

"Harlan Greene? This whole thing was about Harlan Greene?"

"You've heard of him?"

"Damn right I've heard of him. He runs the next county over from where I grew up."

"Then you know what I'm talkin' about."

"More or less."

"Well, he's why we've got to stay away from the bus depot. His people will be watching it for sure. Besides, there isn't one out of there until six in the morning."

"So what do you have in mind?"

"Paducah. I thought we'd drive over there. You can get an express. You'll be at your base in a couple of hours."

Sam considered what the stranger had said. He wasn't sure he was getting the whole story, but the mention of Harlan Greene let him know he was getting enough.

Johnny Gee had his comb out and was working studiously on his hair, smoothing it back, patting it down. He caught Sam's eye and grinned.

"How's the coif lookin'? Think it'll do?"

Sam couldn't help but chuckle.

"Sure. Looks very Jack Nicholson. A cross between distinguished and dastardly."

"Really? You're not kiddin' me?" Johnny Gee touched his gleaming pompadour with a fingertip. He squared his shoulders and extended his neck. His grin faded into a look of sublime satisfaction, and he pocketed the comb.

"Let's blow this popstand, man. Paducah beckons. 'Sides, I don't like sittin' still."

Sam put the Caddy in gear and started out of town the way they'd come in.

"How far is the interstate?" Johnny Gee asked as they passed the last streetlight in Annoyance.

"About twenty miles. We'll pick it up, head south to Paducah. Be there in no time."

"How we doin' for gas?"

Sam checked the gauge.

"Half a tank. That's about a hundred miles in this thing."

"We'll stop outside Paducah. There's a million truckstops down near the state line."

With the car once more at speed, the rolling hills of Illinois disappearing beneath its wheels, headlights poking through the darkness, Sam relaxed. He'd be back on schedule in a matter of hours, back in uniform in just over two days. His uniforms! He panicked. Then he remembered. He'd checked his duffel through to Clarksville, where it would be waiting for him at the baggage claim window at the bus depot. He relaxed his grip on the wheel and cracked the window for some air. There was really nothing quite like piloting a big, overweight, overbuilt, overpowered American car down two-lane roads at high speeds at night. All that invisible land off to the left and right of the car cloaked in mysterious blackness . . . the whisper of the wind in your left ear . . . the silence and calm behind the wheel . . . the soft green glow of the dashboard instruments just below the windshield, through which you saw only a tunnel. . . .

You wanted never to lift your right foot from the gas, never to stop going forward. It was like borrowing a piece of the night, wherever you passed became yours for an instant, and then it was gone, and so were you, into the darkness and over the hill and down the road and out of sight.

There were worse ways to spend an evening. Things had started out a little rough, but it seemed like they'd taken a turn for the better. He glanced over at Johnny Gee.

"Hey, I think we're getting close to the interstate."

Johnny Gee perked up. In the distance were the usual gaggle of fast food plazas and gas stations that populate the curlicues of entrance and exit ramps on the nation's freeways. The car slowed, and they drove into a night zone illuminated, bright as day.

"Turn around," Johnny Gee said.

"What . . ."

He grabbed Sam's arm.

"Make a U-turn, man. Don't ask questions. Just do it."

Sam whipped the wheel and the Caddy made the turn, hanging its front wheel in the dirt. In an instant they were back in the darkness beyond the swarm of commerce around the interchange.

"What's going on?"

"Step on it, man. Get us the fuck outa here."

Sam put his foot to the floor, they crested a hill, and the lights in the rear view mirror disappeared. Johnny Gee stayed on his knees for another mile, peering into the darkness out the back window, then he turned around.

"Take the next right. It'll be coming up around the next bend," he said.

"What'd you see back there?" asked Sam, watching the road ahead, looking for the turn.

"You see that Burger Chef off to the right?"

"Yeah. I saw it."

"Parked right at the exit. Blue Buick. It was the shooters from the diner. They were watching the interstate entrance. I don't think they saw us, the direction we're coming from. Ain't nobody behind us. I think you turned just in time. Another two hundred yards and we'd have been right the fuck in front of them. They woulda seen us for sure. That was some U-turn you pulled. I thought you'd put us in the ditch, fast as we were goin'."

"You said they'd be watching the buses. Now you say they're watching the interstate ramps. How many of them are there, anyway?"

"Harlan Greene? He's got as many goons as he wants, man. He runs a lot of shit in this part of the state. There!" Johnny Gee pointed. "Make the turn."

Sam turned onto a county blacktop, an access road to farms in the area. It was half as narrow as the state road they'd been on, recently surfaced with sand and oil. There were patches, he knew, that could still be slick.

"Where is this thing going to take us?" he asked, adjusting to the changing road conditions.

"We'll head west on these back roads and jump back on

the interstate outside Paducah. I know these county roads. Been on 'em all my life.''

''This was a dirt road not too long ago,'' Sam said. ''What could you possibly be doing out in boonies like this? You don't look like the shit-shoveling type.''

Johnny Gee chuckled and looked over his shoulder.

''I was comin' out here to little bars and luncheonettes most every day for quite a while,'' said Johnny Gee. ''Runnin' numbers. Takin' bets. I had a good piece of territory for a while.''

''You're a criminal,'' Sam said. ''That's how I got into this mess. Both of you are criminals.''

''Sure, I been a con,'' said Johnny Gee. ''But I got out of that business after I got arrested and did a hitch inside. I haven't run numbers or taken bets out here for years.''

''Yeah? What am I supposed to be? Relieved and appreciative that you decided to clean up your act?''

Johnny Gee turned and fixed him with a glare.

''I don't give a fuck how you feel, man. I didn't organize my life around your judgments about what the fuck is right and wrong in this world. What in hell's wrong with takin' a guy's bet on a football game and passing it along, anyway? I guess you never bet a dollar on your college team, put down five on the Superbowl. Huh? You never placed a red-blooded American bet on a red-blooded American blood sport? You never put down a buck in a football pool?''

''I've bet on a few games,'' Sam said. ''I just never thought about the bets . . . going anywhere. I mean . . .''

''Somebody's got to take the bets, man. May as well be me as the next guy, huh? Look. Let's knock this shit off and get this machine down the road.''

''How far does this road go?''

"We gonna come to a series of T-intersections. When you hit them, just keep turnin' left. We're gonna pass through a series of little towns. Keep to the speed limit going in and out. They got two-man police departments, and they just love to pick up some municipal income from speedin' tickets."

"I know what you're talking about. We've got the same little burgs around my hometown."

"They ever get you for speedin', man?"

"Nope. I used to test my race car on dirt farm roads, redline it in every gear, listening to the engine for flat spots in the tune. When you tune an engine right, it's got a certain note it hits in each gear at different rpm. It's like a guitar. You're listening for the same thing . . . a certain harmony, a coming-together of the mechanical noise."

"You make it sound real nice and artistic-like. It must make you feel good to know about stuff like that."

"Yeah, I guess it does."

"I don't know nothin' about cars, but I know somethin' about how to get in and out of shit, and how to keep movin'," he said, without elaborating. "It's useful to know, when the time comes. Its own kinda wisdom." He extracted a pack of cigarettes from his jacket pocket, shook out the last one and lit it. He inhaled deeply, cracked the window, and blew the smoke into the wind.

"This bother you, mister?"

"Smoking? Nah."

"We gotta stop and get me some more Pic's," said Johnny Gee. "I'm out." He exhaled another deep puff into the night and leaned his head back against the seat, closing his eyes.

Sam peered into the dimness ahead. One shallow rise after another, like a gentle earthen roller coaster, the road

itself nearly straight as a ruler, farmlands broken by occasional bursts of timber dark against the night sky and the
dim glow of a nearby farmhouse. He leaned forward to
switch on the radio and caught a glimpse of the rear view
mirror in the corner of his eye. He wasn't sure . . . could
have been . . . it was just a glimmer. He straightened up,
got a fix on the road ahead, and looked into the rear view
mirror dead on, kept watching it, glanced at the road ahead,
back in the mirror at the road unwinding like a ribbon in
the red glow of the Caddy's taillights.

There it was! Just as he crested the hill. Headlights in the
far distance, two little pinpricks of light. A half-mile back
judging by the size of the lights in the mirror.

"Hey. I think we've got somebody behind us."

"What kinda car?"

"I don't know. They're too far away. I can see them every
time we reach the top of one of these little hills, and then
just for a moment. There they are again! See the lights?"

Johnny Gee turned around and crouched on the seat,
looking out the rear window. He'd tossed his cigarette out
the window and gave his full attention to the road.

"Yeah. I got 'em. There they are again. I think the car's
gainin' on us. Looks closer now."

"You're right. They're coming on strong."

"Did we pass through one of those little towns while I
was dozin'?"

"Yes, we did. Tiny place. One blinking yellow light. But I
didn't see any cops back there. The town was shuttered up
tight. Nothing was moving." Sam kept glancing up at the
rear view mirror.

"There they are again. They're moving up. Maybe a quarter of a mile back."

"Put your foot in it and get us the fuck outa here," said Johnny Gee, never taking his eyes off the road behind them. "All we need is a couple of Harlan Greene's boys on top of us this far out on a county road. They catch us, nobody'd find us for a week."

"Maybe it's your friend's brother, the chief of police."

"That ain't Howie's brother back there, man! You better push it, or they're gonna leave us all over the road, man," said Johnny Gee. "They're still comin' on."

Sam looked in the rear view mirror. As he did, a flashing blue light winked at him between the headlights, now about a hundred yards distant.

"It's a police car. I'm pulling over," he said, lifting his foot from the gas. The Caddy began to slow.

"It ain't the cops!" screamed Johnny Gee. "I don't know who it is, but it ain't the cops! Get us outa here!"

"Yes, it is. It's an unmarked car. I'm not going to try and outrun them. I don't want resisting arrest added to a speeding violation."

"Don't you understand anything, man? So it's an unmarked sheriff's car. That don't matter. Harlan Greene owns the sheriff in this county and every other county around here for a hundred miles! That son-of-a-bitch stops us, he'll deliver us to Harlan within the hour. Now get us outa here. Outrun the bastards. C'mon, man. Do it!"

The car was right on their tail now, the strobe filling the interior of the Cadillac with bursts of blue light. Sam kept the Caddy in his lane, but he slowed to fifty-five miles an hour, the speed limit. He didn't know what to do. He knew from what his mother had told him that Harlan Greene was nobody's angel, but the kid was saying the sheriff was owned by Harlan Greene, and that the hoods at the diner worked for him? That was very, very hard to believe. The Caddy slowed to fifty. The other car started to pull alongside.

"Step on it! Get the fuck outa here!" screamed Johnny Gee. "Those fuckers would just as soon kill us!"

The car was abreast of the Caddy. Sam looked to his left. The man in the right front seat stuck a twelve gauge pump shotgun out the window. The barrel was pointed directly at him, only a few feet from his face. Sam pushed his right foot to the floor. He heard the shotgun go off. The Caddy's rear window shattered, filling the interior of the car with flying glass. He reached for the back of his neck. It felt as if a hundred bees had stung him. He grabbed the wheel with both hands, glanced at the speedometer. Ninety-five. One hundred.

"What'd I fuckin' tell you!" It was Johnny Gee, screaming in his right ear. The blue light flashed in his eyes, reflected off the windshield. He could barely make out the road ahead.

"You still think that's the cops back there? You hear any siren? You hear them honk their horn? You hear them yell a warning over their loudspeaker? They just started blastin'. Cops where you from usually shoot you for speedin'?"

Sam glanced over his shoulder. The other car was gaining on them again. He waited until they were a car-length away. He held the steering wheel tightly and jammed on the brakes. The car behind slammed into the Caddy's rear bumper and careened off to the side. The Caddy picked up a couple of car lengths. He looked in the rear view mirror. The shotgun was sticking out the window, pointed straight at them. He jerked the wheel, swerving his left wheels onto the dirt shoulder. He heard the loud report of the shotgun again.

Missed. He swerved back into the right lane and hit the gas. He was doing a hundred and five miles an hour. He aimed the Caddy down the middle of the road. The car drifted aimlessly from side to side, five feet in either direction. He could just barely keep it between the ditches. A hundred and five, a hundred and ten. That was it, all the Caddy could do.

He stayed on the gas, crested a hill, hit one-ten down the other side. He looked back.

The flashing blue light was gone. So were the headlights. He studied the rear view mirror. Nothing back there. Darkness. He eased up. A hundred. Ninety-five. Johnny Gee sat bolt upright next to him staring out the windshield like a zombie. Frozen.

"I think we lost them," Sam yelled over the wind from the blown-out rear window.

"Stay on it. Let's get the fuck outa here," yelled Johnny Gee, still staring straight ahead.

Sam looked in the rear view mirror. Total blackness. They were alone.

Suddenly he was blinded by the flashing blue strobe. The driver of the other car had switched off his lights and crept up on them in the darkness. Now he was pulling into the left lane, starting to come alongside. Sam squinted against the flashes from the strobe. The shotgun went off again. The Caddy shuddered as a blast hit the trunk.

Sam didn't hesitate this time. Everything he knew about driving a modified on a dirt track came back to him in a rush. He tapped the brakes, just enough to let the other car get ahead. Then he hit the gas and pulled abreast of the other car's rear fender. As the guy with the shotgun swiveled to put the Caddy in his sights, Sam yanked the steering wheel to the left, slamming the car's rear fender. The shot-

gun jerked upward and hit the window frame, firing harm-
lessly into the air. The guy recovered, pumped the shotgun,
and aimed at the Caddy. Sam crashed into the other car
again, throwing him into a slide. The car skidded onto the
shoulder of the road and straightened out. The man with the
shotgun was yelling at his driver. This was it. Sam tapped
the brakes, drifting behind the other car. The guy with the
shotgun leaned out the window from the waist up, aiming at
the windshield of the Caddy. Sam pressed his right foot to
the floor. The Caddy slammed into the car's right rear
fender. The car careened wildly off the road, skidded sideways into a ditch and back up the far side nose first into the
air. Then it flipped, landed on its roof, skidded upside down
through a muddy field, and slammed into a line of trees.
Sam heard his left rear tire blow out and the Caddy went
sideways. He threw the wheel into the slide and held on.

6

THE CADILLAC SKIDDED to a halt in the middle of the
road, its headlights shining along a narrow dirt lane at the
edge of a cornfield. Two hundred yards distant stood the
remains of an old farmhouse and outbuildings, weathered
and crumbling, nearly obscured by a grove of oaks and un-
trimmed hedges and vines at the end of the lane.

The two men stared straight ahead without speaking as
the dust settled around the Cadillac, which listed in the
direction of the blown rear tire. Sam's breath came in sharp,
wet gasps. Johnny Gee was rigid. In the distance came the
low muffled wail of a stuck car horn, a mournful reminder of
where they were and what had happened.

Johnny Gee continued to stare straight ahead. He hadn't moved.

"Come on. We've got trouble." Sam poked his arm, and he stirred.

"Where are we?" said Johnny Gee tonelessly.

"We blew a tire."

"What happened to the other car? Those bastards were trying to kill us!"

"They went off the road." Sam pointed out the side window in the direction of the wailing car horn.

"Is that them?" asked Johnny Gee, squinting into the night. "What happened?"

"The car flipped. I saw it hit the trees."

"How many of 'em was there?"

"Two." Sam was talking to himself as much as to Johnny Gee. His speech was tight, forced, and his words came in rapid bursts. "I couldn't believe it. They had a shotgun. They kept shooting at us. I ran them off the road. It looked like an unmarked car, but I don't think they were cops. They didn't want to arrest us. They wanted to kill us."

"What'd I tell you? Harlan's boys don't mess around. Cops or no cops, there ain't no law enforcement in this county. There's just enforcement, period. Ya get what I mean?"

"All of this over a damned debt? Those two guys were doing their best to make sure we'd be bleeding on the side of the road. Are you sure you got the whole story from your friend?"

Johnny Gee looked at the woods obscuring the wrecked car. The horn still blared into the darkness.

"I only know one thing for sure. We got to get outa here," he said. "We gotta keep movin'. These guys don't give up.

There'll be others. We gotta get you to that bus, get you outa here."

"First, we've got to get this car off the road," said Sam, dropping the Caddy into gear.

"Don't we have to change the tire?"

"Yeah, but I think we should have a look at those guys first. I saw the car go over. It didn't look like anybody could have survived the crash, but . . ."

"You gotta be kiddin' me. They're tryin' to kill us, and you want to go hold their hands?"

"I just want to see if anybody's alive. If they are, I'm calling an ambulance at the next town."

"You're crazy."

"You got me into this, but I'm getting myself out. That means I'm not leaving anyone dying on the side of the road. We've got to do what's right here."

"What do you think this is? A war movie? Like, you got to care for the wounded or something?"

"I ran them off the road. I'm going to see if either of them survived. You can stay with the car if you want. I don't care."

Johnny Gee studied Sam. He meant what he was saying. He shrugged.

"What's down there at the end of that dirt road?" asked Johnny Gee.

"Looks like an abandoned farmhouse."

"Will this thing make it down there . . . like, into those trees behind the shack? We better hide the car if we're gonna check these bums out."

"Sure." Sam put the Caddy in gear and it limped down the dirt road. He pulled around the old farmhouse and cut the engine. They were sitting in what was once a backyard. A tire swing hung from a branch high up in a tall oak tree.

An outhouse leaned fifteen degrees from the vertical over on the other side of the oak. A screen door could be heard banging desultorily in the wind. Who lived here, and how many years ago did they leave? Who played in this weed-clogged yard, and who rode that rusting tricycle peeking out from beneath the back stairs? Sam hit the headlight switch and the overgrown yard was plunged into darkness.

"Come on," he commanded. He grabbed the keys and opened the door. The cold night hit him like a slap. He heard the other door slam.

"I can't see shit out here," said Johnny Gee. "Fuck." Sam heard the thud of a body hitting the ground. He walked around the car. He saw an arm sticking out of the weeds.

"You gonna give me a hand, or you gonna stand there?"

Sam pulled Johnny Gee to his feet. No one could have looked more out of place, combing the dirt from a farmyard out of his hair, his sharkskin suit thigh high in rye grass and goldenrod.

"Let's go," Sam called, heading down the dirt road in the direction of the blaring car horn.

They crossed the blacktop and entered the woods, crashing through the undergrowth. Low trees slapped them in the face and brambles tugged at their pants legs. Then, through the trees, they saw the other car's headlights.

It was a black Ford sedan, and it was upside down, sitting on its roof, headlights pointing into the woods, the blue light torn from the dashboard still flashing wildly inside the car. Sam walked gingerly around the car to the passenger side. A man's body dangled half-in, half-out of the passenger window, facing up. The shotgun lay on the ground, a few yards from the body.

"Jesus. Look at this," said Sam in a low, stunned voice. "His hand is gone."

"Guy must have shot himself when the car went over," said Johnny Gee. "Too bad."

"Do you recognize him?"

"Yeah, sure. I know all the shotgun thugs in these parts," said Johnny Gee sarcastically. Sam shot him a look, and Johnny Gee walked away.

He stood over the body, staring. The man was still breathing, but he was unconscious.

"I didn't want this," he mumbled to himself.

He felt an arm around his shoulder.

"Hey, man. It wasn't your fault. It's okay. The dude's an asshole."

"But why is this happening?"

"I know how you feel, man. Most of us just want to get by, you know? Make a few bucks, eat supper, catch a couple of shows on the tube, and hit the sack. Nobody needs this kind of shit. But it wasn't your fault. There was nothing else you could do."

"Where's the other guy?" asked Sam, regaining his composure.

"He's over there," said Johnny Gee. "He's still got his seat belt on."

Sam walked around to the driver's side of the car. He reached in the window, hit the headlight switch and turned off the ignition. The blue light stopped flashing, but the horn kept blaring. He hit the steering wheel a couple of times and the horn stopped. An icy stillness fell over the woods. Sam got down on his hands and knees and stuck his head in the window. In the silence, he could hear the driver breathing.

"He's still alive. Come over here and give me a hand with

him," he commanded. Johnny Gee bent over and grabbed the man's arm while Sam reached up inside the car and flipped a lever on the man's seat belt. He crumbled into a heap on the inside of the car's roof, and the two men pulled him gently from the wreck.

"I've seen this one before," said Johnny Gee. He's the one shot at us when we were carrying Howie to the car. He's from up in Hamilton County. Works for Harlan, I'm sure of it."

"Well, he's still breathing."

"Just barely."

"Do these guys think we've got the money? The fifty thousand? That's why they were chasing us?"

"Who knows what they think? All I know is, we better get the fuck out of here before another carload of them comes along and finishes what they started."

"Maybe we can bring him around, and ask him some questions. I want to know why these guys were trying to kill us, for starters."

"That's a wonderful idea," sneered Johnny Gee. "Then he'll know exactly what we look like, and he'll be able to give a description of the two guys who ran him off the road and shot up his partner. Wonderful. Why didn't I think of that?"

"But *they* were the ones who were trying to kill *us.*"

"And he's gonna admit that to the cops? Golly, officer, I was just chasing these guys and taking an occasional shot at them, when they ran me off the road. That's how the accident happened. Honest." Johnny Gee felt for his pack of cigarettes and not finding it, cursed to himself. "That's beautiful. You must believe in the tooth fairy, too."

Sam grabbed him by the shoulder and pushed him up against the wrecked Ford.

"Don't act wise with me," he said in even tones. "Somebody told these guys to find us and kill us, and I want to know why. I don't buy this story about your friend owing some money, and they were trying to collect. If we don't figure out what's going on here, we're going to be in bigger trouble than we're in already. Now, knock off the sarcastic bullshit, tell me what you think, and tell me straight."

"All I'm saying is, we've got to get the hell away from here. If these guys live, they'll tell anybody who'll listen that we shot at them, that it's our shotgun. You better hope both of these dudes die, and you better hope somebody takes prints off that gun over there and figures out that he shot his own hand off with it. That's the only chance we have, man."

Sam knelt next to the injured man and listened to his breathing for a moment. Then he stood up.

"He's breathing a lot easier now. I think he's going to be okay. I'm still calling an ambulance when we get to the next town."

"You do what you have to," said Johnny Gee.

"Come on. Let's get back to the car," said Sam, walking back into the woods.

"I'm right behind you."

It took ten minutes to get back across the road to the Cadillac. Sam didn't waste any time. He unlocked the trunk and raised the lid. A trunk light came on, illuminating a semicircle of high weeds blowing softly in the wind.

"Here. Take this," said Sam, handing over the jack and base plate.

"What's this shit?"

"You never changed a tire before?"

"Do I look like I ever changed a tire?" Johnny Gee turned down the collar of his suit jacket and examined what was left of the creases in his trouser legs.

"I guess not. Put the jack down and give me a hand with the spare."

Sam tilted the spare vertical in its round depression at the bottom of the trunk. Johnny Gee was wiping dirt from his shoes.

"Step aside," Sam commanded, lifting the spare from the trunk and carrying it to the side of the car. Quickly he assembled the shaft and base of the jack, hooked it to the Caddy's bumper and jacked the left rear off the ground. With the jack handle, he popped the hubcap and began removing the lug nuts from the hub. He pulled the flat tire free of the hub, and put on the spare. Then he spun the lug nuts back on, tightened them up, hit the release lever on the jack and lowered the wheel to the ground. He was lifting the flat tire into the trunk when he saw a clean towel neatly folded at the bottom of the spare tire well. He rested the flat tire on the edge of the trunk, grabbed the towel and wiped the grime from his hands. He was ready to tilt the flat tire into the well when something shiny caught his eye.

"Come here. Look at this."

Johnny Gee leaned over the bumper so he could see.

"What in hell is that?"

"I don't know, man. Boxes of shit. Tools, probably."

Sam let the spare drop to the ground. Five shiny brown boxes, arrayed like spokes of a wheel around the bottom of the spare tire well, had been hidden under the towel. He removed one of the boxes and held it to the light. He snapped the box open with his thumb.

"It's a videotape," he said. "They're all videotapes."

The screen door beat a slow tattoo. The wind picked up, blowing the smell of a nearby swamp across the swaying weeds.

Sam took the rest of the videotapes from the well. He threw the jack in the trunk, and jumped in the front seat. He started the car and switched on the lights.

"Hey, man, wait for me," called Johnny Gee as Sam backed the Caddy in a circle, turning around. Sam hit the brakes. The thin man opened the passenger door and climbed in.

"You were gonna leave me, man. What the fuck is the matter with you?"

"You had no idea these tapes were in the car?"

"I told you what the old man told me. He owed some guys fifty thou, and he didn't have the dough, and the trouble started. I didn't know nothin' about no tapes, man."

"Let me get this straight. You're telling me the old man told you absolutely nothing about this stuff?" Sam held one of the tapes and shook it in Johnny Gee's face.

"Wait a minute. He said this one thing, that he had some insurance, and they knew he had the insurance, and that's why he wasn't worried 'bout them pullin' nothin'."

"And you think these videotapes are the so-called insurance he told you about?"

"Could be, man. Who knows?"

The Cadillac rolled to a stop at the end of the dirt road. Sam leaned forward, resting his forehead on the top of the steering wheel. He took two deep breaths and looked up.

"How do we get off this road?"

"Go right. There's a turn-off a couple miles west of here. We can head south, get outa this county faster that way."

"What do you think is on the tapes?" he asked.

"I don't know. Could be anything . . . Hollywood porno, some dirty home movies . . . Howie's been into a lot of shit over the years."

"I thought you told me he was county leader and sheriff."

"That don't mean nothin'. You're county leader or sheriff in these parts, you can get yourself a piece of any action you want in on. You know what they say about politics. Gettin' elected pays, man. Yes indeed it does."

"You say he told you nothing about the tapes?"

"Not a word. All he told me was, the whole beef was about the money he owed. That's all I know."

"I'm sure these videotapes are what the trouble back at the diner was about. Maybe they belonged to someone else. Maybe they're stolen. Maybe there never was any fifty thousand dollars. Maybe all the time there were just these five videotapes."

"Only way we're gonna find out is have a look at them."

"Now just exactly how are we going to accomplish that at nine-thirty at night in the middle of nowhere?" Sam peered into the darkness trying to see beyond the headlights. Nothing but more farmland. He glanced at the speedometer. Eighty-five.

"Take a left at the end of that fence there," said Johnny Gee, pointing up ahead. Sam slowed and took the turn. The road surface got worse and worse. Rough stretches were interrupted by clusters of potholes and rain gully washouts.

"Where in hell is this going to take us?" he asked, slowing to ten miles an hour to negotiate some flooded low ground.

"There's a town up ahead. 'Less I'm mistaken, they got a video store."

"A video rental place? Out here?"

"Everybody's got one of those recorders nowadays, man. Especially out here. You got your dish, you got your video-tape recorder, you're set for the winter, don't care how much it snows on your ass. You just hunker down and flip on that tube. These people out here don't know how they got along without all this shit. It's the truth. 'Tween cable and those big antennas, the boonies are wired in, man. They got their MTV out here. Who do you think is buyin' all them Spring-steen albums and John Cougar albums? They got their Camaro and their color TV and their stereo, and they are right where you are now at, man. Right here."

The Caddy hit one last stretch of potholes and the road smoothed out. "Watch out. Place is right up ahead."

They rounded a corner and sure enough, up ahead on the left was a brightly lit minimall, a row of three or four stores plonked down in the middle of a gravel lot on the edge of town. The sign at the far end said VIDEO CONNECTION. Sam pulled into the gravel lot.

"Better park this thing by the side of the building, over there in the dark," said Johnny Gee.

Sam cut the engine and doused the lights. "What are we going to do in there?" he asked.

"You let me handle these folks," said Johnny Gee, stacking the tapes and tucking them under his arm. He strode purposefully around the corner of the building to the door. Sam followed close behind.

Five kids were sitting around on the floor watching MTV on a projection TV. Not a single head turned when they walked in. Five faces stayed glued to the gigantic images of leaping guitarists on the screen at the end of the room. The din from four speakers blaring the MTV audio was deafening. Sam and Johnny Gee stood just inside the door for a moment before they were noticed. Finally the video store proprietor, who had a shag haircut similar to that of the lead singer on the screen, unfixed his gaze and waved blankly.

"Hey, dude, what can I get for ya?" he yelled. They could barely hear him.

"Need to use your VCR for a minute, man," yelled Johnny Gee. "Got a couple tapes we need to check the audio on, know what I mean? We heard you got a good setup."

"Hey, dude, check it out. We got some power at Video Connection, man. S'what we're here for. Be my guest."

He pointed to a VCR on a shelf next to the projection screen. A grinning mouth full of yellow teeth peeked through the poodle-like cloud of hair nearly obscuring his face. He had the sunny disposition of a midwestern farmer and the look of a pipefitter from Bay Ridge Brooklyn. The combination was unsettling.

The kid touched a switch under the counter, and the big screen went blank. Five poodle heads turned.

"What time you all close?" asked Johnny Gee. He removed one of the tapes from its brown plastic box. Its label read Ramada Inn. He inserted it in the VCR and turned to the poodles.

"You all don't mind, do you? This will take just a minute." Five heads of hair shook blankly. No, they didn't mind. Something different to check out, man.

He punched play. The screen went fuzzy, and four speakers spewed static at great volume. The kid behind the counter turned a knob somewhere, and the volume went down. Then the screen went blank and a dim image came into focus.

"Jimmy. Check it out. Black and white. The fifties, dude," said a voice from the collected poodles, all of whom were gazing intently at the big screen.

A date and time signature appeared on the lower left hand corner of the screen, counting off minutes and hours. The scene looks like it was shot in a motel: two beds, a small table, wall lamps, shag rug. Extreme wide angle lens. Everything visible from the bathroom door to the dresser at the far side of the room. The camera is looking down into the room from above. There is the sound of a key turning in a lock, and a door opens. A man comes into view, a tall man, maybe six foot four, wearing a wrinkled suit and carrying a briefcase. Another man, also wearing a wrinkled suit, follows.

"How many Ramada Inns you been in, Frankie?" the second man asks the first. "How many Ramada Inns are there? A thousand? A million?"

"Shut up," says the tall man. He puts the briefcase down on the table and collapses into a bucket chair.

"You want me to get some ice?" asks the second man, his back to the camera.

Frankie rubs his face and leans his head back until he is looking at the ceiling.

"Get some ice, Leo," says the big man called Frankie. "Then get the bottle out of the trunk, Leo. You forgot the bottle again, Leo. How many Ramada Inns are you going to forget the bottle in, Leo? Ask yourself that question on your way out the door."

Sound of a door opening and closing. Frankie stands up and walks into the bathroom. Sound of water running.

Sound of a door closing. Sound of a toilet flushing. Sound of door opening. Frankie reappears, sits down in the bucket chair again. Head back. Eyes closed.

Leo seated on bed, reading a newspaper. Frankie in the bucket chair, one hand on a drink, the other arm thrown across his eyes in a gesture of fatigue.

Sound of someone knocking at the door. Leo gets up. Two men appear.

"We've got to stop meeting like this," says the first man. Frankie in bucket chair gets heavily to his feet, rounds table, grasps hand of first man, then the other.

"Sit down. Have a drink," he says with authority. "Leo. Bring me a couple glasses." Leo disappears into the bathroom, reappears with glasses.

"Sheriff, how are you doing?" asks Frankie.

"I think I want a drink," says the smaller man. He is gray-haired, and coiffed in the blow-dry manner. Nattily dressed.

The other man is younger, taller, and defers to the small man.

Frankie pours two drinks. Ice cubes make splashing noises when they're dropped into the glasses. The three men lift glasses and toast.

"To, ah, prosperity," says Frankie.

"I'll second that," says the gray-haired man.

"We've got a few questions," says the gray-haired man.

"I've got all the answers you need right here," says Frankie, patting the briefcase at the side of his chair.

There is a silence. The three men sip their drinks.

"Is it like you said?" asks the gray-haired man.

"Exactly like I said," says Frankie.

"Then that answers our question," says the gray-haired man.

Frankie picks up the briefcase and pushes it across the table to the gray-haired man. He opens it. Cash can be seen inside the briefcase. He turns to the younger man and nods. Closes the briefcase. The two men stand. Frankie rises to his feet. The three shake hands wordlessly.

"Show our friends to the door, Leo," says Frankie.

Sound of door opening, they disappear off camera, sound of door closing.

"Get the rest of the stuff out of the trunk, Leo," says Frankie.

The door opens and closes again, and the screen goes blank.

The poodles sat on the floor, staring at the pale gray screen.

"Hey, dude. What is this show? Some kind of new series?"

Johnny Gee punched eject. The VCR spat forth the videotape.

"Yeah. It's some outtakes a friend gave me," said Johnny Gee. "From a miniseries. It'll be on around Christmas." He looked around for Sam.

"We've got to go. Thanks a lot, man. Watch for it. It's called 'Two On A String.' You'll love it."

"Hey. Anytime, dude," said the proprietor.

Sam headed out the door. Johnny Gee followed.

"That was some kinda surveillance tape. They're all surveillance tapes," Sam said.

"Who are the guys on the tape? Do you have any idea?"

"Those first two guys? Leo and Frankie? I've never heard of 'em. Never seen 'em. The gray-haired guy who took the dough is the sheriff from up in Franklin County. Guy called O'Brien. Had a run-in with him a few years back."

"Who's the other guy?"

"How should I know? Some two-bit politician on the make, looks to me. Slick-lookin' bastard, wasn't he?"

"But . . . whose surveillance tapes are they? And what the hell were they doing in this car?" asked Sam. He looked over at Johnny Gee, and saw him in a new way. He wasn't shucking and jiving now. Sam found himself believing him for the first time all night.

"Don't know. First we got to have a look at the rest of these tapes. We find out who's the producer of this little miniseries, we'll know who they belong to. Or who they used to belong to."

7

THEY PULLED OUT of the minimall, took a quick left, drove down a side street, and picked up the main road on the other side of town. The Caddy clipped along at a respectful sixty miles per hour. No sense in attracting unwanted attention.

Sam's fingers were numb, attached to the wheel like claws. He had a slight twitch at the corners of his mouth. Nothing he had learned in his years in the army had prepared him for this.

He was lost, cut off from familiar roadways both physical and moral. What was he doing? Why did those men back there try to kill him? What were those videotapes all about?

What in hell was going on?

This much he knew:

The whole thing was about the videotapes. Maybe the thing to do was get the tapes to the police, explain to them what had happened back at the diner and when those men shot at him and tried to force him off the road, how he'd found the tapes in the trunk under the spare tire . . . explain the whole damn mess and be done with it and get on down to Fort Campbell and the comfortable, familiar surroundings of the United States Army. Yeah, that's what he'd do.

Sam relaxed and studied the road up ahead. It was a smooth blacktop with dirt shoulders. One long, loping curve eased into another, skirting the edges of gently rounded hills. They were still deep in farm country. He turned the wheel, leaning the big car into another right hand curve. Suddenly, the front end broke loose. The wheel jerked wildly in his hands. He took his foot off the gas, slowing the car to thirty-five miles an hour, then thirty. At twenty-five, the Caddy came back under control.

"The front end is gone," he said. "We must have cracked a control arm. We drive much more than ten, fifteen miles, we're going to lose a wheel, and put this thing in the trees."

"How far you think we could make at this speed? It ain't shakin' like it was."

"We're taking a chance just driving this thing," said Sam. "I don't know how long it'll hold together." He gripped the steering wheel tightly, his eyes fixed on the road ahead. "Wait a minute," he said. "I know a guy. He can't be more than twenty miles from here. Dave Spicer. He owns a gas station. He's got exactly what we need."

"Yeah, and we might be able to take a look at the rest of

these tapes while we're at his place. We got to figure out where we stand with this shit. Know what I mean?"

"Sort of." Sam grew wary. "Spicer's a friend, but . . . I'm not sure I want him involved. We're the ones in trouble. If we show him the tapes, we'll be pulling him in on top of us. He doesn't need this."

"Yeah, well, we don't need it neither, but we got it. I just thought if he's got a VCR, we could use it, that's all."

"We'll see."

"Hey, man, don't get so uptight about it. Whatever you say, goes, okay? Look. You and me are different, see? We just got to deal with that. You're what? Major in the army? That right?"

"Yeah, that's right."

"Major. That sounds real official." A smile crossed the face of Johnny Gee. "You mind if I call you Major, Major?"

"It's okay by me. That's what I am."

"I never met an officer before. I like that."

"There are worse things to be, I guess."

"You got that right. Do you know where you're goin'? I mean, where this guy Spicer's station is?"

"We just keep on the road. There's a turn we make up ahead. I'll show you."

"Which way?"

"Left."

"Which way are we headin'?"

"West."

"Hey, you pay attention, don't you, Major?"

"You bet I do."

"I thought you were gonna say, 'That's what they pay me for.' That woulda worked."

"If we don't get out of this mess pretty quickly, I'm never going to get paid another dime as a major or anything else."

The big car wound its way around another bend, a cold wind whistling at the windows. Sam let it drift up above thirty miles per hour, and the front end started to shimmy again. He slowed it down.

"You don't like to drive this big s.o.b. slow, huh?" asked Johnny Gee.

"Not this slow."

"You ever think how much a car's like a woman, man?"

"What do you mean?"

"You know. They both got hard outsides and soft insides, and every other day you got to spend money on 'em. And both of 'em is considered used after you've had 'em one day."

"I guess I've never made that particular comparison, myself." Sam glanced at Johnny Gee. He was grinning to himself in the dark. What would this guy come up with next?

"You got a wife, man?"

"I used to. It was a while ago." Sam studied the road for a moment.

"Tell me something. What are you getting at?"

"Nothin'. I'm not gettin' at nothin'. Just passin' the time, Major."

The car's front end started to shimmy again. Sam took his foot off the gas and brought it back under control. "What the hell got you asking about my ex-wife, anyway?"

"I don't know. Cars. Yeah. That was it."

"What about you? Have you got a girlfriend?"

"I don't have girlfriends, I have habits," said Johnny Gee.

"What do you mean by that?"

"I gamble, I shoot pool for money, I drink, I smoke, I bet

on horse races. Habits don't argue with you. Habits don't fight with you. You don't have to wait for habits to get in the mood. All habits do is cost you, and they usually cost a hell of a lot less than women."

"That's the rankest piece of self-serving nonsense I've ever heard. You ought to write that down so you'll remember it."

Sam pulled the car up to two aging gas pumps.

"Looks like it's been closed for years," said Johnny Gee. "How long since you been here?"

"It's been a while, I guess. Not since I use to race the dirt tracks around here. Ten years. Maybe more."

Sam hit the horn a short blast. A face appeared in a window. The door to the darkened station opened. A thin man wearing a gray fedora stepped out. His shoes had pointed toes, and they shone in the headlights of the car. He looked so much like Johnny Gee, he could have been his brother.

"Hey. Is Dave Spicer here?" Sam called out the car window.

"Who wants to know?" asked the slight figure in a hoarse voice. His eyes were hidden beneath the brim of the fedora, and the tip of a cigar glowed in the darkness at the corner of his mouth.

"Sam Butterfield. We used to race together."

"He ain't here yet. Come back in an hour." The slight figure retreated into the darkened gas station, which went back to looking as if it were closed for business.

"What was that all about, man? He didn't look like any pump jockey I've ever seen."

"I don't know. I've never seen him before. He must be a friend of Spicer's."

"I don't like this, man. Maybe we ought to go someplace else."

"Calm yourself, Johnny. Trust me."

Sam put the car in gear and drove through the small town, which looked to be in the same shape the gas station was in: darkened, shuttered storefronts, no streetlights, littered gutters, sidewalks cracked and overgrown with weeds. Even the town's lone traffic light was turned off.

"This place has seen better days," Sam said, as he slowed to a stop at an intersection. The stop sign listed at a forty-five degree angle, and was half obscured by a fallen tree limb.

"You've been away too long, man. Farming ain't what it used to be in these parts," said Johnny Gee. "I used to collect around these parts a year ago. No more. Ain't nobody around here got five dollars to bet on a football game this weekend . . . any other weekend for that matter."

Sam pulled into a dirt lot next to a crumbling building on the edge of town. If you weren't looking for it, you'd never find it. No sign. No neon, not even a beer logo in a window. In fact, no windows. The bar was a flat-roofed cinderblock bunker set back from the road about fifty feet. The only hint that the place was open for business was the presence of a couple of pickups and a late sixties Camaro with a jacked-up rear end and fat tires.

Inside, a row of naugahyde booths lined one wall. A juke box was playing Loretta Lynn's "Don't Come Home A-drinkin' With Lovin' On Your Mind," a piece of advice being actively ignored by the half-dozen men standing at the bar and gathered around the lone pool table in the center of the room.

The bartender was a man in his fifties who looked as if he were missing one tooth for every year he'd been pouring drinks. He smiled, exposing a wide expanse of gum. He'd been pouring for quite a while.

"What'll ya have?" he asked.

Johnny Gee leaned close to Sam's ear.

"You got any money?" he asked.

"Yeah."

"Lend me a quick five," said Johnny Gee, his eyes sparkling. He looked like a man who had been on the road a long time and had finally walked in his own front door and was home.

"In addition to everything else, you're broke?" Sam asked incredulously.

"Shh," hissed Johnny Gee between his teeth. "Just pony up the five. I know what I'm doin'."

Sam dug into his wallet and handed over a five. Johnny Gee slapped the bill on the bar and ordered two beers. The bartender fished two long-necked Buds out of a slide-top cooler and opened them. He removed the five and replaced it with three ones. Johnny Gee took a sip of beer, palmed one of the bills, and sauntered over to the pool table. He placed the bill on the end of the table and raised his beer in a mock toast.

"May the best man win this game, 'cause I've got the winner," he said with a smile.

"Has Dave Spicer been in?" Sam asked the bartender.

"Ain't seen him."

"Thanks."

Sam leaned against the bar. He took quick, nervous sips of beer. He was many miles from Fort Campbell and in more trouble than he cared to contemplate. And he was watching a stranger wearing a ludicrous shiny suit prepare to play pool with another stranger in a seedy bar on the edge of some godforsaken little burg. It came over him suddenly, a wave of lonesomeness and homesickness and fright. He felt dizzy and sat down on a bar stool. He looked down at his hand. He was holding the beer bottle so tightly, his knuckles were white. He took a last swig of beer, put the bottle down and looked around. At the end of the bar, there was a narrow hall leading to the restrooms. He could just barely make out a pay phone on the wall at the end of the hall in the darkness.

"What kinda rules you play by here . . . call the eight ball, bank the eight ball, what?" asked Johnny Gee. He was chalking a cue stick and taking a practiced look at the fresh rack of balls. He looked as if he had been standing there for twenty years. His opponent broke the rack and sank the five ball, then missed. Johnny Gee moved into position with a grace that surprised Sam. The cue stick seemed a natural extension of his arm, and he stroked the ball softly, like a caress. He sank two, and missed the fifteen. He stepped back from the table and lit a cigarette. His eyes were fixed on the table, unswerving. He kept up a fluid, witty patter, but nothing broke his concentration. Nothing.

Sam meandered across the room in the direction of the hallway. As he passed the pool table, Johnny Gee caught his eye.

"Put a buck on the table, take the next game, man," he said, chalking his cue stick.

"No thanks," said Sam. He kept walking.

"Where you goin'?" asked Johnny Gee.

"Bathroom," Sam replied, turning his head. "You go ahead and play. I'll be back in a minute."

Sam reached the pay phone and dropped a quarter. He dialed zero and a phone number. The operator came on the line. "Collect from Sam Butterfield," he said, turning his back to the room. It was dark at the end of the hall, but he could see that the wall had been used as a makeshift phone book over the years. It was covered with numbers. Over the phone, in large magic marker letters, was written, "Frankie: call your wife." Next to it: "I did. Last Wednesday."

His mother answered: "Yes, of course I'll accept the charges."

"It's me, Ma."

"Where are you, Sam? Are you in Fort Campbell yet?" His mother's voice came over the line like a soothing, reassuring balm, wiping away the homesickness and fear he had felt just a moment ago.

"I'm not at Campbell yet," Sam said. "In fact, I'm not sure where I am."

"What do you mean by that, Sam?"

"Well, I'm in a little town down in Harris County, right near one of the tracks where I used to race. But I don't know what the name of it is."

"How did you get way down there?"

"I don't know where to start . . . at the diner, or when we blew the tire," said Sam.

"Start at the beginning and take your time, Sam," said his mother. And he did. He told her everything, from the fight in the alley to the wreck on the highway to the tapes. When he was finished, he heard her take a deep breath before she spoke.

"Where did you say you were again?"

"Jerome," he said. "I remember the name now. There's a dirt track not far from here. I ran in couple of races years ago."

"What do you think is going to happen, Sam?"

"I don't know. I'll have to call you again when it's over."

"Please, be careful, won't you?"

"You bet, Ma."

Sam hung up the phone and walked back into the bar. Hearing his mother's voice made him feel better. Somebody new was racking the balls, and Johnny Gee was chalking his stick. The same guys were hunched over the bar. A black-and-white movie flickered on the TV hanging from a set of tire chains screwed into the ceiling.

"Hey, man. You got another buck? Buy me another beer, will ya? I'm on a roll here." Johnny Gee flashed him a wide grin and a wink. His ridiculous shiny suit made a certain kind of sense in the light of the pool table. It made him look trim, and efficient, stripped clean of extraneous detail, ready to do only one thing: stroke a pool cue. The skinny arms of the suit extended into the stick through the grip of his long, slender fingers. If he were a machine, Sam thought, Johnny Gee would be a racing bike, all spindly and bristling with gears and spokes and neat, tight little molded-in welds. Narrow and fast. That's what he was, standing with a pool cue at the table in the dimness. Narrow and fast.

Sam ordered two more beers and leaned against the bar. Johnny Gee broke the rack with one quick jab of the cue. The balls scattered randomly from one end of the table to the other. Two balls went down.

"I'll take lows," said Johnny Gee, placing his cigarette on the edge of the table. He took aim at one of the solid-colored balls and shot. The ball hit the side cushion and banked into a corner pocket. He walked around the table, studying the lay of the balls, although this wasn't particularly necessary. He was lined up to shoot another ball in the side pocket and from there, to roll a third ball down the side rail into the corner. He did this. The man he was playing looked dejected. Johnny Gee missed his next shot, a long one into the corner at the opposite end of the table. He sipped his beer and chalked his cue absentmindedly. The other man made two easy shots and missed. Somebody on the television late movie said, "I wonder . . ." A phone rang.

"Anybody here called Butterfield?" the bartender yelled.

"Yeah, me," said Sam.

"For you."

"What are you doing in town, kid?" said a voice.

"Spicer? Is that you?"

"None other. Been a while. What you been doing with yourself?"

"I'm in a spot of trouble, Spicer, and I wonder . . ."

"Stay where you are, kid. I'll be there in five."

"I'll wait for you in the parking lot, Spicer. I'm driving a Caddy."

"I'll find you." The phone went dead.

Sam handed the phone to the bartender and leaned heavily against the bar.

"I'll have another beer, please," he half-whispered. He was surprised at how tired he was. The bartender delivered the beer and Sam pushed a couple of dollars across the bar.

"You know Spicer, huh?" asked the bartender.

"How'd . . . how'd you know?" Sam stammered.

"Ain't a big town, man. He calls here once, twice a day."

"Of course."

"I said, you know Spicer, huh?"

"We used to race together at the fairgrounds."

"Musta been a while ago. Spicer ain't raced in, I don't know how long."

"Back in the seventies," said Sam, pulling hard on his beer.

"Hey! I remember you! You're that kid from upstate. Yeah, I remember now. You won a few down here, didn't you?"

"A few."

"Old Spicer, he was a demon behind the wheel, hisself, as I recall."

"He beat me about as many times as I beat him. He was something." Sam finished his beer. He felt a hand on his shoulder.

"Hey, man, what was that call all about?" It was Johnny Gee.

"Come on. We've got to go," said Sam. He turned around and brushed past Johnny Gee and pushed open the door at the end of the hallway. It opened onto the parking lot. Johnny Gee followed him.

"Where you goin'? What was that call all about, man?"

"Just come on," said Sam.

The door closed behind them with a soft *whoosh.* Sam climbed into the front seat of the Caddy and rested his head on the steering wheel. Somehow, there had to be a way. . . .

THE CADILLAC STARTED on the first crank. Sam sat behind the wheel staring at the cinderblock wall of the bar.

"You got to tell me what's goin' on, man," said Johnny
Gee.

"Spicer's coming here to meet us," said Sam. "Sit tight."

"Pull out and take the first right, Butter," said a voice
from the back seat. Sam's head jerked around, coming face
to face with the smiling countenance of his friend Spicer.

"Spicer. You scared the shit out of me. How'd you find
us?"

"You said you was in a Caddy, Butter, and this one's the
only Caddy in the lot. Besides, I seen you guys comin' out
the back of the bar, I just jumped in."

"What is this 'Butter' shit?" asked Johnny Gee.

"That's what they used to call me around the dirt tracks," said Sam.

"So tell me about the back window here. I've seen 'em lookin' better."

"In a minute. Where are we going, Spicer?"

"Take this turn. Stay goin' straight down this road for about ten miles, and you'll see a big white farmhouse on your right. Take the drive next to it."

"Where are you taking us?" Sam stole a glance at his friend Spicer. He was wearing an orange International Harvester cap and a plaid-lined blue jean jacket. His face was red and weathered from years of working outdoors. The smile on his face revealed several missing teeth.

"My place," said Spicer. "You got any ideas about fixin' that front end, you may as well forget 'em. Once a Caddy's front end is as far gone as this one, there's no hope."

"I guess you're right about the front end, Spicer," said Sam.

"You seen we got a couple of problems," said Johnny Gee.

"Victor said . . ."

"Who's Victor?"

"Guy you talked to back at the station. He's uh, what you might call my executive assistant." A deep smoker's cough gurgled up from inside Spicer's throat, trailing off in a laugh.

"I still love to say ridiculous shit and laugh myself sick, huh, Butter? You remember how we used to sit around between heats down at the track cracking weak jokes and laughin' our heads off?"

"Yeah. We had some good times, Spicer."

"And we drove some good races, huh, Butter?"

"You ought to know, Spicer. You watched me drive from just off my rear bumper enough."

"Shit."

"Speaking of shit, we're about neck deep in some," said Johnny Gee, interrupting.

"Yeah, I figured you wasn't down here on no social visit," said Spicer. "Old Victor said he heard some shit on the scanner about you guys a few minutes ago. That's why I got him to take me over to the bar, lookin' for you. I figured you'd want to know you was featured as tonight's entertainment on the police bands."

"Scanner?" Sam took his foot off the gas as the front end began to shimmy.

"Police band radio scanner. One of the little things with the blinkin' red lights, picks up all the local cop talk. We got one in the station. Handy little fucker."

"What'd he hear?" asked Johnny Gee.

"Just a description of two white males driving a Caddy that fits this description. I figured it had to be you, from what Victor told me."

"An' this went out over all the police radios around here?" Johnny Gee stuck a cigarette in his mouth and asked for a light. Spicer lit a match. Johnny Gee took a long drag and thanked him.

"That description of you two went out over the sheriff's radio, but all the local law around here monitors each other's frequencies, so they all got it by now."

"What kinda other trouble you got, 'sides the front end and the rear end and the holes in the doors? You got some wonderful alignment there, Butter. This thing feels like it's runnin' on three wheels. So who popped the back window for you?"

Sam took a deep breath and launched into a recitation of everything that had happened since the parking lot at the diner. When he was finished, he stole a quick glance at Spicer, and just as fast, wished he hadn't.

The man in the back seat started coughing and laughing, coughing and laughing, finally sticking his head out the window to get his wind back.

"What's so damn funny?" asked Johnny Gee when the red-faced man returned to normal.

"You're gonna love the operation I got out at the farm, Butter," he said. "When that old station of mine stopped payin' its way, and when the dirt tracks closed, I looked around for somethin' that would get me by, and I found it. Lord almighty, I found it."

"What are you up to, Spicer?" asked Sam.

"Well, the economy done passed up the boonies out here, I guess you seen," said Spicer. "Things are different since you was around, kid. No racing to speak of, 'less you're willin' to travel over to Terre Haute, maybe further, and I'm getting too sore in the joints for that. So first the tracks closed, and then the interstate went through, and they put a mess of them self-serve stations out on the interchange, and I pretty much went bust. I had to come up with somethin' pretty quick, so I looked around for a while, and I come up with somethin' all right. You're gonna love it."

"I'm going to love what?"

"Just wait till you see," he said, starting to laugh again.

"Funny guy," said Johnny Gee with a shrug.

"Is this the farmhouse you were talking about?" asked Sam, pointing to a large white Victorian surrounded by a grove of oaks and tall pines.

"That's it. There's your turn."

Sam pointed the big Caddy down a dirt road not much wider than the car. The front bumper scraped underbrush and crashed through a ridge of tall grass growing down the middle of the road.

"This ain't a road, it's a path," said Johnny Gee. "Where you takin' us?"

" 'Nother coupla miles. Where we're goin' is, uh, off the beaten track, you might say." Spicer collapsed into another gale of laughs and coughs.

"You're not makin' book, and you couldn't grow marijuana if you wanted to," said Johnny Gee. "What you got back here? The most far-out whorehouse in the state?"

Spicer stopped laughing long enough to point across a small field. A beat-up trailer could be seen against the trees at the edge of the field, and next to it sat the biggest satellite dish Johnny Gee had ever seen.

"What the hell . . ."

"You heard of home video rentals?" asked Spicer, directing the question at Johnny Gee. He pointed to a spot next to the trailer, and Sam eased the Caddy to a halt. The three men got out of the car and walked over to the dish, which stood ten feet over their heads.

"We're kinda supplementin' the market back here in the woods. Undercuttin' the competition, you might say."

"That's some dish," said Johnny Gee.

"That's forty-two grand worth of some dish," said Spicer. "And you said somethin' about gettin' a look at them tapes you found?" Spicer unlocked the door to the trailer and opened it. He flipped on the light switch. Industrial shelving covered every wall of the trailer, even the windows, and more shelving stuck into the room like stacks in a library. Every inch of the shelving was taken up with racks of video recorders. Boxes of blank tapes lined the hall to the rear of the trailer.

"I'm a big fan of HBO," said Spicer, breaking into another spasm of laughter.

"You're bootlegging videos right off the dish outside," said Johnny Gee. "That's some clever shit, man."

"We can make two hundred tapes at a time," said Spicer with a sweep of his hand. "All you got to do is load them up, punch the buttons, and throw this switch over here when the movie starts to run." He pointed to a master console at the end of the trailer. Next to it, a state-of-the-art Sony monitor sat on a pedestal between two stereo speakers.

"When I seen them video stores sproutin' around here like weeds, I seen my chance. I told you I found somethin' that would pay the bills. It's clean, it's easy, there's an ever-growin' market, and there's a steady flow of product. They just keep showin' them movies on HBO and Cinemax and Showtime, and we just keep tapin' 'em. Hollywood sells their videos for thirty, forty, hell, seventy dollars. We sell ours for nine ninety-five. All you got to do is push buttons and unwrap tapes. Damnedest thing you ever saw. A fuckin' torrent of money. More'n I ever won at the dirt tracks, that's for damn sure."

"Where did you get all this stuff, Spicer?" asked Sam, taking a seat at the console.

"I had me some phony business cards printed up and flew out to one of them electronics industry conventions in Las Vegas. I hung around there for a couple days, finally made a deal with a guy outa L.A. for these recorders. He had a warehouse full of 'em, models from a coupla years ago, no infrared remote, nonprogrammable. All they do is record and play back. Perfect. That's all I need 'em for anyway. I got the dish from some company near Salt Lake City that was goin' outa business, picked it up for less than half of what it was worth, and they trucked it out here and set it up. I've had this piece of land since the fifties. Never did anything with it, too hilly to farm, even if it was cleared, which it isn't. So I just dragged this old trailer out here and set things up. Victor's the one knew how to do everything, all the wirin' and stuff. He did a nickel 'bout twelve years ago on a larceny beef. They knocked over a good-size savings and loan, and Victor was the one canceled the alarm. He specialized in debugging alarms for years, finally got busted, did his time, and went straight. He was working for me down at the station on automobile electrical systems. A fuckin' wizard, that guy."

"You could have used him when you were driving modifieds, Spicer," Sam said.

"You couldn't be more right about that, Butter. Guys like Victor don't come down the pike every day. Quiet. Don't drink. Keeps to himself. Loves the tube. This setup is perfect for him. All it takes is the two of us. That way I ain't got five guys runnin' around Saturday nights gettin' drunk blabbin' to bimbos about all the free videotaped movies they can get. Keep things small and keep 'em simple is what I always say."

"Hey, man," said Johnny Gee. "I'm gonna run out to the car and get them tapes. Let's have us another look." When he returned with the tapes, he handed them to Spicer and sat on an old wooden milk crate in the corner. Spicer walked into a room at the back of the trailer and returned with a six-pack of cold beer and handed them around.

"This is the one we already looked at?" asked Johnny

Gee, indicating a tape with RAMADA INN typed on the label alongside a list of dates.

Sam examined the tape and nodded his head, yes. He felt like he was at the bottom of a well standing waist deep in mud and looking up. The only way he was going to get out was by understanding what had put him down there to begin with. He cracked open his beer and took a swig. Nothing had ever tasted better. Be thankful for the little things. He remembered that from Ranger school. He was on patrol one night and had come to the edge of the woods, and there before him was a neon sign that read U-NEEDA-REST BAR. Indeed they did. The ten guys on the patrol pitched in and bought four cases of beer and forty cheeseburgers and stumbled under the load back into the woods where they promptly sat down on a couple of logs and finished the entire mess in under an hour, resuming the patrol considerably refreshed and thankful for the little things in life.

"Which one of these tapes should we see first, Major?" asked Johnny Gee.

"What's on the other labels?"

Johnny Gee opened the boxes examined each tape in turn.

"You got the one that says 'Ramada Inn.' This one says 'Mobile Van.' This one says 'Sheraton Springfield.' This one here just says 'The Company' on it, and this one says . . . Jesus! 'Corrine's'!"

"That's the whorehouse up in Springfield, isn't it?" asked Spicer.

"You damn right it is. Let's take a look at it first."

"No." Sam sounded more sure of himself than he was. "I want to know what's going on. Let's watch the one that says 'Mobile Van.' Maybe we'll learn something we don't know."

Johnny Gee puffed his cigarette. He handed the "Mobile Van" tape to Spicer.

Spicer stuck the tape in a machine mounted above the console, pressed a couple of buttons on the console, flipped on the Sony, and sat down in a wicker rocker. The screen flickered on, gray and white like snow, then went black. Again time and date signature appeared in the lower left corner of the screen. August 3, 10 A.M. A man's face appeared.

"Saturday, three August. Rock County, Route Seven," he said.

The camera cut away from the face and pointed out a windshield of a van. A black limousine pulled away from the curb several car-lengths ahead of the van.

"It's a rental limo. See the plate?" Johnny Gee pointed at the license plate.

Spicer chuckled and said, "Wonder who's in that fucker."

The screen went blank for an instant, then the picture returned, this time showing the limo at a greater distance down a two-lane road.

"You recognize anything?" asked Johnny Gee.

"The voice on the tape said Rock County. I haven't spent much time over in Rock County. That could have been any one of a dozen towns there. I don't know which one," said Sam.

"Kinda reminded me of Wilson, but I'm not sure either. You recognized it, Spicer?"

"I raced at the Rock County speedway a couple of times. It's just outside of Wilson, between there and Florence. I'm not sure. Could be Wilson. Didn't the voice say Route Seven?"

"Yeah, he did," said Johnny Gee.

"Wilson's right on Seven. I wonder what they're doing out there."

The screen goes blank again then the picture returned, the limo is in wild terrain, and no farms can be seen.

"Looks like that state forest down there, to me," said Johnny Gee. "Wait a minute. The limo's turning."

The limousine turns off on a side road. The camera jiggles, and the screen goes blank again. When the picture returns, the camera is pointing down a brush-covered hill, a long lens apparently having been attached to the camera. The limousine is in view, at the bottom of the hill on a dirt road, a good distance away from the camera.

"Where they at?" asked Johnny Gee, studying the picture.

"Shh." Sam pointed at the screen.

The limo's doors open. Several men get out. One man is carrying a long cardboard tube. He opens the tube and withdraws a large sheet of paper and spreads it across the hood of the limo. Another man helps him hold the corners of the sheet down. The other men gather around the limo's hood.

"What in hell is that?" Johnny Gee asked.

"Looks like a blueprint," said Sam.

"You recognize anybody?" asked Johnny Gee.

"They've got their backs to us. I couldn't make out any faces." Sam leaned forward as the camera zoomed closer.

"It's a blueprint," Sam said. "I can see it now. That guy on the other side of the hood in the suit, he was the driver. I think he's just a chauffeur."

"One of 'em is pointin' across that field," said Johnny Gee.

The camera pans. The field has been staked by surveyors, and the stakes are tied together with plastic ribbon.

"You make any sense of that shift?" asked Johnny Gee.

"They're gonna build something out there, and whatever it is, it is gonna be big." Spicer drew on his cigar and coughed softly.

The camera pulls back, revealing the entire field. One set of stakes runs in a straight line over a small hill, disappearing in the distance. Another set runs at a right angle along the dirt road for a quarter mile, following the road into a woodline.

The camera zooms back on the men at the limousine. One man is doing most of the talking. He is wearing khaki trousers and a khaki shirt. The other men are wearing suits. The camera stays on the men at the limousine for a few minutes, then the screen goes blank.

When the picture returns, the man in khaki is rolling up the blueprint and shoving it back into the tube. The men in suits are walking across the field along one of the staked-out plastic ribbons. The chauffeur is leaning against the limousine, talking with the man in khaki.

The camera pulls back to take in the whole scene. The men in suits are standing in the middle of the field talking and pointing. One of the men, a fat man who looks like he weighs at least three hundred pounds, takes a cigar out of his pocket and lights up. He steps away from the other three men. They talk among themselves for a few minutes, then walk over to the fat man. There is some talk among them, then one of the men shakes hands with the fat man first, and with the others. The four men start walking back toward the limousine. The camera zooms in on the four.

"I seen the fat one before," said Spicer.

"You've seen him?" asked Sam. "Where? When?"

"Yeah. I seen him. Long time ago. Can't exactly recall where."

"Do you know who he is?"

"Can't rightly recall. All I know is, I seen him once."

"What in hell are these guys doing in a field in Rock County?" asked Sam. "And why is somebody shooting the whole scene on videotape? I can't figure it."

"Me neither," said Johnny Gee.

Everyone turned back to the Sony.

The four men are dilly-dallying in the field, taking their time walking back to the limousine. They've conducted some kind of business. Something is going to be built on the field. But what? And who are they?

The camera zooms in as they near the limousine.

"Do you recognize any of 'em?" asked Johnny Gee.

"I only seen the fat one. Rest of 'em mean nothin' to me."

The men are getting into the limousine when the screen goes blank again. The picture returns with a view of the limousine on the two-lane road, shot from the hillside.

"Hit the fast forward. I want to see where they're going," said Sam.

Spicer hit a button, and the screen flickered crazily. There was a whirring noise as the machine raced ahead.

"Stop the tape. Let's have a look," Sam said.

"Pussy next," said Johnny Gee. "I wanna see who's doin' what to who at Corrine's."

"I want to see what else is on this tape, first." Sam shot Johnny Gee a look.

"Okay, but pussy next," said Johnny Gee, grinning. "You got to play fair."

Spicer hit the stop button, then hit the one marked play. They turned to watch the Sony.

The screen flickered and went white. Time and date signature, lower left corner. August 5, 7 A.M.

White. Still white. Then the camera pulls back to reveal the white side of a garbage truck. The truck is idling on a street next to a chain-link fence, waiting to turn right through a gate into a huge lot next to some kind of industrial complex. A low, flat-roofed, dark-colored building seems to go on forever, running off the left edge of the screen. A hydraulic crank arm opens the gate, and the white garbage truck turns into the lot. The truck has commercial plates.

The chain-link gates close, and the camera moves down the street, pans the side of the industrial building. No windows. No doors. Just aluminum siding.

"Place looks like a giant dumpster," said Johnny Gee, taking a drag on his cigarette. "I've seen jails that looked better."

A door appears at the left of the screen. The camera begins to zoom in on the door.

"Eeeeeep-eeeeep-eeeeep-eeeeep!" A loud buzzer sounded as the Sony's screen went blank.

"What in hell is going on, Spicer?" yelled Sam. "That sounds like a damn fire alarm."

"That's my automated recordin' system," said Spicer. "Means a movie is comin' on. Give it a minute. There it is."

The familiar logo for HBO flickered on the screen and began its video special effects swirling dance. The sound came up. Synthesizer music.

"Lemme check the schedule. Yeah. Here it is," said Spicer, bent over the HBO schedule.

Behind them two hundred video recorders whirred and began taping.

"What's the movie, Spicer?"

"It's that Elmore Leonard thing, ah, *Stick* with Burt Reynolds. I ain't taped it yet, so I had this thing set on automatic to pick it up at ten-thirty. I heard today the thing ain't movin' so hot at the stores. I think I'll cut my losses right here and now."

Spicer got up and moved to the console. He punched a couple of buttons and the whirring noise of the video recorders closest to them ended.

"What did you do?"

"I just canceled half the machines. I was gonna make two hundred copies. Now we'll just have a hundred to sell. Don't make no difference anyhow. They don't move, we'll just tape another movie over this one and put new labels on the fuckers. What a business, huh? What'd I tell you?"

"Can you start our tape again and put it back on the Sony? Or do we have to watch *Stick*?" asked Sam.

"Easy." Spicer punched a button, and the Sony went blank. He punched another, and the VCR on the console kicked into gear and the olive drab industrial building reappeared on the screen.

"Door's got somethin' written on it," said Johnny Gee.

"Can't read it," said Spicer.

"I can't either," said Sam. "Stop the tape."

"Wait a minute. Somethin' else is comin' on." Johnny Gee nodded at the Sony, as the screen flickered, went white, then gray, then blank.

TIME SIGNATURE. AUGUST 7, 8:27 P.M. Out of focus, focusing, focusing.

Building appears. Big building. Nighttime. Lots of lights. Semicircular drive. Cabs waiting. Spotlit shrubs. Airport limo. Camera pulls back. Tall building, with balconies. Lots of balconies. Lots of rooms. Lots of lights.

"It's a hotel," Johnny Gee said, taking a swig of beer. "Downtown Sheraton, up in Springfield. See the sign in front?"

"Looks like any one of them shitholes to me," said Spicer, choking on his words, coughing and laughing, coughing and laughing. "Know what I call them big fancy hotels? Buck-pluckers. That's all they do to ya. Pluck bucks from your wallet. And what for? A fuckin' yard for a bed and a bath? Who are they kiddin'?" Spicer dissolved into spasms of coughing, his cap falling over his face.

"They put a chocolate on your pillow at night, Spicer. That shit costs money." Johnny Gee poked Spicer. "Kinda dough you're makin' with this scam, you gonna be able to afford a damn hotel suite, man."

"Not this little red rooster," said Spicer. "I get up too early in the mornin' to be fooled by that shit."

"You know what a suite is, Spicer? Huh?"

"No. I'll play dumb. You tell me."

"A bed and a bath and a pussy. That's why they call it sweet."

Spicer doubled over laughing. "Your friend, Butter. I'm startin' to like him. You got to get yourself in deep shit, you could do worse for company."

"Come on, you guys. Something is happening," Sam interrupted. They watched the Sony.

A black limousine is pulling up the drive to the hotel. A stretched Checker cab moves out of the way. The hotel doorman opens the limousine's rear door. A short man in a gray suit steps out and says something to the doorman. The doorman moves to the side. Then a tall man steps out of the limousine. He is wearing a tan suit, and he pauses to straighten his lapels and brush something from his sleeve.

Camera zooms in on the scene at the hotel door. The man's hair shines in the lights from the awning overhead. The man leans in the door of the limousine, saying something to the driver. He stands up and straightens his suit again. Then he walks into the hotel.

The screen goes blank, flickering gray-black, gray-black. Then it lights up; hotel, drive, lights, shrubs, doorman.

"How'd you like to have that job," said Spicer.

"What job?" asked Johnny Gee.

"Doorman. Standin' around all day, all night in a fuckin' monkey suit, openin' doors, tippin' your hat, takin' fifty cents here, a skinny buck there. Now, there's some real dignity in that gig, for sure. Can you feature that?"

"Probably clears more than the major here. How much you make, man?"

"Knock off the bullshit, will you?"

"Doorman's probably union, probably makes as much as you do. How's that make you feel?"

"I don't care one way or the other."

"Listen to this shit. Our major here ain't makin' as much as a fuckin' doorman, and he don't care one way or the other. Man could get sent to fuckin' Nicaragua tomorrow, and he don't give a shit that he's gettin' paid like the help at the Downtown Sheraton."

"He's probably makin' more than the poor dudes in the van," said Spicer. "How'd you like that job, sittin' all fuckin' day in a hot fuckin' van, lookin' through a little video lens, can't even get out and stretch your fuckin' legs. Whatdaya figure? They pee in their coke cans?" Spicer doubled over coughing and laughing, coughing and laughing.

When he recovered, he said: "We're just joshin' you, Butter. I got great respect for those in the nation's service. We both do. Isn't that right?"

"Yeah. We ain't serious. I can't remember the last time I was serious."

"Shut up. The camera's zooming in on something," Sam said. His eyes had been glued to the screen the whole time.

"What do we got here?" asked Johnny Gee. "I don't see nothin'."

"Another car. See it?"

"That one? On the right?"

"That's the one. See? They're focusing on the license."

"They sure as hell are."

The car pulls to a stop at the door, and a slight, balding man gets out. He hands a dollar to the parking attendant and watches as the attendant drives off.

"See him?" asked Johnny Gee.

The camera zooms closer.

"Recognize the fucker?"

"I'm not sure . . ." said Sam.

"He was in the field lookin' at all them stakes and shit. The bald guy."

"Oh, I've got him now."

"What time does it say on the screen?" Johnny Gee squinted and shook his head.

"Nine-oh-three P.M."

"Same day?"

"Same day. August seven."

The screen goes blank again.

The picture reappears: same scene, front of the Sheraton. The bald man is waiting for his car to be driven around. He gets in it and drives off. Time signature: August 7, 11:45 P.M. Screen goes blank.

Hotel appears again, in daylight, revealing the departure of the man with the shiny hair. Time signature: August 8, 9:32 A.M.

"Those poor fuckers in the van sat out there in front of that palace all night waitin'. What a gig." Johnny Gee stubbed his cigarette out in a wagon wheel ashtray and shook his head. "They're just plain torchin' taxpayers' dollars on this thing, that's for sure."

"We don't even know that these are police tapes," said Sam.

"They ain't cop tapes, whose are they?" asked Johnny Gee.

"They could be industrial espionage. I read an article once that said big companies do it all the time."

"Do what?"

"Spy on each other."

"Lemme check the picture quality on my movie," said Spicer, punching a button on the console. The VCR stopped, the screen went dark, then a bright color picture appeared. Burt Reynolds was walking across the lawn of a big estate somewhere in southern Florida. A beautiful blue bay was in the background. Burt was striding purposefully toward the camera. A girl appeared. Burt strode purposefully in the direction of the girl.

"I think we have seen enough of Burt," said Sam.

Spicer punched the button, the screen went dark, then popped up gray-black again.

"What the hell's going on now?" hissed Johnny Gee, cigarette between his teeth. He was pointing at the Sony.

New time signature: August 10, 11:42 A.M.

A limousine is turning a corner about a stop light away from the surveillance van. The van takes the corner, following the limousine at a respectful distance. The limousine is heading into an industrial area along a river somewhere. The roadsides are littered with wood and metal scraps that have fallen from truck beds. Most of the buildings along the road are brick with rows of skylights like pup tents along their roofs. They come from an era when industries groaned and clanked and whistled, but now the riverside buildings are silent, and most of them appear long closed, their facades wounded by broken windows and cracked and faded corporate name signs, weeds poking through cracks in their parking lots, gates unlocked, fences broken. The limousine rushes past the brick buildings heading for a cluster of cylindrical oil tanks at the end of a road at the edge of a river.

The oil tanks are surrounded by low berms of compacted earth, and the limousine can be seen making its way around the first tank and the second, then it disappears. The van pulls up outside the gate to the tank complex. No corporate name sign.

The screen goes blank.

Picture back: A telephoto lens shows the back of the limousine and the door to a double-wide in the background of the shot. A sign next to the door reads HARDHAT AREA.

"What do you figure that place is?" asked Johnny Gee. "Some kind of oil refinery?"

"Those are storage tanks," said Sam. "There isn't any refining equipment there."

The door to the double-wide opens, and out steps a short man in a gray suit, followed by a man wearing a windbreaker and a hardhat. Then a tall man appears, blinking in the sun.

"Hey! That's Frankie, from the other tape!" said Johnny Gee. "You remember. The big guy makin' the payoff in the Ramada."

"Who's the other guy . . . the one in the suit?" asked Sam.

"Isn't he one of the guys at the hotel?"

"I think you're right. The little guy, who got out of the limo first."

"That's the one. The other fucker looks like he works there."

The three men stand talking at the side of the limousine for a few minutes, then the short man in the gray suit and the tall man called Frankie get in the limousine and drive off. The man in the hardhat walks over to a pickup truck, starts it up, and drives off. The camera swings back to the door of the double-wide. There are no other signs of life at the tank complex. The screen goes blank.

"What do you think that was all about?" asked Sam.

"Guy's touring the waterfront, lookin' for a location for his new restaurant," said Spicer, coughing and laughing.

"I'm serious."

"Who knows?" said Johnny Gee.

"Whatever they were doing, it had something to do with that field down in Rock County. The bald guy was in the field, and he was at the hotel. Now this guy was at the hotel, and he's standing around with Frankie from the Ramada. It's all connected somehow."

"Let's put on another tape. Here. Corrine's cathouse next," said Johnny Gee, handing the tape to Spicer. "I been hearin' about that place for years. I heard once they got girls from seven different countries there. Guy told me they spend a grand a week on fuckin' underwear. Whew."

"No. I want to see the one that says Sheraton," said Sam, flipping through the videos. He pulled out the Sheraton tape and gave it to Spicer, taking the one marked Corrine's from Johnny Gee.

Spicer popped the Mobile Van tape out of the VCR and slipped the Sheraton tape in its place. He punched play.

The screen comes up gray, flickers, then the interior of a hotel room appears on the screen in black and white, shot through a wide angle lens. Time signature: August 7, 8:15 P.M. The minutes begin to tick off. 8:16. 8:17. 8:18.

The room looks like an ordinary living room. No bed. Kitchenette counter in the foreground. Dinette table and chairs. Sofa along left wall. Coffee table. Three bucket chairs. Lamps atop tables at either end of the sofa. Hanging lamp over dinette set. No signs of human occupation.

"Looks like one of them suites," said Spicer, doubling over laughing and coughing. "How much you figure they get for one of them suites?"

"I don't know. A hundred. Hundred and twenty? It's the Sheraton, man. You pay for the name," said Johnny Gee.

Sound of door opening, closing. Sound of refrigerator opening in kitchenette, out of view of camera. Refrigerator closing. Water running in sink. Water off.

Sound of door opening again. Man's voice, authoritative:

"Step out in the middle of the room and say something, so we can get a sound level, Stillman."

Another man's voice: "Can I get a beer?"

First man:

"In a minute. Sit down on the sofa and say something. We've got to get our levels set."

Second man:

"What do you want me to say?

First man:

"Recite the alphabet. I don't care."

Sound of door closing.

Frankie appears on camera, at the lower left edge of the screen. He turns and looks up at the camera.

"It's Frankie!" said Sam. "He's got his hair slicked back, and he's wearing a suit, but it's him."

"What's he doing?" asked Johnny Gee.

Frankie Stillman walks over to the sofa and sits down. Starts reciting the alphabet. Gets to the letter O and says:

"That enough? You guys got enough?"

Sound of door opening.

Man's voice:

"That's fine, Frankie. Now keep your shit together until the others get here. One beer. I told you. You've got to be straight for this."

Stillman looks in the direction of the voice:

"One beer?"

"Looks like Frankie ain't none too happy," said Johnny Gee.

The man called Frankie Stillman is sitting on the sofa, beer in hand, staring at the wall on the other side of the room. He takes a swig of beer. He stares. Another swig. More staring. Time signature: 8:30 P.M. Phone rings. Man called Frankie Stillman picks up the phone.

"Yeah? So? What are you giving me this problem for? Solve it yourself." He hangs up.

Silence. Listening. Foot tapping edge of coffee table. Sits down. Takes swig of beer.

Sound of knock at the door. Man called Frankie Stillman stands up, walks off camera to the door.

Sound of Frankie Stillman's voice:

"Jimmy. C'mon in. Been expecting you. Want something to drink?"

Sound of another man's voice:

"What are you having?"

Sound of Stillman's voice:

"Beer. We've also got Scotch, bourbon, you name it. What'll it be?"

Other man:

"Bourbon will be fine."

Stillman:

"On the rocks with a splash?"

Other man:

"That will hit the spot."

Sound of refrigerator opening, ice hitting glass, liquid pouring, faucet on and off.

Frankie Stillman appears on camera, sits down on the sofa, same spot. He is followed by the man with shiny hair, bourbon on the rocks in his hand. He takes a seat in one of the bucket chairs, and begins to swivel the chair back and forth, left and right.

Johnny Gee stood up and stretched.

"Stop the tape for a minute, will you, Spicer? This is gettin' good, and I got to take a leak. Don't want to miss anything."

Spicer hit the stop button and sat down. Johnny Gee ambled into the back of the trailer toward the bathroom.

"I wish I had a better idea of what's going on," said Sam. He crushed his empty beer can and pitched it into the empty box.

"I know what you mean, Butter. You look at this shit one way, it's kinda funny. You look at it the other way, it's scary."

"What's scary?" Johnny Gee walked back into the trailer's control room and sat down.

"Butter and me was just talkin' about these tapes. It's kinda scary, not really knowin' what's goin' on." Spicer scooted his chair closer to the console. "Like, who's spyin' on who? Who's the big shot runnin' the show?"

"Who cares?"

"I care." Sam fixed Johnny Gee with a stare and didn't

move. "We've got to figure out who made these tapes, and why. Somebody tried to kill us for these tapes, and from everything we've seen so far, I'm as lost now as I was two hours ago."

"You got a point, man. Let's watch the rest of this stuff in the Sheraton. Every time old Spicer punches up a tape, we get a little closer, don't you think? To figuring out where we stand, I mean."

"Yeah."

"Go ahead, Spicer." Spicer hit the play button.

The room pops into view.

The man called Frankie Stillman and the man with the shiny hair are still sitting with their drinks.

"What time are the others coming?" asks the man with the shiny hair.

"They should be here any minute. What time is it?"

"A little after eight-thirty."

"The man's already here. He arrived this afternoon, took a room downstairs. He said he doesn't want to make the drive home tonight."

"Who are we waiting on?" The man with the shiny hair checks his watch again.

"The man's lawyer. Harvey Pugh. You met him last week."

Stillman gets up and walks over to the window, moves the curtains aside, and looks out.

"Yes, of course. Harvey Pugh. Interesting man. How long does he know our friend?"

"Years. The man and his father were partners, then Harvey's father died, and the man put him through college. They've been together ever since. Like father and son, you know?"

"You can trust him, then. Pugh, I mean." The man with the shiny hair checks his watch, takes a sip of his bourbon.

"Of course I do. You do business with the man, you do business with Harvey. Harvey handles everything for him. Even talks for him. They're like the same person." Stillman takes a swig of beer and sits down on the sofa again.

Phone rings. Stillman picks it up.

"Yeah?"

Stillman listening intently.

"Jimmy's already here. You all come on up."

Stillman listening.

"We'll be waiting for you."

Stillman hangs up the phone.

"That was Harvey. They're on the way up. They'll be here in a minute."

Room falls silent. Both men sip their drinks.

"Fascinatin' conversation, huh?" said Johnny Gee, pointing at the screen. Neither man moved a muscle. "Coupla real party animals. Frankie's just thrilled to be there. The other dude looks like he sat down on a sixteen-penny nail."

"Shh." Sam held his finger to his lips, still watching the screen.

Sound of knock at the door. Man called Frankie Stillman gets up to answer it.

Sound of Frankie's voice:

"Hey, you old buzzard. How are you doing? You're looking well."

Sound of another voice:

"Real good, Frankie, real good."

Sound of Frankie's voice:

"Harvey. Good to see you."

Sound of another voice:

"Same here, Frankie. How are things in Chicago?"

Sound of Frankie's voice:

"I can't complain."

Sound of Harvey Pugh's voice:

"That's good to hear. Seems to me I heard something about them empaneling a grand jury up there."

Sound of Frankie's voice:

"They're always gonna empanel a grand jury in Chicago. I stopped paying attention to that shit years ago."

Camera picks up the backs of two men entering the room.

"It's the fat dude!" said Johnny Gee. "He looks twice as big up close. Where you figure he gets them suits? You could pitch that suit in the woods and sleep under it."

Spicer yanked his cigar out of his mouth and started laughing.

"That's the guy I seen before. Sure is," said Spicer.

Harvey Pugh sits down in one of the bucket chairs. He's a short, slight man with a bald head and a freckled face and almost no chin.

"Dude looks like an accountant," said Spicer.

The fat man collapses on the sofa, breathing heavily.

Sound of Frankie's voice from the kitchenette:

"You gentlemen care for a beverage?"

"I'll have me a Coke," says the fat man.

"The same," says Harvey Pugh.

Frankie delivers the Cokes and sits down.

"The purpose of this little get together . . ." says Frankie.

"We know what the purpose of this meeting is," says Harvey Pugh. "That right?"

"That's right," says the fat man.

"We want to know how things went with O'Brien and Friedman the other night. That right?"

"That's right," says the fat man.

"Very well," says Frankie. "They were on time, and we were on time. And they left happy."

"And Friedman's going to pass along a taste to Jones and Walters and the other guy. What's his name? The chairman of the committee." Harvey Pugh consults some notes in his lap.

"To Jones and Walters. I'm meeting with the committee chairman myself. He's playing hard to get," says Frankie.

"We want to know when all the, uh, legislative transactions have been accomplished. That right?"

"That's right," says the fat man, taking a sip of Coke.

"Now, Jimmy," says Harvey Pugh, turning to the man with shiny hair. "Your people are happy with the site. Am I correct?"

"Very," says the man with the shiny hair. "We're prepared to go through with the closing as soon as the governor signs the bill."

"And we're not expecting any problems there," says Harvey Pugh. "That right?"

"That's right," says the fat man.

"The senate's scheduled to act on the bill right after Thanksgiving, and we should get some action from the house the week after that. And the governor's been very cooperative. That right?"

"That's right," says the fat man. He finishes his Coke.

"You want another?" asks Frankie Stillman.

The fat man nods his head. Frankie gets up and walks off camera in the direction of the kitchenette.

"What's with those two?" asked Sam, indicating the figures on the TV screen. "All that business . . . 'That right? That's right.' Over and over. I've never heard anything like it in my life."

"It's some weird shit, is what it is."

Frankie Stillman returns with the Cokes and sits down.

"How about your people?" asks Harvey Pugh, looking in the direction of Frankie Stillman.

"My people are rock solid," says Frankie. "We're prepared to take our share of the mortgage, if it means the kind of jobs we've been talking about."

"It will," says the man with shiny hair. "We expect to be doing business in a three-state area before the end of next year."

"Sounds good to us," says Harvey Pugh. "That right?"

"That's right."

"How about another drink, boys?" asks Frankie Stillman, standing up. "I think this calls for a little celebration."

"I'll have another Coke," says the fat man.

"Same here," says Harvey Pugh.

"Bourbon for me," says the man with shiny hair.

Frankie Stillman disappears from view into the kitchenette. Sounds of refrigerator door opening and closing, ice cubes hitting glasses, pouring liquid. Frankie returns with the drinks and passes them around.

"To the future," says Frankie, raising his glass.

"Hear hear," says the man with shiny hair.

Harvey Pugh stands up.

"My daddy always told me land was as good as money in the bank," says Harvey Pugh. "That right?"

"That's right."

"To money in the bank," says Harvey Pugh.

"That's right," says the fat man.

SPICER HIT THE VCR stop button.

"What do you make of that shit?" asked Johnny Gee.

"I think they were talking about that land with all the surveyor's marks we saw on the other tape," Sam said. "On the other tape, they visited the land. On this one, someone is selling it, and someone else is buying it, and I think the seller and the buyer were right in that room in the Sheraton."

"Which one is which?" Johnny Gee studied the glowing tip of his cigarette, flicked the ash into the wagon wheel.

"The fat man is selling, and the other guy is buying."

"After some law is passed in Springfield."

"And that's why they were payin' off those dudes in the Ramada Inn. They were buyin' votes."

"Right."

"This is gettin' downright interestin'," said Johnny Gee. "Let's take another look at that Ramada tape, see who else is gettin' paid off."

"How'd you like this shit?" asked Spicer. "Long as you all got these tapes, you got somebody's nuts caught in a vice, for sure."

"These tapes have a whole bunch of peoples' nuts in a vice," said Sam, a grin passing across his face. "Now I understand why they'd even be willing to kill for them. If these tapes get out, a whole lot of powerful people are going to take a very big fall."

"Yeah, but the fact that we got the tapes and not them has got *our* shit hanging in the proverbial sling, too," said Johnny Gee. "We got 'em and they want 'em, and from the looks of things, I'd say we ain't the only ones who got plenty to fuckin' worry about."

Sam put the tape marked "Ramada" on top of the console. Spicer popped the Sheraton tape from the VCR and slipped in the new tape. He punched play.

Blank screen. Then, Ramada Inn room.

Time signature: August 12, 7:49 P.M.

Sound of door opening, closing.

Man appears, camera shooting him from high on wall near door. Walks into room, looks around, walks over to window, pulls curtains aside, looks out.

"That's the same room in the Ramada as before," said Johnny Gee. "And there's our boy Frankie. He looks happy to be back."

Sound of door opening. Sound of man's voice:

"We've got to get a sound level, Frankie. Say something."

"Don't you guys have the equipment set up from before?" Frankie Stillman turns from the window toward the camera.

Sound of man's voice from door:

"We pulled our stuff out of here on the fifth, the day after the meeting with O'Brien and Friedman at the Sheraton. We didn't even know you were going to meet with this guy until yesterday."

"So sorry about th ," says Stillman. "You want me to say anything else?"

Sound of man's voice from door:

"That's okay. We've got our level. Where are you going to sit?"

"Same as before." Frankie Stillman indicates the table and chairs in the corner.

Sound of man's voice:

"What time is your boy due?"

"Eight-thirty. That's what he told me on the phone yesterday."

Sound of man's voice:

"Okay. Do it just like before. Here's the money."

Sound of something hitting the floor.

Frankie Stillman walks toward door, off camera.

Sound of door closing.

Frankie Stillman walks back into room carrying a black briefcase, puts it on the table. Switches on the TV, flips channels. Stops on "Wheel of Fortune." Lies down on the bed, hands behind head.

Screen goes blank.

"I wonder who he's meeting with this time?" asked Sam.

"They said something about payin' some dude when they were at the Sheraton shindig," said Johnny Gee.

"These guys must get tired of hotel rooms," said Spicer, blowing a big smoke ring. "That guy Stillman ought to be thinkin' about gettin' himself a nice scam where he can spend some time at home. Fuck all that runnin' around." Spicer grinned expansively, looking around at his trailer setup. He leaned his head back and blew another smoke ring.

Same scene pops up, time signature: August 12, 8:27 P.M.

Frankie Stillman is still on the bed. On the television, two cars are careening around corners at top volume.

Sound of knock on the door.

"Just a minute," says Stillman, getting to his feet. He switches off the television and walks off camera in the direction of the door.

Sound of door opening.

Sound of Frankie Stillman's voice:

"I've been expecting you, and you're right on time. C'mon in."

Sound of door closing.

Two men walk into view, one of them Stillman, who walks directly to the table and takes a chair.

"Have a seat," he says to the other man, indicating the chair across from him. "You have a long drive?"

"Couple of hours," says the other man, whose back is to the door, and whose face still isn't visible.

"I know this is inconvenient, but there's no sense in taking chances," says Stillman. "Around Springfield, things are so . . ."

"Public," says the other man.

"You got it. Public. Exactly." Stillman fingers his tie, looking everywhere but directly at the man across the table from him. "I'd offer you a drink," he says, "but I didn't get a chance to stop on my way here."

"That's okay. I've got to drive back tonight myself," says the other man. He's wearing a suit, and has a full head of dark hair, combed just over the ears and cut to the collar in the back.

Stillman reaches under the table and comes up with the briefcase and places it before him on the table.

"My understanding is that things are going well in Washington," says Stillman, looking right at the other man for the first time.

"They are," says the other man.

"In Springfield, too. I'm told the bill will be reported out of committee the first week after Thanksgiving."

"That's correct."

"That will come as good news to my people," says Stillman, patting the briefcase.

"I hope so," says the other man.

"What's in here will come as good news to the finance director of your election committee," says Stillman, smiling broadly now, patting the briefcase.

"I'm sure it will. Statewide campaigns have become, how should I put this, prohibitively expensive recently. Sometimes I wish we could pass a law against television advertising by political candidates, and return to the days of speeches at Kiwanis clubs and American Legion posts." The other man takes a deep breath. "Just wishful thinking, I guess."

"In the meantime, we need good people like you in government," says Frankie Stillman. "We can't let a little thing like money stand in the way of progress, can we?"

"That's what I've always said."

"I hear the polls look good. This time next year, you'll be in the governor's office, no problem."

Frankie Stillman shoves the briefcase across the table. The other man opens the briefcase. Stacks of cash held together with rubber bands fill it.

The other man snaps shut the briefcase, stands and extends his hand to Frankie Stillman. The two men shake. The other man turns to walk to the door.

Sam jumped to his feet, his eyes still fixed on the screen of the Sony. He shifted his weight from one foot to the other as he watched the man in the suit and Frankie Stillman walk off camera in the direction of the door. He heard the sound of the motel door open and shut, then he watched the man called Frankie Stillman walk back into the middle of the motel room, turn directly toward the camera lens, and say:

"You got enough on the Congressman, the two-faced little prick? Can we go home now?"

The screen went blank.

Sam kept staring at the blank screen.

"What's up, man?" asked Johnny Gee.

". . . I was raised to believe in guys like him. If you can't believe in a United States Congressman, who can you believe in?"

"Yourself." Johnny Gee said the word and looked away. He thought for a moment, then he said:

"You come into this world, all you got is your naked little body and your name. When you leave this world, that's all you are gonna take with you. You can't take your house or your car or your bank account. All you really got in the meantime is yourself. It ain't much, but it's enough, Major."

"That's a pretty bleak way of looking at things," Sam said, watching the other man.

"Most of the time, all you got to look at is pretty fuckin' bleak."

"You two philosophers want to watch any of the rest of this shit?" asked Spicer, pointing to the stack of surveillance tapes. In the background, the VCRs could be heard clicking off. The Burt Reynolds movie had ended.

"I still want to see the whorehouse tape," said Johnny Gee. "At least that tape will be funny. I wonder who they caught with their trousers down. C'mon, Spicer, put that fucker on the machine and let it roll."

Spicer picked up the tape marked Corrine's and slid it into the VCR. He punched play and sat back.

Blank screen, flickering, flickering. Time signature: Sept. 3, 10:15 P.M. Black and white.

Camera looking down on room from ceiling overhead through wide angle lens. Door to room at bottom of screen. A mahogany armoire to right of door. Another door next to armoire on right edge of screen, half open, showing sink in bathroom. Kingsize bed at top of screen, covered with a fur throw. Large mirror on wall along left edge of screen. Persian rug on floor. Armchair in corner. TV set at bottom of bed directly under camera lens, VCR on top of TV.

"Look at that shit," said Spicer. "They got the television set up to watch porno in that cathouse."

Minutes ticking by on time signature. 10:16. 10:17. 10:18.

Sound of voices outside the door, muffled. Sound of door opening.

Sound of woman's voice:

"You just go right on in and sit down, and I'll be right back."

Sound of man's voice:

"I want the same girl as before, now. What's her name?"

Sound of woman's voice:

"Don't you think I know what you like by now? You just relax. Wendy will be right with you."

Man walks into room, looking around, loosening tie. Walks over to bed, presses on mattress, smiles to himself.

"Who's that? We seen him before?" Johnny Gee squinted at the screen. The man's face wasn't completely visible from the overhead camera. He walked over to the armchair and sat down, his face now fully visible.

"I know I seen him before. I just can't place him. Wait a minute. Nah. Can't place him. How about you, Major? Can you place him?"

"I'm not sure . . ."

Man sitting on chair, fiddling with his tie, looking around.

He's about forty, receding hairline, dark features, long, straight nose. He's wearing a suit and dark loafers with tassels.

Minutes tick by. 10:21. 10:22. 10:23.

Sound of door opening.

Young woman walks in, dressed in short skirt, high heels, leopard-print camisole top. Man stands up.

"Hi, Wendy," says the man, sounding a bit hesitant.

"Hi, Mr. Bosco," says the woman.

"Call me Lou, like before," says the man.

"Fuck! It's Lou Bosco!" said Johnny Gee. "He was one of the guys beating on us at the diner!"

"Shh," Sam said, pointing at the screen.

Another young woman is coming through the door, this one with a big bouffant hairstyle, wearing a satin robe with a fur collar and high heels.

"Who's this?" asks the man. The two young women stand next to each other, posing.

Woman walks into the room, dressed in a short skirt and red blouse. She has a distinctive streak of gray in her dark hair, which is short and swept back in a modern style.

The woman walks into the room and stands directly beneath the camera, so all that can be seen is the top of her head, her shoulders, and her hands as she gestures.

"I brought you a little surprise, Lou," says the woman in the suit.

"Well, what have we got here, Sheila?" asks the man, expressing mock surprise.

"This is Brenda. Now go on and say hello to Mr. Bosco, Brenda."

The second young woman glides over to Lou Bosco and rubs her hand along the side of his thigh. "Glad to meet ya, Mr. Bosco," she says in a husky whisper.

"I hear you all have got lots to celebrate tonight. I don't think you'll have any trouble celebrating with Brenda and Wendy." The woman in the suit turns and walks out the door, closing it behind her.

"Just a minute," said Johnny Gee. "Reverse the tape. Show me that again."

"Which shot?" asked Spicer.

"Where the woman is walking in the door, when she stops. Right there. Can you freeze it?"

"Sure," said Spicer. He froze the frame.

"That's Sheila all right," said Johnny Gee. "She's got a few miles on her, but that's Sheila."

"What?"

"See the little scar on her cheek?"

"Yeah."

"I was there when a dude clipped her, opened her up. Blood all over the place."

"What'd you do?" asked Spicer.

"I picked up a pipe and split his head."

THE THREE MEN stared at the image frozen on the Sony's screen.

"Kill the tape," said Johnny Gee.

"Are you sure you . . ." asked Spicer, hitting the button on the VCR.

" 'Course I'm fuckin' sure it's her. I had a thing going with Sheila for a year . . . almost two years. Kind of an angle we come up with on our own. She was hookin', like usual, you know? And what we'd do, we'd watch out for really straight guys who were in the dough. She'd find a way to catch a look at their wallets and get a look at their driver's license and memorize the address. Then I'd cruise by, check it out, follow the guy to work, get an angle on how much he had to lose. Sometimes the guy would be a local banker, sometimes a lawyer, always the pillar-of-the-community type dudes, they were the ones we hit. Anyway, once we had the guy specked, I'd start generatin' letters, sendin' them to his place of business first, then to his house. We never threatened anything, just sent letters askin' for a job, askin' for references, anything to rattle the guy. Sheila, she'd sign the letters. What we'd do, we'd rattle the guy good with maybe twenty letters, so his wife was askin' what was goin' on, maybe his boss was wonderin' why he's gettin' so much mail, then Sheila'd arrange to meet the guy on the street, catch him on his way to lunch, somethin' like that, and she'd tell him maybe she'd stop askin' for references and shit if she had enough scratch to get outa town, like maybe a grand, maybe two. They'd usually come across. If they didn't, we just moved the con to the next guy and ran the same thing."

"Where'd you pull the con, Johnny?" asked Spicer.

"We were in Akron for a while, then Cinci, then Miami, then Zanesville, Wheeling, Peoria, Cleveland, Cape Girardeau . . . we moved around. We even jacked up a banker in Hannibal. Jeez. I remember when we drove outa town I told Sheila I felt just like Huck Finn, and she said, who? She didn't have a clue."

"What made you stop?"

"You can't run a con like that very long. You got to keep movin'. Even then it's gonna catch up with you. It was good while it lasted, though. Sheila. I ain't thought about her in months. She was somethin', though. I met her at Corrine's place in Springfield, and she wasn't a day over seventeen, man. I had some minor shit goin', nothin' big, but I was gettin' by, operatin' out of a bar on Market Street called the

Short Stop, down near the train station. She was hookin' for Corrine's and hung out in the bar when she wasn't at the whorehouse. We got to be friends, you know? She had me over to her place a coupla times for spaghetti, and one time, on a Sunday, we drove out in the country to a lake for a picnic. I remember. We had chicken salad sandwiches and chips and beer. I had a hell of a nice short in those days, a '65 Mustang. It was like she'd tell me her troubles, I'd tell her mine. 'Fore either of us knew it, we were runnin' that shit on her super straight johns. It was better than workin'. Know what I mean?"

"I'm afraid I do," Sam said.

"You get it on with her?" asked Spicer.

"Me and Sheila was friends and everything, you know, but we wasn't lovers. I mean, she was gettin' into a lesbo thing. Lotta hookers go the other way, you know? And I was busy, man. I was savin' up so I could get my own little book to run, and I had my short, and I had ambitions. We was both movin' fast. Lots of stuff gets away from you. I never really thought about it much. She drifted on, and I drifted, we stayed in touch for a while, then I lost track of her."

"Tell me about this place in Springfield," said Sam.

"The whorehouse?"

"What do you know about it?"

"Hell, everybody knows about Corrine's. I don't know how it got the name . . . maybe someone named Corrine ran it once. Been there forever. It's a big old house up on the north side of town."

"How long ago were you there?"

"Must be almost a year, now. At least that. It's some place, lemme tell you. Got silk fabric on the walls, and mirrors on the ceilings, and fancy furniture, you know, with velvet cushions and the like. Corrine's has always been a first-class establishment. It had to be. Every goddamned politician in the state's gotten his rocks off on those four-poster beds over the years."

"Politicians?"

"Don't you know anything, man? What you think these dudes do when they leave their little home districts and head off to the capital to conduct the state's business? You think 'cause you're elected state rep, those votes mean you got to keep your pants zipped? Christ. Corrine's is an institution. It's like, you're not really sworn in until you been up to Corrine's with the boys to get your pipes cleared. It's, what you call it . . . rite of passage."

"So how do you figure this whorehouse . . . Corrine's . . . became involved with these videotapes?" asked Sam.

"She owed somebody."

"What do you mean?"

"You run a place like that, man, you're always gonna owe somebody. How you think that joint has stayed open all these years? All these pols in and outa there every session of the legislature, it's gotta be protected. Besides, Corrine's has always served a kinda noble function in state government."

"What might that be?"

"Well, it's kind of a variation on the old you-scratch-my-back, I'll-scratch-yours thing. You know. With the lobbyists and all. You vote my way on this bill, and I'll see you tonight at Corrine's, and the party's on me."

"They use whores to buy votes?" Sam's voice sounded as incredulous as he was.

"Hey, loose women been valid currency in Springfield for years, man. Get over it. The sky ain't fallin'. They had places like hers in Athens and Rome, man. You musta studied about it in college."

Sam paused before he spoke, spinning his empty beer can in a circle on the floor with the toe of his shoe.

"How close were you to the woman who runs this place?" he asked.

"Not very. My action was with Sheila and she was just workin' there then. What can I say? But we was tight for a long while . . . I mean, tight as you get with a hooker. She went back to Corrine's when we split up. Now it looks like she's runnin' the place."

"Do you think she'd tell you who's behind the tapes? I mean, who is taping whom?"

"The question is, does she know anything? I don't know. She was pretty sharp. She'd probably help us out, for old times, like."

"What are you driving at, Sam?" Spicer looked at him warily, puffing on his cigarette.

"Technically, if we're in possession of evidence of a felony, and I think we are, it's our duty to turn it over to the proper authorities. But the problem here is self-evident: with so many 'proper authorities' on these tapes, who do we turn them over to?"

"So where does that leave us?"

"I was hoping maybe your friend Sheila could help us tell the good guys from the bad guys, but I understand what you're saying about her. Why should she jump ship in a storm? You might be an old friend, but given the stakes here, that's probably not reason enough for her to tell us what we need to know."

"You're right about that, Major," said Johnny Gee. "So what do you think we ought to do?"

"I say we wrap up these tapes and mail them to the state attorney general and be done with them."

"That ain't a bad idea, Sam. I can do that for you, first thing in the morning," said Spicer.

"As for me, I'm a major in the army. Who's going to believe I have anything to do with political corruption in the state of Illinois? I'm not that worried about it. The army is a great insulator. People have a natural reluctance to accuse an officer in the service of his country. Moreover, we've committed no crimes. I jumped in to help you and Howie tonight because the two of you were getting the shit pounded out of you, and you needed help. That isn't a crime. They shot at us, we didn't shoot at them. All I wanted to do was what was right, and I did it. I've got nothing to be ashamed of."

"I see what you mean. So what are you sayin'? We leave the tapes with Spicer and bolt?"

"Essentially, yes. I'm due at Fort Campbell on Monday morning, and if I'm not there, I'm AWOL. For an officer of my rank, that's a serious offense. So I'm going on to Campbell. I'll be glad to tell my story to any law enforcement authorities who want to hear it when the time comes, *if* the time comes. I'll be more than glad to give whatever testimony I have to give if charges are ever filed against the men who beat you up and shot at us. But I'll be damned if I'm going to get charged with AWOL and ruin my career in the army. This is the thing I'm getting at: as long as I wear the uniform, I belong to the army. My allegiance is down there at Fort Campbell. I'll give whatever testimony is necessary after I've reported for duty."

"What do we do now?"

"I thought Spicer could drop us off at the bus depot down

in Paducah. You can catch a bus somewhere . . . anywhere but back home . . . and I'll catch one to Campbell."

"Yeah, that sounds okay, but we've got a problem," said Johnny Gee.

"What's that?"

"You forgot about the all-points out on us that Spicer said he heard about. You know what? We'll never make it out of this county. We're dangerous as long as we're vertical and talkin', man."

"That is a problem."

"I can get you guys outa here, Butter," said Spicer. "No problem."

"How, Spicer?" asked Sam. "I've watched you blow by me and disappear around the turn in quite a few races, but I don't quite see how you're going to disappear the two of us."

"I've got a pickup over there behind the dish," said Spicer. "Got a camper on the back and everything. I could stash you two back there until we're out of the county. Make it look like I'm headin' out huntin'. Nobody'll give me any trouble."

Sam glanced at Johnny Gee and turned to Spicer.

"If you say it will work, that's good enough for me, Spicer," he said. "Give me a couple of minutes. I've got to get my stuff out of the car." He stood up and headed for the door. Johnny Gee followed.

Outside, Sam reached into the Caddy's back seat for his overnight bag.

"What do you think, Major? You think we've got a chance?" asked Johnny Gee.

"Spicer knows this country better than the ruts on the dirt tracks we used to drive," Sam said. "If anybody can get us out of this county, he can."

"I sure as hell hope so."

"Let's go back inside and get the tapes." Sam grabbed his overnight bag and they stepped back into the trailer.

"Give me a minute to set things up for the next taping," said Spicer. "And I got to leave a note for Victor. He'll be by in the morning."

Spicer pointed toward the back of the trailer.

"You two can give me a hand reloadin' the recorders. Just grab some blanks in the hallway and pop out the Burt Reynolds movie and pop in a new tape."

They reset the recorders, and Spicer took a minute to fiddle with the buttons on the console. "There's some foreign flick comin' on at two in the morning, somethin' about the gods bein' crazy. They say it's doin' pretty good business."

"Who's 'they,' Spicer?" asked Johnny Gee.

"The trades, that's who. I get *Variety* and *Hollywood Reporter* every day in the mail. I'm always watchin' the grosses. That way, you can get some idea what's gonna sell on videotape, although tape sales don't always follow box office that close."

Sam put the five surveillance tapes on Spicer's console.

"I think you ought to wrap them in brown paper and send them straight to the attorney general in Springfield. Type, don't write, an address label, and don't mail them from a post office. Just slap three bucks worth of stamps on the package and drop them in a mailbox. I don't think it's a good idea if anybody sees you sending a package to the state attorney general. It's the kind of thing people would remember."

"I got you, Butter," said Spicer.

They were on their way out the door when Johnny Gee grabbed Sam by his collar.

"I think you better take a look at yourself in the mirror, 'fore we go much further," he said.

Sam looked down at his pants, dirty and stained from changing the tire on the Caddy. He glanced at his hands. The same. "Maybe you're right," he said. He headed for the john. When he came out, he had changed his clothes and shaved.

"Have a look at the major," said Johnny Gee. "Looks like a page outa some magazine."

Sam was wearing a pair of khaki pants, a plaid shirt, and a heavy plaid overjacket.

"I got this stuff from L. L. Bean. It's cheaper than most stores."

"What the hell is L. L. Bean?" asked Spicer. "You come some distance from your days behind the wheel of a modified, Butter."

"Forget it," said Sam.

Spicer led the way as they tramped through the high grass surrounding the satellite dish. Behind the dish, tucked into the woodline, was an old gray Dodge pickup with a homemade camper over the bed.

"C'mon," said Spicer, leading the way to the pickup. It was a '55 Dodge, no rust, primered, but covered with mud. The fenders were dented, the front bumper was missing, and a foot-long crack marred the windshield.

"This thing gonna run?" asked Johnny Gee.

"Don't let the looks of the outside fool ya," said Spicer. He opened the hood.

"Christ. You've got a Chrysler hemi in this thing," said

Sam. "Two fours and a crossfire manifold, headers . . .
what else has this thing got?"

"Four-speed, quick-change rear end, three-quarter race
cam, gas shocks, V-class radials. It's a sleeper. Victor helped
me set it up. We use it to move our videos. You don't wanna
get stopped with five or six thousand bootleg tapes, ya
know? In this thing, you plain don't get stopped."

"It looks like a refugee from a junkyard on the outside.
Hasn't had any body work in twenty years."

"Yeah, but we tore it down from the ground up underneath. Rebuilt the entire runnin' gear, frame, everything.
Thing corners like a fuckin' Corvette, and loaded down full,
it's faster than any cop car in the state."

"I believe it," Sam said.

Spicer closed the hood, walked around back of the truck
and opened the camper. Inside, the truck bed looked as if it
were piled full of wooden crates. Spicer lifted a hidden handle and the entire back of the pile of crates lifted up on
concealed hinges, revealing a hollow space where the crates
should have been.

"You guys get back here and I'll close this thing up and
throw a tarp over it."

"Looks like a setup I've seen used for cigarettes and
shine," said Johnny Gee.

"Cigarettes, bootleg videos, don't make no difference. It
would work for anything."

"C'mon. Get a move on. We got to get you to Paducah
'fore the sun comes up. They're lookin' for your asses now,
but by daylight this county is gonna look like a war zone,
there'll be so many cops."

Spicer grabbed a shotgun lying inside the hollow pile of
crates and threw it into the front seat of the truck. He pulled

his International Harvester cap down over his eyes and buttoned his plaid-lined jean jacket.

"How do I look?" he asked. "Look like I'm gonna get me some rabbits come sunrise?"

"You're the genuine article, Spicer. If I was a rabbit, I'd be scared shitless lookin' at you," said Johnny Gee.

"Go on and get in there," said Spicer, indicating the truck bed hiding place. "You'll find a coupla blankets and an old quilt you can wrap up in. I figure it'll take me an hour or so to clear the county, then you all can ride up front."

Sam and Johnny Gee climbed in. Spicer closed the door on the hollow crates, then he buttoned up the camper. When he started the truck, the deep rumble from the big engine's headers could be felt through the truck bed.

"This thing sounds like a goddamned dragster," Sam said.

"Yeah? Well, it rides like a goddamned pickup truck," said Johnny Gee. Spicer was bouncing the truck down the dirt road at a good clip, and the two men in the back were feeling every rut and hole in the road.

He hit the paved road and took a left, the truck picking up speed, losing some of its deep exhaust note as he shifted into third and fourth gear. The truck stopped and turned right, stopped again and turned left, then got quickly up to speed.

"He's goin' around that little town back there," said Johnny Gee. "I hope he knows what he's doing."

"He knows. Quit worrying."

The truck ran at speed for quite a while, then slowed. The two men in the back heard a knock on the back of the cab. "Road block," called Spicer. "Don't make any noise."

The truck stopped. The two men in the back heard Spicer's voice first:

"What's the trouble, officer?" he asked.

Then they heard another voice:

"Where are you headed, sir?"

"Goin' huntin' in the Shawnee National Forest," said Spicer. "Figured I'd get me some rabbits, maybe a squirrel or two."

"You're getting an early start," said the voice.

"I like to take my time."

"Have you seen anyone on the road tonight?"

"You mean walkin' along the road? Nah. Not a soul."

"What have you got in the back?"

"Farm implements. It's my business."

"Let's have a look."

Sam and Johnny Gee heard Spicer open the driver's door, step out, and walk around to the back of the truck. Then they heard him open the tailgate and the camper's rear window.

"What's in the boxes?" asked the cop.

"Farm implements. I sell tractor hitches and winches."

"Let's have a look," said the cop.

The two men inside the hollowed-out space lay still, listening in the dark. They heard Spicer pry open the top of one of the crates. Light from a flashlight flickered through the cracks in the crates.

"Jesus, how many hitches have you got back here?"

They relaxed.

"About four hundred. It's a good business. Damn things are always breakin'. I come along and replace 'em. Cost about twenty-five dollars. You can make a good livin' sellin' hitches and winches."

"I guess you can. Okay. Close it up. Sorry for the trouble, sir."

"No problem," said Spicer.

They heard Spicer close the camper, then he got back into the truck's cab.

"You mind if I ask what you're lookin' for tonight, officer?" asked Spicer. He started the truck and let it idle.

"Couple of guys wanted for a killing, one about thirty, thirty-five, and the other in his twenties. White males."

"No kiddin'. Well, good luck."

"We'll get them. We've got them bottled up in the county. We're watching every road in and out of here. It's just a matter of time."

"I'm sure you're right, officer. See ya," said Spicer.

The men in the back felt the truck shudder as Spicer eased off the clutch and onto the gas. He drove for another hour, then pulled off on a side road. He stopped the truck, opened the camper, and lifted the hidden door to the compartment.

"You all can get out now. I don't think there's gonna be any more road blocks. We're clear of Harris County."

They climbed out the back of the truck and stood shivering in the dark.

"What the hell did you do back there?" asked Johnny Gee. "I thought for sure that cop was going to find us."

"I put a false bottom on these two crates here," said Spicer, tapping the crates closest to the back of the pickup bed. "And I filled them with tractor hitches I bought at the hardware store in town. No way you can tell it isn't a whole crate full. That's the second time I had to pry one open. I got stopped for speedin' once and did the same thing. In daylight. They never suspected a thing."

Spicer closed the camper and the three men got in the cab. "Pour me some of that coffee there," said Spicer, pointing to a thermos next to the floor shift. He turned the truck around and drove back to the road they'd been on before. Within a few seconds, the truck was doing seventy-five miles an hour toward Paducah.

"Which way are we goin'?" asked Johnny Gee.

"We're gonna stay right on this 640, then pick up 138 outside of Five Points and take it straight into Paducah. That way, we pass through only a couple little towns on the way. I figure we'll be there about one-thirty, quarter to two."

The old gray pickup rocketed down the two-lane road into the night. A small town blinked by, its lone red light flashing yellow, storefronts darkened, gas station shuttered, drive-in movie marquee reading "closed for the winter." Another town: a four-way stop, two churches, and a shut-down chicken processing factory. Miles of fresh-plowed farmland luminous in the darkness. Another farm town, its lone police car idling lights off, on a side street . . . Spicer cruising the truck down Main Street five miles an hour under the speed limit. Back on the gas outside of town, and soon in the distance the faint glow of Paducah on the horizon.

12

THE BIG GREYHOUND bus rolled into Clarksville, Tennessee, on U.S. 31 from the north, through a satiny strip of cinderblock motels, beer joints, bowling alleys, used car lots, and auto parts stores lit up so brightly it seemed like day. The main drag was a neon evocation of the American dream, a four-lane playland where a beat-up jalopy and a tank of gas promised possibility, and a wallet full of hard-earned dollar bills sang satisfaction. Old 31 had changed over the years to accommodate the needs and desires of the modern age: fast food chains had uprooted mom-and-pop drive-ins and luncheonettes; gas stations had turned into bunkered computerized pay-first-and-pump-your-own service plazas selling everything from gas to beer, to bait, to ammo, to rubbers; drive-in movies had transmogrified into quad-plex-mini-cinemas. Still, the old highway gleamed and glistened, comfortable and somehow homey like a big out-door living room, bright and warm and inviting, shouldering aside the loneliness of the night with neon and chrome and promises in the dark.

Major Sam Butterfield, Jr., got off at the bus depot and retrieved his duffel from the baggage claim room. It had been there since the previous evening, having arrived on the bus he missed back at the diner. It was nearly six in the morning, and the sun was coming up, when he hailed a cab and headed for the post headquarters at Fort Campbell. He reported to the duty officer at six-thirty and handed over his orders.

"Ranger, huh, Major?" asked the bleary-eyed duty officer, a captain who had been up all night and was looking forward to a day off before reporting back to his own unit.

"This time out, anyway."

"You got one hardass commander in that colonel . . . what's his name?"

"Duchamp. Lieutenant Colonel Duchamp."

"I heard they run five miles every morning, and ten on Mondays. You ready for a five-mile run in fatigues and boots tomorrow morning, sir?"

"I don't think anyone, anywhere, anytime, is ready for five miles every morning, Captain."

"Well, you've got twenty-four hours to rest up, sir. I suggest you take a room over at the BOQ for the time being. You can't clear through finance and personnel on Sunday. The duty vehicle will take you over. You'll find the BOQ next to the Officers' Club. It's the two-story brick building that looks like a twenty-year-old Holiday Inn." The captain chuckled, picked up the phone, and summoned his driver.

Sam picked up his bags and followed the enlisted man.

"Pretty fancy, huh, sir?" said the fatigue-clad enlisted man, indicating the staffcar idling at curbside.

"I see it runs."

"Oh, it'll get you there, sir."

Fort Campbell was a pleasant, if unremarkable, army post. Broad, tree-lined avenues led through the main post, through the section of huge Victorians with expansive lawns reserved for the post commandant and his colonels, past the hospital, the commissary, the day care center, the junior high, the grade school, but most of all, past one howitzer after another mounted on concrete blocks, barrels aimed forever skyward at some imaginary enemy just over that hillock, or through those trees over there. Fort Campbell was an infantry post, which trained and housed infantry soldiers, enlisted and officer alike. But an infantry Ranger battalion at Fort Campbell, despite its nominal status as "infantry," was bound to be received by the non-Ranger boys like a burr under a saddle. Major Butterfield steeled himself for the sometimes not so good-natured ribbing that was bound to go on between the Airborne Infantry Rangers and the men of the infantry who were neither Ranger nor airborne.

He threw his bags in the corner of a nondescript motel-like BOQ room and flopped on the bed. Within a minute, he was asleep.

The next morning, he put on a set of fatigues, dug his boots out of his duffel and gave them a quick polish, donned his black beret, and headed downstairs.

"How do you get to the Three-Sixty-one?" he asked the enlisted man at the BOQ desk.

"Are you just reporting in, sir?"

"Yes, I am."

"I'll call you a cab, sir. The Three-Sixty-one is way over on the other end of the post, in the old barracks. There hasn't been anybody over there for years. It's about thirty miles away."

"Thanks."

The cab passed through the main portion of the post, where huge motor pools loomed like deathstar parking lots, with row upon row of armored personnel carriers seeming to disappear into the distance. Over there, a company or two of massive M-1 main battle tanks, state of the art, its freshly hosed-down slant nose and slab sides glistening in the early morning sun.

Motor pool after motor pool, endlessly olive drab, endlessly iron, endlessly, mournfully huge and threatening and expansive. Major Butterfield yearned to get out there where a pair of boots, a pack, a bayonet, and a rifle were all that were called for on a field of battle.

The cab drove through a sandy pine forest, past a few firing ranges, through another pine forest, and into a clearing that contained the remains of an old World War II training encampment: a dozen rows of two-story wood frame buildings painted a bilious shade of puce green, set along a grid of gravel roads. A gate at the entrance to the encampment proclaimed: HOME OF THE THREE-SIXTY-ONE RANGER BATTALION. DRIVE ON IF YOU DARE. It was Lieutenant Colonel Duchamp's outfit all right. In fact, there they were, the entire battalion, double-timing down one of the gravel roads, coming out of the woods at the end of their five-mile run, clad in boots, fatigue pants, and T-shirts with Ranger tabs on the chest. The colonel was out front. He called, "Baaaaattalion! Halt!" and every company, every last platoon, halted at once. The colonel dismissed them and walked over to Sam. It was a cool morning, and he hadn't even worked up a sweat. He was a big man, over six feet two, with broad shoulders and a thick but not flabby waist. He had a steel gray crew cut, and a tanned, heavily lined face. If you glanced at him, you'd say he was from the Ozarks, or perhaps the Kentucky hill country. In truth, he was born in Chapel Hill, North Carolina, son of wealthy southern textile manufacturers. He disappointed the family by taking a pass on Harvard and instead went to West Point, graduating in 1969. This was his second battalion command. He'd been offered a cushy, prestigious job in the Pentagon, in the office of the chief of staff of the army, but his tan said he liked life best when his battalion was in the field. He was only forty-two, but the wrinkles came with the military command. There was little doubt, looking at the big man with his hands on his hips and the Ranger tab heaving on his T-shirted chest, that he just loved it.

"Major Butterfield reporting as ordered, sir." Sam saluted smartly.

The colonel returned his salute and shook his hand.

"Good to have you back in a battalion with me, Sam," he said, smiling with genuine affection.

"Well, sir, it's a long way from Fort Lewis, but it's sure good to be here."

"Are you ready to take over as executive officer?"

"Yes, sir, I am. If I were really to tell you the truth, I'd rather have a company under you, but rank caught up with me, I guess."

"You already had a platoon under me, Sam."

"Yes, sir, and that was the best damn company in this man's army."

"Well, Major, welcome to the best damn battalion in this man's army."

The colonel led the way to one of the company mess halls, long, one-story buildings centered in each of the four company areas. When the colonel entered, one of the troops yelled "tenshut" and the place leapt to attention. The colonel waved his hand and said, "At ease." The room relaxed.

They went through the mess line, got their breakfasts, and sat at the first available table. There was no wooden barrier between the enlisted and officer areas of the mess hall, Sam noticed. It was a sign of Lieutenant Colonel Duchamp's command. We fight together, we eat together, said the colonel.

"No more of those goddamned battalion messes," he said, digging into his chow. "It took some bargaining, but I demanded a battalion area where they still had company areas and company messes. This is what we got."

"It looks pretty good to me," said Sam. At Fort Lewis, they had been quartered in college-style dormitories with huge college-style battalion mess halls, the whole battalion plonked down on a piece of asphalt, not a blade of grass to be seen. This was primitive, but this was better. Much better. Here platoons lived two to a building, and three of the old wood buildings formed a company area around the mess hall and company headquarters. It was silly, but the whole business . . . being out in the woods, collected together in platoons and companies, the battalion off by itself living an existence that was a virtual anachronism in the modern army . . . it seemed somehow cozy and wonderful.

The colonel briefed Sam on what had been happening since he'd gotten there a couple of weeks ago—the training schedule, the class schedule, equipment shortcomings, AWOL (there were only two, and they had returned after one day), the attitude of the troops, the skill and leadership abilities of the officers. It was a good battalion that was about to get better. A lot better, it seemed to Sam after the colonel had finished. They carried their trays to the KP slot and walked into the company area.

"I want you to take a few days to clear post finance and personnel and get settled downtown. I . . . uh . . . noticed in your paperwork that you are no longer married."

"I noticed, too, sir."

The colonel laughed and clapped Sam on the back.

"Well, the BOQs suck," said the colonel.

"I noticed that, too, sir."

"You're staying in one?"

"I got here yesterday, sir."

"You should have given me a call, Sam," said the colonel with mock sternness. "You could have stayed at our place."

"I was too pooped, sir. And it was early yesterday morning. I didn't want to bother you on Sunday morning."

"Your car arrived yet?"

"Still waiting, sir. It should be here in a couple of months."

"I'll have the battalion duty vehicle drive you back to the BOQ and downtown. You can rent a jalopy on the strip for ten bucks a day at a place called Rent-a-Wreck."

"I saw it coming in, sir."

"Then get busy. I'll expect you back here on Wednesday morning at reveille. Oh, yeah. A lot of the unmarried lieutenants are staying at an apartment complex called the

Dorchester. It's some kind of singles garden apartment deal with a pool and something called a goddamned party room."

"Yes, sir."

"I wouldn't recommend it."

Major Butterfield grinned.

"They're paying twice their housing allowance for half the space you could get about five miles down the highway south of the post. There's a trailer park down there renting nice double-wides."

"I'll take a look, sir."

"I'll see you in forty-eight hours, Sam. Correction. Make that forty-six hours."

Major Butterfield saluted, and the colonel double-timed off in the direction of battalion headquarters. A staff car materialized, driven by an impeccably clad young Ranger trooper. Sam climbed in. This time, fired-up from breakfast with the colonel, it seemed to Sam that the drive back to the main post was over in a moment. In another moment he was down on the strip and behind the wheel of a rented Ford. He headed south down the strip on the lookout for a trailer park on his left. He found it right where the colonel said it would be. It was a decent enough place, about forty double-wides interspersed with a few twelve-by-sixties. Nice asphalt roads, a smattering of pines here and there, and a little pool inside a chain-link fence in the middle of the place. A sign said it was the PULL-ON-IN TRAILER COURT, obviously a reference to its earlier days as a transient park.

After what had happened to Sam on Saturday night, everything seemed almost too easy. He looked at three double-wides and then went back to the first one and took it. The trailer was parked in a little grove of pines at the far left corner of the park. It was ten bucks a month more than the others, but it had a washer-dryer, two bedrooms, a dishwasher, and a covered carport. What more could a divorced major ask for? He gave the man in the Peterbilt cap and cowboy boots a month's rent and a month's deposit. He inquired as to the whereabouts of a bank, a supermarket, a laundry where he could get his fatigues starched, a liquor store . . . the necessities. The man from the trailer park filled him in and welcomed him to Clarksville as he pocketed the neatly folded hundred-dollar bills. He asked about a phone. The man pointed down the street at a booth.

"Thanks," said Sam. He knew he was in an off-post town for sure now. They love your money but they couldn't care less about all those nameless, placeless military faces just passing through. The trailer park cowboy would be there with his hand out for the rent on the first of every month, but you'd be lucky if he'd get up off his fat ass and pick up the phone and call the cops if he saw your car getting boosted. Jesus. Civilians. It was hard to believe he'd ever been one.

He called his mother collect. She was relieved to find out that the nightmare of Saturday night was behind him, that he'd arrived safely at Fort Campbell and reported to his unit.

"I'm not sure what it was all about, Ma, but I'm glad as hell to be out of there," said Sam.

"Sam, look." His mother's tone was alert, sure. He remembered, it seemed so long ago and he guessed it was, that as political as his father was, his mother was always the one he turned to for practical advice, the how-to-get-along-in-the-world stuff every boy needs more than he knows.

"From what you told me, you did the right thing, Sam. Anything even marginally involving Harlan Greene . . .

well, the more distance you put between yourself and that man, the better."

"I don't know how deeply he was involved, Ma."

"You said he was the one the old man mentioned, right? The one who loaned him the money?"

"Yes, he was the one."

"Did you see him on any of the videotapes?"

"I wouldn't know, Ma. I've never seen him."

"He's as big around as a hot tub and just about as sweaty. Did you see anyone who looked like that?"

"Yeah. There was a big fat man on two of the tapes. On one, he was surveying a field somewhere down south of our place, down near the Shawnee National Forest, in Rock County, as well as we could determine. And the other time he was in a hotel room in Springfield, only he didn't say much."

"Did he have some jerk with him that kept saying, 'That right?' and he would answer, 'That's right'?"

"Yeah. Exactly."

"That was Harlan Greene, Sam. That's what he does at every meeting of the County Commission. One of his jerks gets up and talks for him, and he sits in the back of the room drinking a Coke, and every once in a while, the jerk turns to him and says, 'That right?' and Harlan says, 'That's right.'"

"Look, Ma, do you think you're going to be all right? I mean, those guys were trying to kill us the other night. If they could have, they would have."

"What did you do with the surveillance tapes? You said you sent them to the attorney general?"

"They're going in the mail today."

"That ought to put the lid on Harlan Greene. I wouldn't

worry yourself too much about me, Sam. Harlan Greene knows if he tangles with me, he's going to have his hands full. Your father and I made his life miserable for years, and I can do it again by myself, if need be. There's one thing you've forgotten about politics, or maybe you never learned."

"What's that, Ma?"

"As much friction as politics causes, you've got to have insulation between yourself and the heat. And the only way you're going to get it is by getting involved. Well, I've been involved for *years,* and by this time, I've got myself a hide built up thick as a buffalo's. Your daddy taught me, Sam. Nothing is not political. I'm sure that sounds stupid, but it's what I learned from him, the years we were together, and if it was good enough for him, it's good enough for me."

"I'm sure you're right. I'm just not sure Harlan Greene agrees with you."

"Look, Sam. Everyone around these parts knows we've been enemies for years. He won't pull something stupid. Let some time go by, Sam. We'll know soon enough whether or not we've got trouble. In the meantime, I think you ought to get yourself settled in down there and I think you ought to call Betsy. I know she'd like to hear from you."

"And may I ask how you came upon that little nugget of wisdom, Ma?"

"I spoke to her yesterday. She said she'd heard you had been around, and she just wanted to know if you knew about the reunion you've got coming up. Your class reunion from S.I.U."

"I know about it."

"Good. I'll tell her when I call her in the morning."

"Ma, look. You're not going to get me and Betsy back

together. What happened between us happened a long time ago."

"Nothing like memories to make the heart grow fonder, huh, Sam?"

"Ma . . ." The phone went dead.

Sam stared at the receiver for a moment and thought about what his mother had said. Maybe she was right. Maybe he ought to just put the last seventy-two hours behind him and sink himself neck deep into the battalion. It did feel good to be back in the warm bosom of the army, where everything was spelled out for you in black and white. These are the good guys, our guys, and those are the bad guys, their guys. This is what Rangers do to bad guys: they hunt them down and kill them. It made a kind of dark sense, the army did. What you did was live your life waiting and training for the day that you'd go out and put your skills to use on a field of battle where there would be only one winner and one loser, and everybody knew which one we would be. It was a comforting notion to those wearing fatigues and boots every day that if God wasn't on your side, he sure as hell was looking over your olive drab shoulder.

He headed back to the post to go through the bureaucratic nightmare that was post finance and post personnel, a bewildering maze filled with sluglike civilian federal civil servants who held the purse strings and the keys to the lockers that contained your records, which in the army amounted to your entire career. He had heard horror story after horror story about guys who had gotten mad during the finance/personnel nightmare and yelled at someone. Before you knew it, your finance records couldn't be found, which meant that copies had to come from some bunker beneath

Indianapolis, of all places, and that little paper shuffle was known to take at least three months.

During which time, in the absence of such records, you could not be paid.

Then, of course, there was your 201 personnel file, the loss of which could find you reassigned virtually anywhere, not to mention the potential loss of any letters of commendation, copies of which might not have yet found their way to your big 201 file in the sky at the Pentagon.

So the civil service slugs were not to be fucked with, and fuck with them Major Butterfield did not. He was a good boy, and in a mere five hours, from noon until five, the twenty minutes of work necessary to clear finance and personnel got done. He felt lucky. He still had all his limbs, all his records, half his sanity, but he had no patience left at all. He drove back to the double-wide staring across white knuckles on the steering wheel. On the way he stopped for milk, eggs, beer, wine, and such. He pulled into the carport just in time to see headlights behind him.

THE CAR BEHIND him cut its lights, and Sam's eyes adjusted to the dark. It was a red Audi coupe. The driver's door opened, and a tall fatigue-clad figure stepped onto the gravel drive.

"Hey, Butterfield! That you in there?" a woman's voice called.

Sam climbed out of the car and squinted to see who it was.

"It's me, Sam. Hillary Conyers." The figure strode into view. She approached six feet tall in bloused boots, and her full head of blond hair had been French braided and tucked up under her cap, which sported a major's leaf just like Sam's. She walked into the porch light, and smiled. Her face was tanned and adorned with pale lipstick and a minimum of makeup, in the manner prescribed for women in the military. Still, she was as beautiful as Sam remembered her, and it was obvious that she hadn't lost any of the spunk she'd had as a lieutenant.

"I heard you reported in yesterday, Sam, so I called your unit and your colonel said you might be out here. How'd you find this place, anyway?"

Hillary Conyers had been stationed at Fort Benning with Sam when he went through the Basic Course. They'd had a mad, passionate, just-out-of-college affair during the two months of the Basic Course, then Sam's first duty station a couple of thousand miles away had separated them, and they lost touch. Sam, of course, had gone on to get married and divorced, and a quick glance at Hillary's ring finger confirmed that she was currently single as well.

"Jesus, Hillary, what are you doing here?" asked Sam incredulously. "We haven't seen each other in . . . how many . . ."

"Ten years. It's been a long time. I'm assigned to post headquarters. Public information officer. That's how I knew you had signed in. One of my jobs is to check the book for new arrivals every once in a while, see if we can place an item in hometown newspapers . . . you know the routine. Major Sam Butterfield reports for duty at Fort Campbell, etc., etc. He will be serving with the blah-blah battalion. Fascinating stuff an information officer gets to crank out."

"Well, come on in, Hillary. Jeez, I don't know what we're doing standing out here in the cold."

Sam led the way into the double-wide. Hillary closed the door and doffed her cap, and a long braid unfolded. She reached back and plucked a tie from the braid and ran her fingers quickly through her hair, which fell around her face in soft folds.

"You want a beer?" Sam opened the refrigerator and held up a couple of bottles of Beck's. "It's not the real German stuff, but it's close enough for government work."

Hillary nodded and took one of the beers. Sam fumbled in a drawer and came up with an opener and cracked the caps off both bottles.

"What shall we drink to after all this time?" he asked, still a little stunned at the appearance of someone out of his deep past, especially someone like Hillary Conyers, for chrissake.

"Let's drink to your beautiful quarters," said Hillary, laughing. "What have we got here? An actual, for-real bark-a-lounger, as in, what dog in his whole sorry life would ever sit on this thing?" She pointed to a particularly hideous naugahyde recliner across the room, and Sam laughed aloud.

"And over here, what do we have? Your obligatory Ethan Allen sofa in a delicious brown and orange plaid. What would you call this decorating scheme, Sam? Early American Trailer Park?"

"Yeah, that's about it," he laughed.

"And the kitchen. Are these actually gold flecks in this formica counter? Or are they perhaps gold-*filled* flecks? Isn't this interesting. There appears to be an Egyptian motif to these cabinets . . . or is it Greek? I think these are the first green columns I've ever seen. Green columns on orange cabinets. Mmmm. Definitely classically inspired. Definitely."

Sam laughed. He tried a sip of beer, and then spat it across the room as he started laughing again.

"We've got a green stove, a yellow dishwasher, and what is this color? A wine-colored refrigerator? What an interesting notion. I see the plan. The appliances match the colors of the linoleum floor. How exciting. And the linoleum floor is set off by windows done in rubberized nylon drapes that are . . . my goodness. What color is this, Sam? Could it be fuchsia? Yes, I think it is a fuchsia. It's a kind of stone-washed fuchsia, or is it just faded?"

"Hey . . . c'mon . . . Hillary," Sam stuttered between guffaws. "I just got here."

"We must call *Metropolitan Home,* Sam. They won't waste a moment sending a photographer. I can see it now. The military bachelor pad look. Is it real, or is it camouflage?"

Sam, still laughing, staggered across the kitchen and wrapped an arm around Hillary's fatigue-clad shoulder.

"C'mon, Hillary. You've got to stop. I'm getting a pain in my side. Have you had supper yet?"

"Of course not. I just got off."

"You've got to know where we can get a good steak around here. We'll get drunk as skunks and try to understand the last ten years of our lives. What do you say?"

"I say welcome to Campbell, Major," said Hillary. She leaned over and planted a wet kiss on his lips. "Don't get me wrong. I've got nothing against bachelor pads. In fact, I've got one of my own on the other side of town."

"I was wondering . . ."

"Wonder no longer, Major Butterfield. I'm footloose and fancy-free once again."

"You're divorced, too?"

"Two years."

"C'mon, girl. I'll use some of the Temporary Duty Pay they're giving me and buy us enough martinis to jumpstart our memories. You tell me about yours and I'll tell you about mine and maybe we can make sense out of what I'm doing in a trailer park at this late date in life."

"I know just the place," she said. "But first, we've got to stop at my apartment so I can change."

"Lead the way, Major Conyers," laughed Sam as he followed her out the door.

The next morning Sam crept out of bed at four-thirty. Hillary didn't have to be at headquarters until eight, but he had to make the five-fifteen reveille run. He pulled on a freshly laundered set of fatigues, laced up his boots, jumped into the Ford with sleep still in his eyes and raced for the battalion area. He made it.

After five miles of sweat-stained double-timing along dirt roads winding through the woods surrounding the battalion area, he and Lieutenant Colonel Duchamp sat down to breakfast in the C-Company messhall. The colonel was slow talking and rather slow moving, but Sam knew there was a massive resolve beneath the gentility. Duchamp was gung-ho with a drawl.

After breakfast, he took Sam back to the battalion orderly room and introduced him to the sergeant major, the personnel NCO, and the captains who served as S-1, S-2, S-3, and S-4. Then he called in his company commanders one by one for meetings with the new executive officer. The battalion was a congenial, businesslike place. Everybody had a job, and every job got done with a minimum of flapping and slapping. That was about as much as you could expect of the army: minimum hassle doing the myriad make-work jobs asked of you. Duchamp's battalion was going to be a good place to work.

Sam's office was a small space off the orderly room with an interior door connecting with the colonel's. It was furnished with government-issue institutional sturdy desk, chair, bookcase, typewriter table, typewriter. All were metal, all were painted puce green and black, all were so well worn they probably dated back to World War II. He sat behind his desk, put his feet up. He remembered when Lieutenant Colonel Duchamp used to say a platoon leader ought to be able to carry his desk in his pocket, and for two years under Duchamp when he was company commander, that's exactly what the then Lieutenant Butterfield did. Everything there was to know about his platoon—in fact, about his entire life —was tucked inside his fatigue shirt pocket in a three-by-five-inch notebook.

But now here he was in an office again, at a new desk, in a new job in a new unit, and even, as it had turned out, with a new/old girlfriend he hadn't expected but whom he had taken to his bed like a prospector too long away from a waterhole.

He heard a knock at his door.

"Enter," he called out.

The door opened. Lieutenant Colonel Duchamp loomed in the doorway.

The new executive officer leapt to his feet and stood at attention.

"Out here in the orderly room, Major. I want to have words with you."

Sam walked into the orderly room where it appeared all of the battalion officers and senior NCO's had gathered. Was this some kind of initiation rite in the Three-Sixty-one, he wondered.

"Take off your fatigue shirt, Major," commanded the colonel.

"Sir?"

"I said take it off, Butterfield. No questions. Do as I say."

He unbuttoned and doffed his shirt. The colonel took it from him. He reached behind him and the sergeant major handed him something.

"Put this on," commanded the colonel, holding out a fresh shirt.

Sam did as the colonel said. When he was finished buttoning and tucking in the fresh fatigue shirt, the colonel held out his hand.

"Congratulations, Major Butterfield, and welcome to the Three-Sixty-one," said the colonel with a big grin.

Sam glanced at his shirt. Sure enough, the unit patch had been sewn on the left shoulder. Then the colonel handed him a small blue box containing two battalion insignia.

"The orderly room crew chipped in and picked these up for you at the quartermaster's," said the colonel.

"Thanks . . . guys."

"Nothing to be said, mister," said the colonel. "Get back to work. There will be an officer's call at the O-Club at eighteen hundred hours, gentlemen. We have a brand new XO in our midst who needs to be exposed to the Three-Sixty-one way of doing things. This of course calls for something of a celebration. The Three-Sixty-one will celebrate this evening, gentlemen, and we will show these non-Ranger sons-of-bitches how a Ranger wets his whistle. Any questions?"

"No, sir!" came a chorus of voices.

"Dismissed," commanded the colonel.

Sam retreated to his office and sat at his desk.

The rest of the day went by in a blur—a tour of the battalion area with the sergeant major, a visit to each company headquarters and introductions to the first sergeants, tour of the motor pool, a quick trip out to the firing range. Before he knew it, eighteen hundred hours was upon them, and the battalion repaired to the Officers Club to raise not a few glasses to their new member, and raise a little Ranger hell in the presence of their compatriots. Much singing. A few rather confused speeches on the subject of Rangerhood. More singing. More paeans to the wonders and mysteries of Rangerhood. Some frisbee-like tossing of the Ranger beret across the O-Club bar. More singing.

He called Hillary from a pay phone and arranged to meet her back at the double-wide.

In the days and weeks to come, he would remember thinking later that night, as he and his old flame cooked spaghetti, that things hadn't been this good for him in years.

The next day the paperwork started. This was the domain of the executive officer: paperwork and more paperwork— status reports, strength reports, motor pool tool counts, arms room weapons counts, pay records, personnel updates, reports of surveys on missing equipment, requisitions for new equipment to replace that which was missing—on and on it went in a never-ending snow flurry of gibbering military attention to detail in a manner which asserted, however ridiculously, that in the army no detail was too small to deserve its own separate and equal piece of paper, or poop-sheet.

Still, not everything in the army of the nineties was to be found on a typewritten piece of paper. The battalion was engaged almost daily in training missions, most of which involved being the "aggressors" against other units as they roared around the far reaches of the Fort Campbell reservation. Just a month after Sam showed up for his new job, the entire unit was loaded on C-141 Starlifters—gigantic Air Force cargo jets—and airlifted en masse down to Panama to attend the two-week Jungle Warfare Course. When they returned from Panama, the XO buried himself in paperwork, because at any time the battalion could be alerted and parachuted into some new hellhole for yet even more training, which is precisely what happened two weeks later when they joined Operation Bootstrap, three weeks of training maneuvers at Fort Bragg, North Carolina.

Sam and Hillary spent most of their time driving between her apartment and his double-wide. The unpredictable schedule of the Ranger battalion put a strain on their burgeoning affair, but they managed to spend most weekends together. While Sam was in Panama, she surprised him by ripping up the shag in the double-wide and having some neutral-color industrial carpet installed. Over the two weeks he was on maneuvers at Fort Bragg, she managed to sneak in an order for new curtains.

When his car finally arrived at Port Elizabeth from Germany, they flew to New York for a long weekend and took their time driving back, taking two-lane U.S. 50 most of the way. It was in the driver's seat of the Porsche, with Hillary asleep beside him on the way back, that Sam began to wonder what was actually going on between them. Two divorced people, lovers long ago and once again, thrown together on a typical middle-of-nowhere army post . . .

He didn't really know how he felt about her. It wasn't love, exactly. It was . . . hell, he didn't know what it was, but it sure felt good.

Spring came. One afternoon, Hillary came over and they

planted roses and periwinkles around the concrete patio, and in the double-wide's backyard put in a dozen rows of vegetables. When they were finished, the sun was setting and the patio and garden almost looked homey. Hillary fixed a pitcher of martinis and Sam lit the barbeque. They set the picnic table with a linen tablecloth and a couple of hurricane lamps, and were halfway through two T-bones and a bottle of Cabernet when Hillary reached across the table and touched his hand.

"Sam, there's something I want to talk to you about. . . ."

Oh, no, here it comes, he thought.

"I've enjoyed the last six months with you more than I can tell you, Sam."

"I feel the same way, Hillary. I mean, the last few years haven't been the richest time in my life, and getting to know you again . . . well, it's been great, Hillary. Really something great."

"We're so much alike," said Hillary. "We're both majors in the army. We both like cars. We like to travel. We like to garden. It's really kind of amazing, isn't it? Running into each other after all these years, halfway moving in together, seeing each other all the time. Who would have thought . . ."

"I know. I remember thinking when I got my orders to Fort Campbell, how was I going to meet someone down *here?* Then, that first night, I turned around and there you were."

"And you didn't waste any time either, did you? You took me downtown, wined me, dined me, got me drunk, and drove me back here and threw me on the bed and kept me up half the night, then you had to get up and go on one of those damn reveille runs. I still don't know how you did it."

"I don't either," Sam laughed. "I guess maybe I'm not as old as my 201 file says I am."

"Sam, I just think . . . I don't want . . ."

"What are you trying to say, Hillary?"

"I'm trying to say, I *think* I'm trying to say that I don't want either of us . . ."

"To get hurt."

"To get hurt."

"I think I know what you're getting at," said Sam, taking a sip of wine. "We've been spending a lot of time together, but you're not ready and I'm not ready to get married again right away. Am I right?"

"That's what I'm trying to say, Sam. I really love being with you . . . hell, I really love you, Sam. But we're both grown ups. I think maybe it would be good for both of us if we began seeing other people as well."

Sam took a deep breath. "I can't tell you how relieved I am to hear you say that, Hillary. I mean, another marriage just doesn't come up on the screen for me right now. I don't know if it's the age we're at, or being majors, or what, but I feel in between things right now, you know?"

"I feel the same way. I'm coming up for reassignment at the end of this year, and I didn't want . . ."

"I know what you mean, Hillary," Sam said. "Let's enjoy each other's company and be glad the army saw fit to reacquaint us here at Campbell."

She leaned across the table and kissed him. "Me too, Major Butterfield. Me too. Now, your turn to do the dishes, or mine?"

* * *

It was an hour past lunch, the executive officer was full of Yankee pot roast and fruit salad and peas and carrots and Black Forest cake, and he'd felt himself nodding over his by now poopsheet-strewn desk once or twice when he heard the third, or was it fourth knock at the door of his office.

"Enter," mumbled the beleaguered poopsheet-besotted executive officer.

The sergeant major stepped in, closed the door behind himself, and stood next to Sam's desk at ease.

"Sir, there's some weird character out here in the orderly room askin' for you." The sergeant major was a man of short, well-rounded stature whose operative theory of army life seemed to have encompassed never having let anything get in the way of a good meal. His looks were deceiving, however. He was from a place called Deer Lodge, Montana. He had spent the first twenty years of his life in the mountains, and the next twenty in the Rangers. He was fast on his feet, and they said he could move as quickly vertically as he could horizontally. One look at the man's Popeye forearms, and Sam was willing to believe anything.

"Who is it? Did he give his name?"

"No, sir. Just said he had to see you right away."

Sam glanced into the orderly room.

"Where is he?"

"Got him stashed in a chair over by the coffeemaker, sir. He's shakin' so bad he can barely stand up."

"Send him in," Sam said, piling the papers cluttering his desk in one corner.

The sergeant major disappeared. When the executive officer looked up, Johnny Gee was standing before him in a skinny gray sharkskin suit, puffing nervously on a cigarette. His eyes were sunk into deep black pockets, and his hands shook visibly.

"What in hell are you doing here, Johnny?" asked Sam, kicking the door closed with his boot. "You look terrible."

"They shot Spicer, man. I got no place else to go. You're the only person on this fuckin' earth I can trust. I had no choice. I'm sorry. I don't want to fuck up your stuff, man, but I'm just so fuckin' scared, I didn't know what else to do."

"What were you doing there?" Sam gaped at the nervously twitching form of Johnny Gee and considered the situation with abject amazement. First you get a new job, then happen upon someone from your past and settle into something comfortable and good, and now *this*. The apparition before him wasn't part of the plan. He got a sinking feeling in the pit of his stomach, and a cold sweat broke out on his forehead.

"I found him early this mornin'. I was going over to his place to borrow a few bucks. And there he was dead. Just took him out in the woods next to his trailer and tied him to a tree and shot him in the head. And they're after us."

"Us?"

"Yeah. You and me. I don't know how, but they got our names. Spicer musta given up our names 'fore he died. He was all beaten up and shit. They musta beat it outa him. Spicer never woulda given you up otherwise. They know who we are, man. Ain't no doubt about that. The word is on the street. They're gonna do us the same as they did Spicer. They know we seen those fuckin' tapes, man, and nothin' is gonna stop 'em."

"Spicer told us he was sending the tapes to the attorney general. That was all taken care of months ago."

"You read anything in the paper about any investigation? Any arrests? Don't you think you'da seen somethin' by now if Spicer done what he said he was gonna do? They're after us, man. You got to believe me. They got Spicer, and now they want us."

"Who is 'they'?"

"How should I fuckin' know, man? Whoever was after our asses that night you jumped in and helped me. Whoever them tapes belong to. Whoever is connected up with all them big politicians and shit. How am I 'sposed to know? All I know is, Spicer's tied to that tree, shot in the head. I got myself outa there fast as I could. I had to. I'm on their goddamned spring cleanin' program, man. So are you."

"When did you find him?"

"This mornin', 'bout six o'clock."

"How'd you get here?"

"Boosted a car. Drove straight here."

"You *stole* a car?"

"What else was I 'sposed to do, man? Call a cab? Don't worry. I stashed it downtown behind a closed-down factory building. They won't find it for a month. I didn't drive it on the post here, man. I caught a bus from town."

"I can't believe this. I just can't believe it," Sam said, holding his head in his hands.

"What can't you believe, man? They shot fuckin' Spicer. They shot him, man. With a big fuckin' gun. He is *dead,* man. And he didn't have nothin' to do with this thing. All he did was help us out of a jam, and they killed him for it. And it was our fault."

Sam looked up at Johnny Gee. He was right. Spicer had

nothing to do with the tapes, nothing to do with the fight at the diner, nothing to do with the car they ran off the road so many nights ago. All he did was come through for an old friend, and he got killed for it.

Sam thought back to the days they'd raced modifieds together. Spicer had taught him how to set up his suspension and tune it differently for tenth of a mile, quarter-mile, and half-mile tracks. He'd taught him about track conditions, how to vary tire rubber compounds to get the best traction. And one time, when Spicer had failed to make the feature race and Sam's motor had blown in his preliminary, Spicer had lent him his motor. The two of them ripped it out of Spicer's car and mounted it in Sam's between the prelim and the feature. Sam won the feature, and the thing was, Spicer was as happy about the win as he was.

Then, years later, he had climbed into the back of Spicer's truck and Spicer had driven him out of the county, away from the swarm of cops who had been looking for him on a spurious drug rap. Without the unquestioning friendship of Spicer, Sam never would have made it to the bus from Columbus to Ft. Campbell. He would have been AWOL, in deep trouble with the army. He probably wouldn't be sitting where he was right now, in the exec's office in a Ranger battalion. He was numb at the thought.

"Jesus, Johnny, he's really dead?"

"You'd better believe he's dead, man. I stood right there by that tree this mornin', 'bout as far as I am from you. They shot him in the head, and they beat him close to death 'fore they did it. Lookin' at him, I started cryin', man. And it's been years since I cried. Years." His eyes began welling up with tears, and he wiped them on his sleeve.

"I'm sorry, man. I know I'm steppin' on your stuff here, but I had to come."

The tears stopped, and Johnny Gee looked at Sam.

"We've got to do somethin'. All my life, I been runnin' from stuff. When things would go bad, I'd just pick up and split, land somewhere else, and start the same shit over again. I never once faced nothin' down. I let somebody else pick up the pieces of the mess I made. I was always runnin', always runnin'. That's what I done this time, too. I run down here to you. I didn't know what else to do, man. Runnin' is all I know."

Johnny Gee hung his head for a moment, then looked up at Sam again.

"That's why you got to help me, Major. I don't wanna run no more, and I don't think runnin' will do me any good this time, anyway."

"Sit down," Sam said, pulling up a chair.

Johnny Gee sat down and puffed on his cigarette.

"What are we gonna do? Spicer's dead. He didn't do nothin', and he's dead. What are we gonna do?"

This is it, thought Sam. This is that thing they told you about in Ranger school, the thing the army spends years preparing you for. The time would come, they said, when you'd have to stand up and toe the line and make a decision that would determine whether people lived or died. Not just your own life, but the lives of others as well. If you're a combat commander, you might do it every day. But in regular life, when there is no war to fight, most men never face the day when their lives and those of others are literally on the line. Most men spend years arranging things so this kind of moment will never come.

Well, it's here, he thought. It's now.

He stared at the skinny man in the gray suit, who was lighting another cigarette from the tip of his last one, wiping his eyes with his sleeve, tapping his pointed-toe shoes on the floor. He felt a strange affinity with this man called Johnny Gee. He couldn't quite put his finger on the reason why, but he reminded him of a guy he'd raced against when he first started running his Chevy on the dirt tracks of southern Illinois. He was a country boy, maybe ten years older than Sam, and he loved racing with all his heart. He worked two jobs, and poured every cent he earned into his car. He'd been racing for a dozen years, and Sam knew that he'd turned up only once in the winner's circle. Only once had he proudly taken that extra lap with the checkered flag flying from the window of his car. As hard as he tried, and as much money as he spent, winning races somehow consistently eluded him. He'd spin out on the first lap, or run out of gas in the forty-lap feature, or smack into a four-car pile-up he didn't cause. He was an excellent mechanic, he was up on all the latest stock car technology, and his car was always as well prepared as any on the track, but nothing ever went his way.

"Bad luck chases him around that dirt oval like an ex-wife with a writ," Sam heard another racer say one night.

The same might be said of Johnny Gee, he thought. He was a nice enough guy, and as small-time hustlers go, he was probably among the better of them. He had a good sense of humor, and the admirable quality of loyalty, in a kind of backhanded way. Spicer had been the same way. Nothing was ever truly on the up-and-up with Spicer, but when push came to shove, he was there for you. When Sam thought about it, a good number of the guys he went to high school with were just like those two—not terribly bright, a bit down at the heels, but loyal as a hungry puppy with his nose pressed against the screen door on the back porch. He'd had friends like Spicer and Johnny Gee in high school. His best friend in high school, in fact, reminded him a lot of Johnny Gee. He had died in a Friday night car wreck two years after they graduated. Somebody else was driving.

He sat there, staring at Johnny Gee and thinking about his friend, Chester Davidson. He remembered, when his mother wrote him of his friend's death, thinking what a shame it was that the world didn't treat the Chester Davidsons better than it did. It wasn't fair that Chester had died, and all the others in his class—among them several violent raving local lunatics who belonged at least behind bars if not in Chester's place beneath the ground—were still living. He remembered how helpless he felt reading his mother's letter about Chester's death. What could he have done for his friend if he were still back home in Illinois? Keep him from riding around with a carload of beer-swilling assholes? Probably not. But sitting in his barracks three thousand miles away, who knew? After Chester was gone, what consolation could he have afforded Chester's parents? Not much, probably. As it was, he couldn't even attend the funeral. It wasn't fair, he'd thought back then.

It wasn't fair that Spicer was dead, either. But this time, there was a big difference. He wasn't three thousand miles away and he wasn't a lieutenant who couldn't get away on leave. He was a major in the army. He was experienced. He could *do* something.

"Wait here," he told Johnny Gee. "I'll be right back."

Back at Fort Lewis, Duchamp had been a pretty understanding guy. More than once, Sam had gone to him with personal and professional problems that had confounded him. Many of the solutions Duchamp suggested or approved were anything but "by the book," reflecting a reckless, adventuresome streak that was not always appreciated by his superiors. But what Sam had to say today was going to crowd the corners of the colonel's tolerance.

"Where's the old man?" he asked the sergeant major.

"He's out for the rest of the afternoon, sir."

"Where is he, sergeant major?"

The sergeant major caught the edge of desperation in the XO's eye.

"He's checking out the obstacle course, sir," said the sergeant major.

"Thanks, sergeant major," said Sam, flying out the door.

"You're not supposed to take your vehicle out there," the sergeant major called after him, but he was long gone.

He grabbed Johnny Gee and jumped in his Porsche, and headed down a narrow blacktop through the pines toward the battalion training area.

"Where we goin'?" asked Johnny Gee, still nervously smoking one cigarette after another.

"To see the colonel."

"What . . ."

"Shut up," Sam commanded. "I've got to think about this thing."

They drove in silence several miles into the woods and turned off on a dirt road leading north. A mile later, they came upon the colonel's jeep parked by the side of the road. Sam could see the colonel and his driver walking through the obstacle course, checking the tension on a rope here, examining wooden structures for protruding nails there. He parked the Porsche and instructed Johnny Gee to stay with the car. As he approached the colonel he saluted smartly and asked permission to speak with him alone. The colonel dismissed his driver.

"What's on your mind, Sam?" asked the colonel.

"I don't exactly know where to start."

"Start at the beginning," said the colonel.

So he did: "I was sitting in this diner having dinner on my way down here, sir," he began. He told the colonel the whole story. When he was finished, the colonel fished a cigar from his fatigue jacket pocket and took his time lighting up.

"How come you didn't say anything about this when you reported in?" he asked.

"I thought it was over," Sam said. The two men were sitting on the end of a log that was part of one of the obstacles. To their left was the vertical scaling wall, and to their right, the rope swing over the mud pit. The only sounds in the pine forest were the rustling of needles in the wind and an occasional, mournful bobwhite calling for its mate.

"What do you propose to do, Sam?" asked the colonel, pinching the end of his burnt match to make sure it was completely extinguished.

"I'm going back," he asserted, pointing to Johnny Gee, who could be seen sitting in the front seat of the Porsche, staring straight ahead and chain-smoking.

"I'm not certain you understand the consequences of what you want to do," said the colonel. He tapped a quarter-size ash from the tip of his cigar and ground it into the dirt with the toe of his jump boot.

"What would you do?"

"I think we ought to go straight from here to the post provost marshal, report the crimes to which you are a witness, and let him handle this thing through channels."

"I'm sure that's the right thing to do, sir, and I want to do what's right. But the point is, the channels have broken down. Those tapes were sent to the state attorney general months ago, and nothing has happened. Some of the men I saw on them are the most powerful politicians in the state of Illinois. How do you know the provost marshal won't make his report through channels, and once his report reaches Illinois, one of the channels ends up being controlled by someone on a surveillance tape, by one of the bad guys? We don't. That's why I've got to go back there. I've got to figure out who can be trusted and go through him to the proper authorities. There's no other way. I'm sure of it."

The colonel took a long drag on his cigar and exhaled, watching the smoke drift up toward the pine trees.

"I wish I were still as sure of things as you are, Sam," said the colonel. "I was, once."

"Does that mean—"

"That doesn't mean shit, Sam," barked the colonel. "I don't approve, nor do I condone what you're about to do. For one thing, you seem to have forgotten what I told you. Politics and the military *do not mix.* When they do, the combination is explosive. If you get caught up in the middle of some political scandal in Illinois, your career is going up in smoke. *Finito. Kaput.* You won't be eligible for a position flipping burgers at the post exchange, if that happens. You've been in this man's army for over ten years, Sam. You're halfway home. You've got a fine career, potentially a great career ahead of you."

Sam was mute. He knew the colonel was right. He was taking an enormous chance, but it was a chance he had to take.

"Sign out at battalion on an ordinary pass. You've got some leave-time racked up, haven't you?"

"Yes, sir."

"I'll convert the pass to leave if you're gone past the weekend."

"Yes, sir."

"Be careful out there, Sam. Those people don't give a shit about any code of honor or sense of mission or duty. All that counts out there is money and power. Don't forget it."

"I won't."

"Vamoose. I don't want to know where you're going or what you're going to do. Get." The colonel shooed him away like a stray dog. Sam lit out for the Porsche and found Johnny Gee nervously puffing on a cigarette. He stopped at a pay phone and called Hillary, asking her to meet him at the trailer.

"Who, or what, is that creature in there?" she said when Johnny Gee was using the bathroom down the hall of the double-wide.

He started to explain his reasons for going back to Illinois, but gave up when his own explanation stopped making sense to him. It wasn't something he could put easily into words, he told her. He stuffed a change of clothes and his dop kit into a small overnight bag.

"I think I understand, Sam," she said. "But I think you ought to consider very carefully what this might mean to your career. You've got a perfect record, Sam. This is the kind of thing that could ruin you for good."

"All I know is, a man was killed yesterday because of me, Hillary. And I don't want to walk away from something I started and didn't finish."

"Well, Sam, there are channels you can go through . . ."

"You may be right about those channels in the abstract, but what I witnessed wasn't abstract. It was real. And the other thing that's real is this: they killed Spicer. He helped me out when I needed help. It wasn't his business, and now he's dead because of the fact that he helped me and Johnny Gee get away. I asked him for help, and he gave it, and now he's dead. You know something? Some men go all the way through their lives and never have a friend they can count on when the hammer comes down. You and I both know what it's like not to have been able to count on your own spouse. Well, Spicer was there for me, and I'm going to be there for him. I'm not going to let him down. I won't do it."

Hillary stood up and took both of his hands in hers.

"Take care of yourself out there, Major. Take care of what's-his-name. And remember: those civilians don't play by the same rules as us."

Johnny Gee emerged from the bathroom, hair freshly slicked back, a cigarette dangling from his lips. Sam thought he detected a waft of his own aftershave lotion coming from the skinny man as he walked past.

"Nice crib you got here, man," he said.

Sam leaned over and kissed Hillary as Johnny Gee walked out the door.

He hesitated at the door. Her face was turned toward him, but she was still standing where he had left her.

"I'll call you, Hillary. Thanks."

Hillary listened until she couldn't hear the whine of the Porsche's engine any more.

THE DRIVE FROM Fort Campbell to Springfield stretched through the afternoon into dusk. Sam flipped on the head-lights. The inside of the Porsche glowed from the soft light of the dash instruments. To his right, Johnny Gee reclined against the headrest, snoozing.

"Hey, Johnny, wake up. We've got to talk. I want to make sure we've covered everything."

"What do you mean, man?"

"To begin with, what do you think Spicer did with the tapes?"

"Who knows? He probably sent them off, like he said he would. You really think the attorney general's gonna get serious about 'em when half the dudes on the tapes are his political buddies? Huh?"

"I don't know, Johnny. I really don't know. Maybe we ought to go to the attorney general ourselves. We could tell him what we saw on the tapes, and tell him we think Spicer was killed because of them."

"What good is that gonna do us? If he's got 'em, and he's sittin' on 'em, all he'll do is deny it. If he doesn't have 'em, it'll sound like we've been smokin' funny cigarettes, hallucinatin' an' shit."

"Going back to the sheriff is out of the question."

"Harlan Greene's best friend? Yeah, that'd do us a lot a good."

"Okay, Johnny. You go ahead and get some rest. I think I know what we should do first."

Johnny Gee leaned back and dropped off to sleep as Sam pointed the nose of the Porsche into the darkness. As they crossed the Illinois state line, he turned off the interstate onto a two-lane state road heading north. After an hour, he turned left, then right onto a county blacktop. They passed through several small farm towns and Sam turned once again, right this time off the blacktop onto a gravel farm road. Soon the familiar white fence appeared on his left. He turned into the drive, shifted into first, and pulled up the hill to his family's farmhouse. A light went on in an upstairs window. Sam cut the engine and shook Johnny Gee.

"Where are we, man?"

"At my mother's house," said Sam. "Come on in."

"What time is it?"

"Just past ten." The front door opened and Sam could see the bathrobe-clad figure of his mother in the porchlight. Sam climbed out of the Porsche and hugged her.

"You don't have to tell me," said his mother as she pulled away, studying her son with a grave look. "It's about Harlan Greene, isn't it, Sam?"

"Yes, Ma, it is." Sam introduced Johnny Gee and the three of them repaired to the kitchen. His mother put a pot of coffee on the stove and carried a bowl of fruit in from the dining room. They sat around the kitchen table waiting for the coffee to perk as Sam explained what had happened over the past twenty-four hours.

"I've been expecting you to show up here for about a week," said his mother when he had finished.

"Why is that, Ma?"

"I've been hearing things."

"What kind of things?"

"Harlan Greene's up to something, Sam, but I don't know what it is. There's all kinds of stuff going on over in Hamilton County. It was in the newspaper that the governor's been down here twice in the last month, but I know for a fact that he visited Hamilton County at least one other time, and I heard he was down in Rock County, too. Isn't that one of the places you said you saw Harlan Greene on those tapes?"

"Yeah, Ma. They were surveying a big field down there. He was with several other men."

"Well, he's up to something, I can tell you that much. I don't know what it is, but it's probably something like a new highway, or maybe they're going to dam up another river and flood out another reservoir. You know how they keep those things secret until they're announced. . . ."

"So their buddies can buy up land along the route where the interchanges will be. Yeah, I remember Dad complaining about that when they dammed up Rend Lake and built Interstate 57 years ago. The whole thing was fixed, he said. If you wanted to put in a McDonald's or a Holiday Inn, you had to lease land from Paul Powell's friends."

"Paul Powell?" Johnny Gee poured three cups of coffee and carried them to the table.

"You probably don't remember him. He was secretary of state for years, one of the most powerful men in the state. He was kind of the Mayor Daley of downstate Illinois. When he died, they found eight hundred thousand dollars in small bills tucked away in shoeboxes in his hotel room in Springfield. For twenty years he got a piece of every public works project built down here. They used to say the only man more powerful than Paul Powell was the president, but then the president couldn't get your road repaired or a bridge built. Paul Powell had the kind of power that counted. He could get people elected and he could get things done, roads and bridges built, new post offices and city halls funded."

"And Harlan Greene learned everything he knows at the feet of Paul Powell," said Mrs. Butterfield. "He didn't miss a trick. After Paul Powell went up to Springfield, whenever he needed the strings pulled down here, Harlan did the pulling. Harlan's power base, being county Democratic chairman over in Hamilton County, is the same position Paul Powell held for twenty years before he ran for secretary of state. Of course, his influence spread far beyond the county, and so does Harlan's."

"Ma, the reason I've come back here isn't just Harlan Greene. You remember the man I told you about who helped us? The guy I used to race against, Dave Spicer, from down in Jerome? Johnny found his body yesterday in the woods near his trailer. Somebody beat him to death, looking for the videotapes we left with him."

"Sam . . . you don't—"

"I don't know what to think, Ma. Old Spicer didn't have any enemies. Why else would someone want him dead? And now Johnny's heard the word is out they're looking for us."

"Who is 'they,' Sam?"

"I don't know, but it could be Harlan Greene and his boys, and given your history with him, I wanted you to know what's going on. I don't want any trouble, Ma, but something's got to be done. That's why I came back."

"I understand, Sam. But what are you going to do?"

"The first thing is, we're going to try and find out who's looking for us, what's going on. Then we're going to find out what happened to the videotapes we left with Spicer. And we're going to try and get them to the proper authorities."

"If it's Harlan Greene you're after, Sam, the only way you're going to get him is politically, you know that, don't you?"

"What do you mean?"

"I mean, with the kind of power that man has, the only thing he understands is political power. The law doesn't intimidate him. If he doesn't like the law, he has new laws written that he *does* like. The protection surrounding him comes from the law. He owns every sheriff's department for ten counties around. What he wants done gets done. And anybody who gets in his way gets crushed."

"Then who do you think made those surveillance tapes he showed up on? From the looks of them, he was the target of the surveillance. If he's so powerful, who's big enough in this state to go up against him? The governor?"

"I don't know, Sam. All I know is this: the only power that will bring him down is the power that built him up.

Political power. No matter what you do, you've got to re-member that."

"You sound just like Dad, Ma. Politics. Politics. Nothing gets done without politics. That's what he used to say over and over."

"And your father was right as rain, Sam."

"He was right as far as he went," Sam said. "But he ignored Clausewitz's dictum, that where politics ends, war-fare begins. And I don't care if it takes going to war, I'm going to find out who killed Dave Spicer, and they're going to pay the penalty."

"Why don't you boys get yourselves some sleep," said Mrs. Butterfield, laying an affectionate hand on Sam's shoul-der. "It sounds to me like you're going to need it."

The next afternoon, Sam and Johnny Gee drove north toward Springfield, the Illinois capital located almost squarely in the middle of the state. Although they could have taken an interstate at least part of the way, they avoided the fastest route and stuck to state and county roads, which in central Illinois farm country followed section lines, running due north/south or east/west.

It was time to see Sheila.

She was an outsider who knew all the players inside. She had the additional value of being the only contact they had. Whether she would help them separate the good guys from the bad guys . . . that remained to be seen.

Sam, for one, was not accustomed to the concept of hooker as reliable source. Having watched her performance on the surveillance tape, he was far from convinced of the goodness of her motives in cooperating with those doing the videotaping of Lou Bosco and two hookers romping around the kingsize bed.

"What can I tell ya', man?" said Johnny Gee, a pint of Black Velvet whiskey in one hand, a Picayune cigarette in the other, strung out on fear, mouth twitching, hands shaking, knees pumping up and down.

Sam crouched behind the wheel of the 944 and drove. In an hour, they'd be in Springfield. They had to *do* something. They needed somebody in reserve. His mind kept going back to what he'd learned in the army. Never reveal your total strength to the enemy. Never approach an objective with all of your forces. Always . . . *but always* . . . keep forces in reserve.

"We're not going to diddlybop in there without somebody outside as backup," Sam said. He glanced at the speedometer. They were doing seventy-five, a comfortable cruise. You could barely hear the Porsche's little four-banger purring away up there under the hood. There was no wind noise. A country station burbled at low volume on the radio.

They could see the lights of Springfield illuminating the sky on the horizon. Johnny Gee had finished the pint of Black Velvet and was deep into his second pack of Picayunes. His hands had stopped shaking, and a wide smile had returned to his thin features.

"Okay, man, I got an idea," said Johnny Gee. "Which way we comin' into town?"

"On 29."

"Good. You get near the center of town, look for MacIntyre Street and hang a left. I'll show you the way from there."

"What have you got in mind?"

"You want backup? I'll get you backup. I know what you mean, man. These guys are playin' for keeps."

"Reach under your seat and hand me that bag," Sam instructed.

Johnny Gee felt along the edge of his low-slung seat and pulled out a neatly folded grocery bag.

"Weighs a fuckin' ton, man. What's in there?"

"Give it to me."

Johnny Gee handed him the bag. Sam put it in his lap and unfolded it with one hand. He reached inside.

"What the fuck is *that?*" Johnny Gee recoiled against the car door.

"It's my army issue .45," Sam said, holding the massive gray steel pistol in his right hand. He handed the bag to Johnny Gee. "Stick this back under your seat."

Johnny Gee peered into the bag.

"What's the rest of this stuff?"

"Five more full magazines. I've got one loaded already."

"You aren't plannin' on *usin'* that thing, are you, man?"

"Only if I have to."

"Man, I got me a bellyful of Mexican courage, but I don't know about this gun shit," said Johnny Gee. "You didn't say nothin' about takin' a gun before we left, man."

"I didn't have to. The .45 is always under the passenger seat, except when I'm home. Then I take it inside."

"That's . . . that's . . . that's not what I mean, Major," stuttered Johnny Gee, searching for the right words. "I mean, you didn't say nothin' about *shootin'* anybody."

"I don't plan to."

"Then why you got the gun?"

"The .45 is for the possibility that someone might try to shoot me, or you, for that matter."

"Defensive, like."

"Defensive."

"Oh."

They hit Springfield, and near the center of town took a left on MacIntyre, drove a couple of blocks, took a right, and stopped. A small awning over the door next to the car had plastic letters spelling BILLIARDS sewn into the edge of the canvas. Both letters and awning had seen better days.

"This is the place?" asked Sam.

"The very one," said Johnny Gee.

"Do you want me to come in with you?"

"Your presence . . . aahh . . . might make the patrons kinda nervous, if you get what I mean," said Johnny Gee.

"I'll stay with the car."

"This won't take long."

Johnny Gee sauntered under the awning and through the door into smoky dimness, relaxed amidst the greenish glow of the pool tables and the soft click of the balls so familiar to him. A big black man behind an old brass cash register stood as he entered. Johnny Gee shot his cuffs and glanced down at his shoes. They'd seen better days.

"How you doin', Tiny?" asked Johnny Gee, leaning against the cash register.

"My name ain't Tiny, honky," said the big black man, folding his arms across his chest, which was wider than the scrolled and engraved brass cash register.

"Yeah, well, my name ain't honky," said Johnny Gee. He watched as the big black man moved to his left, coming out from behind the register.

"You ought to know you ain't got no business in here,"

said the big black man. "This is a colored pool hall. This place ain't your place." He stood next to the door with his hand on the doorknob.

"You better be findin' your way outa this part of town," said the big black man.

"I was just lookin' for Moon," said Johnny Gee. "He still play here?"

The big black man took his hand off the doorknob and folded his arms again. He stood a foot taller than Johnny Gee. He was wearing baby blue jogging pants and a baby blue T-shirt, and he smelled of lavender aftershave.

"Who wants to know?" he asked. His voice was surprisingly squeaky for a man of his size.

"Johnny Gee. Me and him were, ah, roommates for a while, you might say."

"You the dude from down south Moon always be talkin' about? The skinny dude with the mean stick?"

Johnny Gee stepped back and pirouetted once.

"The one and only," he said.

"Gimme just a minute."

The big black man stepped behind the cash register and picked up a phone and whispered. Then he pointed to the back of the pool hall.

"Moon be through that door. He say come on back, he be glad to see you." The big man smiled widely at Johnny Gee. He had all of his teeth, and they were very white, except for the ones in front, on which had been engraved the letters "T-I-N-Y" in gold. Johnny Gee walked through the nearly empty pool hall. Only a couple of games were in progress, being played by older gentlemen wearing fedoras and snap brims and suits with wide lapels and baggy pants. The place looked like a page out of a dusty, yellowed copy of a men's magazine from the fifties.

He reached the back door, knocked once. The door opened. A short black man with gray hair came out and motioned that Johnny Gee should put his hands over his head, which he did. The short black man patted him down for weapons, reached inside his jacket, and took his wallet. He checked the wallet and handed it back to Johnny Gee.

"Razor blades," the short black man said to Johnny Gee, nodding at the wallet. "Dudes takin' to carryin' razor blades right in a damn wallet." He shrugged and nodded toward the door. Johnny Gee walked through.

"My man! Skinny Minny Johnny!" The voice came from somewhere in the dimness at the end of the back room. Johnny Gee squinted, but he couldn't see anything. He waited at the door for his eyes to adjust to the dark.

"Moon? That you?" he asked.

"You right about that," said the voice. "C'mon over here and sit down wit da Moon. Long time no see, my man."

Johnny Gee walked in the direction of the voice. He saw nothing but darkness for his first ten steps. Then, at the end of the room, he saw the man the voice belonged to. He was seated on a velvet sofa with two young black women, one on either side of him. He was wearing a red silk suit, a black shirt, and a white tie. A gold medallion hung over the tie. On his feet were a pair of cream-colored kidskin loafers with black wingtip toes.

"You are lookin' good, Moon. How do you feel?" asked Johnny Gee as he approached.

"Never better, my man. Where you been keepin' yo'se'f? Ain't seen you in a couple years, must be."

Moon stood and took Johnny Gee's hand and led him to a

leather armchair. The room appeared to be empty except for a round card table, the armchair, and the sofa. Johnny Gee sat down.

"Girls, this here is Johnny Gee, who I ain't seen since we done some time together. Johnny, this here is Rowanda and this here is Rolene. They twins."

Johnny Gee shook hands with the girls, who didn't look a day over eighteen and who were wearing matching green leather minidresses and knee-high white boots. Rowanda giggled. Johnny Gee could smell the bubblegum on her breath.

"Girls, why don't you take a little walk and let me talk to my man, here," said Moon.

"We ain't got nothin' to do-o-o," whined Rolene.

"Do yo' eyes and yo' lips," hissed Moon. The girls walked across the room and huddled in a corner.

"Whatchew got on yo' mind, Johnny?" asked Moon.

"I need you to come with me up to Corrine's place," said Johnny Gee.

"Corrine's place? You lookin' fo' pussy? You got all you can use right here, man," said Moon. He pointed at the girls, who were standing in the light by the door.

"I could *use* some pussy, but I don't *need* pussy," said Johnny Gee. "What I *need* to do is to talk to Sheila. Me and her ran a con together a few years back. I just now found out she's runnin' the big cathouse in the capital city. Somethin's come up, and I've got to see her. But I ain't been up here in Springfield in years, man. I don't know the lay of the land no more, you know? I need some coverage."

"You in some kinda trouble? I seen you lookin' better. Even in the joint you had some color. You be white as my socks!" The big black man threw his head back and laughed.

Johnny Gee grinned nervously.

"Trouble is what I've got," he said. He sat down and filled his friend's ear for ten minutes. The big man nodded once or twice, then squinted into the darkness and called his girls. They arrived in a fog of five-and-dime perfume. The big man peeled two bills off his roll and handed them the money.

"You all amuse yo'se'fs for a while. I got some bidness to take care of," he said. The girls took the money and sashayed into the pool room.

"What you be needin', Johnny?"

"I'm not real sure, Moon. I guess it'd be nice if you rode along with us, kinda noticeable-like. And the major, he keeps talkin' about us needin' backup."

"You want to discourage the local talent from takin' too close an interest in yo' shit, is what you mean."

"That sounds about right," said Johnny Gee.

They walked into the front room of the pool hall and found Sam, corralled by Tiny. Tiny turned his head, and Moon gave him a signal. He stepped aside.

"That's the biggest person I've ever seen in my life," said Sam, who was standing in the door of the poolroom. "You didn't tell me this was a black place," he said.

"You didn't ask," said Johnny Gee.

They climbed in the Porsche, Johnny Gee squeezed cross-wise into the jump seats, Moon in the front. Sam cranked the engine.

"Where to?" he asked.

"Thirteen twenty-eight Yardley," said Johnny Gee. "Out near the north edge of town."

"Sheila . . . ain't she the one used to write you in the joint?" asked Moon.

"You wanna call a birthday card and a Christmas card writin', yeah, she was the one."

"Yo' girl done moved up in the world, if she runnin' Corrine's, Johnny. Yardley ain't no beat downtown street. Yardley be *uptown.*"

Sam hit the lights and turned the corner. "Which way do you want to go? Out the interstate?"

"Nah. Stay off the interstate. Take High Street."

The drive to the north edge of town took them past the tree-lined grounds of the state capitol. Just on the other side of a small city park, Sam took a right, slowed down, and began checking house numbers.

"Seven hundred block. Six more to go."

"This Yardley?" asked Johnny Gee.

"Yes indeed," said Moon mockingly.

The houses lined the street in two neat rows. Most were wood-frame Victorians with porches and cupolas and gabled roofs, but some were squarish fieldstone structures with gently sloping roofs and dormer windows, a style that was popular in the 1920s. A few had gone to seed, been cut up into rooming houses and apartments, and clusters of mailboxes hung next to their front doors. One or two looked abandoned.

A few blocks down, the street changed. Garbage cans were neatly aligned next to driveways. Fresh paint adorned wood trim. Front porches had a porch swing at one end and a wicker glider at the other. Cars parked in driveways tended toward the Volvo/BMW end of the automotive spectrum. Lawns had been mown and raked, and children's toys and bicycles were neatly arranged at the far end of driveways, behind locked gates.

"Corrine's has moved to the yuppie side of town," said Johnny Gee. "I'll bet these Volvo drivers are just delighted to have this joint in the neighborhood."

"Them Volvo drivers don't have nothin' to say about it," said Moon.

Halfway down the thirteen-hundred block, a tall stone fence appeared on the right and ran a third of the way down the block. The house on the other side of the fence couldn't be seen behind the trees and rhododendrons in the way. At the end of the fence, stone pillars framed a cast iron gate. A television surveillance camera was bolted to the top of one pillar, aimed at the bottom of the other pillar where a buzzer system intercom was mounted.

"This place looks like the front gate to Greenville," said Moon.

"What's Greenville?" asked Sam.

"The state pen," said Johnny Gee.

Sam pulled the Porsche up to the gate and idled the engine.

Johnny Gee unfolded himself from the jump seat and stepped up to the intercom.

"Is this thirteen twenty-eight Yardley?" he called into the intercom speaker, pressing the talk button.

The television camera panned from the driveway and aimed itself directly on the intercom.

"Who's speaking, please?" said a woman's voice, Thai, lilting.

"Johnny Gee. I want to see Sheila."

Pause.

"Are you expected?" asked the voice in the same sing-song tone.

"Nah. I just got to see her. Tell her it's Johnny Gee."

Pause.

"One moment, please."

"What's going on?" asked Sam.

"I told them I want to see Sheila, and they said to wait a minute."

"Sir?" The metallic sing-song voice called from the inter-com speaker.

Johnny Gee looked up at the camera.

"Yeah."

Pause.

"Is that your vehicle?"

"Yeah."

Pause.

"Is there anyone else in the vehicle?"

"Yeah. Two guys. Friends of mine."

Pause.

"I don't know whether we will be able to accommodate your friends."

"Listen to me. We're not looking for a party. I gotta see Sheila and my friends are comin' with me. Now if there are any questions, tell her to talk to me over this thing."

"What's the problem?" asked Sam. He felt for the .45 under the seat, and tightened his fingers around its grip.

"I don't know. Some bitch is sayin' you guys can't be fuckin' accommodated or somethin'."

They stared out the windshield of the car for a few moments, and the intercom crackled again.

"Johnny?" a woman's voice said. "Johnny?"

"That's Sheila," said Johnny Gee.

"Sheila? That you?"

There was a pause.

"It's been a long time, Johnny. Get in the car and tell the driver to back up a few feet. I'll open the gate."

Johnny Gee wrestled himself inside, Sam backed up, and the huge iron gates opened. He put the Porsche in gear and they drove through.

IT WASN'T A house, it was an L-shaped stone mansion set back a hundred yards from the street at the whip end of a winding gravel drive lined with privet hedge. The drive curled around a fountain and branched off into a smaller drive that led around the side of the mansion to a two-story garage that was at least as big as the rest of the houses on Yardley Street.

Sam braked the Porsche to a stop at the circle, front tires throwing gravel into the fountain, which was spotlit and had a marble cupid spouting water in its center.

"Jesus, look at this place," said Johnny Gee.

Ivy climbed the walls of the mansion, twirling itself around cupolas at both corners of the "L." There were at least thirty windows on the two front sides of the mansion, and lights shone through gauzy curtains in most of them. Two low steps led to the front door, twice the size of a normal one, of oak and leaded glass. The door opened. A girl in a black and white miniskirted maid's uniform stood in the entranceway. A huge staircase could be seen behind her, disappearing into the upper reaches of the house. She motioned them in.

Sam killed the engine and turned off the headlights.

"Why don't you wait here, Moon," he said, handing Moon the keys. "You ever drive one of these?"

"I drive a Mercedes," said Moon.

"Good. Get behind the wheel. If anything happens you don't like, start the engine and hit the horn and be ready to go."

"You got it."

Sam reached under the seat, pulled out the .45, and stuck it into his belt at the small of his back. Moon jumped out and took the driver's seat. Sam and Johnny Gee walked to the door.

The girl at the entrance greeted each of them with a cheery, "Hi, my name is Christine. Is there anything I can get for you?"

Neither said anything until Johnny Gee broke the silence.

"Quite a place. Where's Sheila?"

A door slid open along the left wall, and the woman they had seen on the surveillance tape stood in the doorway.

"Hi, Johnny," she breathed, her voice soft, cigarette-husky. "Why don't you and your friend come on in here." She stepped aside to reveal a comfortable Victorian parlor, wallpapered in dark red. Two sofas faced each other in the middle of the room, surrounded by a half-dozen chairs that had gold lions' paws for legs and eagles' heads for arms. The sofas were covered in deep royal blue crushed velvet, and the chairs in real leopard fur. The windows were draped in dark blue velvet with silver tassels. There was a fireplace, and two Tiffany lamps showed their colors atop a mahogany secretary.

The woman wore a long black velvet skirt and a white blouse with full, billowing sleeves and lace cuffs and collar. Her black hair was swept back at the sides, and the gray streak shone in front. She was prettier than she had looked on the black and white videotape, with a prominent, aquiline nose, high cheekbones, and thick eyebrows. Her skin was a lovely olive shade, her cheeks had an expertly applied pinkish glow, and her full lips sported a pale shade of pink lipstick. You could tell she was wearing makeup, but you couldn't tell what she was concealing.

She looked hard at Johnny Gee.

"You've got a lot of gall coming in here like this." Breathy tones had been replaced by nasal hissing. "What kind of game do you think you're running, Johnny? You think you can just ring my buzzer, and I'm supposed to jump through hoops for you because we had a thing going? Huh?"

"Sheila . . . I . . . I—" Johnny Gee stammered.

"You're hot, Johnny. You and the other asshole both. Every pistol-packing jimmy-dick schmuck for three states around is looking for you. The word's out, Johnny. You're so damn hot I should open a window to cool the place down. What did you do? Knock up the governor's daughter . . . by accident?"

"Real funny, Sheila." Johnny Gee straightened up and stopped stammering. "Nice to know you still got the instincts of a fuckin' rattlesnake."

Sheila chuckled and shook her head. She took a seat at one end of the Victorian sofa facing the fireplace.

"You'll never learn, will you, Johnny. You're always going to be small time, and you're always going to find trouble if trouble doesn't find you first. I pegged you a long, long time ago. I might have been young, but I wasn't stupid. I knew a loser when I saw one."

"We didn't come here to rehash the past," Sam said, looking intently at her. "Get over it—"

"It's okay, Major," Johnny Gee interrupted. "You got to understand: I got the two of us busted, back when we was together. It was my fault. But to her, the story's always been the same. She always figured I ratted her out."

The scowl on Sheila's face did not relax. Her left hand rested next to a button on the end table.

"I didn't tell them cops shit, Sheila. I don't care what they told you. I've never ratted anybody out in my life. I sure as hell didn't rat you out."

"You're a small-time fuck, Johnny. And I think I can say that with some accuracy, despite the fact that I never let you fuck me. I ought to turn you over to Harlan Greene right now." Her hand was hovering over the buzzer.

"Wait a minute," said Sam. "We've got somebody outside. If I don't show my face in that door in two minutes, there's going to be hell to pay."

"What's going on here, Johnny? You're Batman, he's Robin? You've got to be kidding me if . . ."

"Shut up. Johnny, go get Moon."

Johnny Gee bolted out the door and returned a moment later with Moon.

"You better listen to his skinny ass, lady, 'cause he be tellin' you the god's truth," said Moon, glaring at Sheila.

"We done a long stretch in the joint together, and I seen him do some dumb shit, and he had one hell of a lot a chances, but Johnny here, he never done ratted nobody out."

Sheila studied Johnny Gee's face. Then she stood up and tugged on a satin rope hanging on the wall next to the fireplace.

"Let me get you something to drink," she said. A girl in a minidress maid's outfit appeared. "Get them whatever they want," she said off-handedly.

Johnny Gee asked for a beer. Moon backed quietly against the door and folded his arms. Sam shook his head no. The girl disappeared through a door that closed soundlessly behind her.

"What have you done, anyway, Johnny? I've seen some shitstorms around this capital, but I've never seen it fly like this. There's a high-priced contract out on you. Your friend, too. It was a stupid move, coming here. How did you know this place wasn't being watched? How did you know some of Harlan's boys wouldn't be here tonight?"

"We weren't sure it was Harlan Greene that's lookin' for us," said Johnny Gee.

"Oh, Jesus. I don't believe it," said Sheila, shaking her head. "Harlan Greene's turning the whole fucking state inside out hunting you down, and you don't know it's him you've pissed off. That's rich, Johnny." She chuckled to herself and ran her hands through her hair. "So what did you do? You still haven't told me."

"We've seen the tapes, Sheila," Sam said.

Sheila glanced at him, then looked inquiringly at Johnny Gee.

"Is that the truth?"

"You bet, baby."

"How did you—"

Sam cut her off.

"That's none of your business."

"I just wanted to know where—"

He cut her off again.

"Look. The point is, we've seen them. We want to know who they belong to. Let's put it this way. We want to know what's going on."

Sheila looked from Sam to Johnny Gee, her astonishment showing in her gaping mouth.

"You've seen the tapes! I can't believe it! Those goddamned tapes! No wonder Harlan wants your asses. You could do more damage than you could with—"

"With a .45," said Johnny Gee.

"Oh, hell, *a lot* more damage than *that.*"

"I told you," said Sam. "We want to know what's going on. You're on the tapes. A good number of scenes were shot right here in this house, through the ceiling. What's going on?"

"How am I supposed to know? They're hot. *You're* hot. That's all I know."

"Bullshit, Sheila," said Johnny Gee. "You don't do nothin' without coverin' your ass six ways from Sunday. Who came in here and set up them cameras? Who's behind them tapes? We got to know, Sheila. Don't you understand?"

"I told you. I don't know. All I know is, Harlan wants them bad enough to—"

"To kill for them," said Johnny Gee. "They killed one guy already. They tied him to a tree and beat him half to death, then they shot him through the head. He had nothin' to do with them tapes. He knew nothin'. He done nothin'. He didn't deserve to die. If anybody deserved to die, it was *me,* goddamnit. Not Spicer."

"Harlan Greene is behind the tapes?" asked Sam.

"I don't know who's behind the tapes. The only people I dealt with were the technicians who installed the camera in the room upstairs. I didn't know who they were working for. I didn't ask. In this business, you don't ask too many questions."

"It's a safe guess that Harlan Greene has an interest in the tapes if he wants them bad enough to kill for them, wouldn't you say?"

"It's a safe guess he's got an interest in everything in this state that isn't nailed down," said Sheila. "Highway contracts, public works projects, dams, zoning ordinances, everything right down to and including ten percent of the contract to provide toilet paper and hand towels to public rest rooms in high schools and out there on the interstate. He's a very busy man. He's a very wealthy man. He's a very dangerous man."

"We know that much," Sam acknowledged.

"And he's a man who's after our particular asses?" asked Johnny Gee.

"That's what I hear!" said Sheila.

"So what's on the tapes that could damage him so severely that he's willing to kill to get them back? It wouldn't be his interest in a large public works project, would it?" asked Sam.

"You catch on fast," said Sheila.

"Tell me something. Who gets paid off so this place can operate out in the open like this?"

"One of Harlan's boys. Ten percent. He's got one of his squinty-eyed little geeks here every week checking my fucking books, excuse the pun. How else you figure an operation like this stays open in the state capital of Illinois? Good will? You've got to have protection in this business, and you've got to have it in a lot of other businesses. Protection like that costs money. It costs ten percent."

"And that ten percent buys a wink and nod from the city police, the county sheriff, the state patrol . . . ten percent buys the local D.A.'s office?"

"You got it."

"What about the state attorney general? Does he turn a blind eye and a deaf ear, too?"

"Hell, I've got a half-dozen clients from the attorney general's office, and the county prosecutor himself was here, let me see . . . two nights ago. I don't pay much attention to them. They pay attention to me."

"Jesus."

"Other than Harlan Greene and the governor, the rest of them are small potatoes."

"You know Harlan Greene?"

"I know him."

"You know who he owns?"

"I'm not sure what you mean."

"I mean, who's loyal to him. Which sheriffs. Which D.A.'s. Which local police chiefs."

"Yeah. I know most of them."

"We want a clean one."

"What?"

"We want you to tell us the name of a clean cop, a clean D.A., a clean sheriff. We want somebody who doesn't owe Harlan Greene. Preferably, we'd like someone who doesn't even *know* Harlan Greene. But we'll settle for a law enforcement official who's not bought and paid for."

"You don't want much, do you?"

"I'm only asking for what I've believed my tax dollars have been paying for all the years I've spent serving my country, not even living in the state of Illinois. An honest public official. That's all I ask."

"I don't know. It's going to take me a while to think about this one," she said.

"That's all we're askin', Sheila," said Johnny Gee. "Just think about it. We just need to talk to somebody we can trust."

"Will you do it?" asked Sam.

"Yeah. I'll do it."

"We'll be in touch," said Sam. He stood up and walked out the door.

A few minutes later Johnny Gee squeezed through the door of the Porsche into the jump seat and lit up a Picayune.

"What went on back there?" asked Sam.

"Nothin'," said Johnny Gee. "We was just talkin' over old times."

THE MORNING SUN was peeking over the horizon when they arrived at Lake Egypt, a long Y-shaped body of water tucked into the hills on the edge of the Shawnee National Forest. The cottage sat in a glade of pines on a point of land at the fork in the Y, so the lake stretched into the distance on either side. A length of dock had been pulled out for the winter and sat forlornly on the shore, a few feet away from the water.

Sam and Johnny Gee were not sure what was going to be happening for the next few days, or indeed if anything would happen. They were going to wait a day, then they would call Sheila. If she had something or someone for them, they would act. If not, they would wait some more.

Moon, for his part, had business to attend to, some of which may or may not have concerned the twin sisters, Rowanda and Rolene. Sam and Johnny Gee had dropped him off at the pool hall with the understanding that he was available if they needed him. If Sam had been at first unsure of the bona fides of Johnny Gee, he had felt immediately at ease with Moon. You could have taken Moon, put sergeant stripes on him, and air-dropped him into any army unit extant and he would have found himself not just a place, but a career. He might have been slicker than oil on glass, but he was *straight* oil on *flat* glass, of that much Sam was certain.

The cottage by the lake had belonged to Sam's grandparents, and he had spent summers there as a kid, before his interests turned to dirt track race cars. Now it belonged to his mother, and she'd rarely visited the place since his father died. It was a simple wood-frame structure with a screened porch on the front and large windows on the sides overlooking the lake in two directions. Sam parked the Porsche under the tree and unlocked the front door with a key that was hidden under a rock next to the porch. He disappeared inside for a moment, then the porch light came on.

"Had to throw the master switch on the fuse box," he said. "Come on in. I'll turn on the heat. The place will be warm in a few minutes."

Johnny Gee walked through the front door. There was one big front room that had a cathedral ceiling and exposed beams. The kitchen opened into the front room on the left, and a doorway next to the kitchen led to the back of the cottage. A large stone fireplace filled one corner. The big room was furnished simply, with wicker chairs and a twig-style sofa with flowered cushions. The bare wood floor was a little worn in spots, and it was coated with a layer of dust. Two pastel rugs were rolled up and stored out of the way along a side wall. Light came from three iron standing lamps that had shades made out of old geological survey maps. The place was homey in the best sense of the word.

Sam pointed out the guest room, suggested Johnny Gee get some sleep, stretched out on his grandparents' old four-poster, and fell right out.

Night had fallen by the time he woke up and fixed a meal of canned soup and Cokes, the only provisions that had been left the last time anyone visited the cottage.

When they were finished, he straightened up the kitchen and changed clothes. He was wearing a sweatshirt with a big RANGER tab on the chest as he strode to the front door.

"I think we'd better hop in the car and drive over to Hodgkins' general store and get some food. We might be here a while."

"That sounds like a good idea, man."

The drive to the store took twenty minutes over gravel roads and two-lane blacktops. When they got there, Sam said hello to Mr. Hodgkins, whom he'd known since he was six years old. They bought a case of beer and three sacks of groceries and made the drive back just as quickly. After they had unloaded the groceries, Sam sat down on an old wicker armchair next to the phone.

"I think I'd better call Betsy," he announced.

"Who is Betsy?"

"My old girlfriend from college. I've been avoiding this call for months, but at this point, I don't think I have any choice."

"What in hell does your college girlfriend have to do with anything?" Johnny Gee was stretched out on the twig sofa, hands laced behind his neck, smoking a Picayune. A can of beer was balanced on his flat stomach, and his feet were crossed, his two-tone shoes on the sofa's wooden arm.

"She works for the governor. Runs his outreach office in the south, twenty counties in the state. She might be able to explain why the governor has been coming down here so often recently." Sam dug into his wallet and pulled out a slip of paper.

"You got the phone number right there, huh?"

"My mother gave it to me months ago. She's been leaning on me to give Betsy a call and ask her out."

"But you already got the chick down at Fort Campbell. What is she? She's an officer, like you?"

"Yeah, she's a major, divorced, just like me."

"That happen all the time in the army? Divorces, I mean."

"Let's put it this way. The military life isn't for everyone, I guess. You know, moving once every two or three years . . . it's pretty disruptive. The housing isn't the best in the world, and the pay's not all that great. You've got to love it to stay in."

"And you love it, huh, Major?"

"I love it, Johnny."

"Then why'd you come back up here, man? You coulda blown me off, told me to pack my ass out to Arizona or somethin'. When I come down to your base the other day, I figured I had a shot, but not much of one. I mean, all this shit is, is trouble."

"I've got to tell you, I gave it some thought."

"Then what made you take the chance?"

"As an officer in the army, your biggest nightmare is that you'll get somebody killed because of your own ignorance, or because of a mistake you made, or because of some circumstance you failed to plan for. You live with it every day. Everybody knows being in the army isn't selling insurance or pumping gas, everybody knows the nature of the business could get you killed. All these young men in your command, the only choice they've got is to look up to you and trust that you won't fuck up. I've never been in combat, but men are killed all the time in training accidents. I've been in the army over ten years, and I have yet to lose a single soldier in a training accident, car wreck, or any other way. But I lost Spicer. I pulled him into this thing, and because I did, he was killed. You can't imagine how that makes me feel."

"Hey, man, I don't feel none too wonderful about Spicer myself. It was me got you and him into this thing in the first place."

Sam reached for the phone.

"Look. Whatever happened, we're both involved now, and we're going to see somebody go to jail for Spicer's death. Now, let me make my call."

"Sure, man. Go ahead."

Sam dialed Betsy's home number and waited while the phone rang once, twice. She picked up on the third ring.

"Hello?"

"Betsy, it's Sam. I'm sorry to be calling you so late . . ."

"Sam. I just heard from your mother. She said you might be calling. What's wrong, Sam? Your mother told me you were in some kind of trouble. Where are you?"

"I'm at my grandparents' old summer cottage on Lake Egypt. Remember? I brought you down here once when we were in high school."

"I remember the place. God, that was a long time ago, wasn't it?"

"Seems like another life."

"I'll say. Your mother told me the man they found dead in Jerome the other day was a friend of yours. I looked up the story in the Carbondale paper. The police got an anonymous tip and found his body tied to a tree in some woods. . . ."

"Yeah. Did she say how he got killed? Did she tell you about the surveillance tapes?"

"No. All she told me was that you're trying to find the man who killed your friend."

Sam went back to the beginning and told her everything. When he was finished, there was a long pause before Betsy spoke.

"So you think Harlan Greene is behind your friend's murder?"

"He's the one who's looking for us. He's the major player on the surveillance tapes I saw. You put two and two together and it comes up Harlan Greene."

"He's a very powerful man in this state, Sam. I'm sure you know that."

"Yeah, and I know he's been crooked since he used to work for Paul Powell."

"He's never been indicted. No one has ever proven that he's taken a dime, much less been mixed up in a murder, Sam. He was the key downstate person in Governor Taylor's election committee, he's always been very close to Secretary of State Offinger and the attorney general, Michael Kennedy. People may talk about him being corrupt, but as far as those men are concerned, come election day, he's their best friend."

"Unfortunately, I know what you say is true."

"What about these surveillance tapes? What happened to them?"

"Spicer was supposed to send them to the attorney general."

"To the attorney general! And you never heard anything more about them?"

"Nothing."

"Well, neither have I, Sam. And I think if anything like the surveillance tapes you're talking about had been received by the attorney general, the governor would certainly know about it, and I would have heard about it by now."

"What are you saying? Spicer didn't send them?"

"I don't know what I'm saying. I guess I'm saying I don't understand. This all sounds very, very strange to me. . . ."

"You think I'm making this up, Betsy? Come on."

"I don't think you're making anything up, Sam. That's not it at all. I just think the whole thing sounds farfetched."

"I *saw* the tapes, Betsy. They're not a figment of my imagination. They exist. Harlan Greene is right there, talking about paying off state reps and state senators for some big vote. He's right there, standing in the middle of some field they're surveying down in Rock County. I don't know what it all adds up to. I was hoping you could help me with that."

Betsy was silent for a moment before she answered.

"I can't do anything tonight, Sam. But when I get to work tomorrow morning, there are some calls I can make. I've got a friend who works for the IBI . . ."

"The IBI?"

"The Illinois Bureau of Investigation. They're an arm of the executive branch. A guy who worked on the governor's campaign with me . . . he was the downstate advance man . . . he works over there now. I'll call him tomorrow morning and feel him out, see if he's heard anything about videotapes."

"Jeez, Betsy, that would be great," Sam said. "But be careful, will you? I don't want you getting in any trouble over this."

"Don't worry. I think I know how to take care of myself by now."

"I guess you do at that," said Sam.

"This whole thing would be a lot easier if you still had those tapes."

"I told you. I left them with Spicer, and he was to send them to the office of the attorney general. As far as I know, that's where they are."

"Okay. We'll just have to take it from there."

"I'm sorry to burden you, Betsy. I should have thought of calling you when I had the tapes in my possession."

"Where will you be tomorrow about ten o'clock?"

"I'll be here." He gave her the phone number for the cottage.

"I'll call you at ten exactly, Sam."

"Thanks, Betsy."

She hung up.

"Hey, Sam?" It was Johnny Gee. He was standing next to the counter separating the kitchen from the front room, sipping a beer.

"Yeah?"

"I think there's somethin' I ought to tell you that I haven't told you, sort of."

"What's that?"

"I heard you talkin' to her about the tapes, and she musta been askin' you where they were, because you kept tellin' her Spicer already sent them off."

"So?"

"He didn't send all of 'em."

"What do you mean by that?"

"I mean, I kept one."

"You did *what?*"

"I kept one of the tapes. I figured with us splittin' up and all, if there was any trouble, I'd need it to deal my way out."

"Christ, Johnny. Where is it? What did you do with it?"

"Well, that night way back when, I stuck it down the back of my pants when you guys weren't lookin', and I just took off with it when we split up. I've been real careful. I never kept it in my room or nothin'. I kept movin' it around."

"Which tape is it, and where the hell is it, Johnny?"

"It's the Sheraton tape, where they're all in that hotel room, remember? I got it stashed in a bus station locker."

"Where?"

"Over in Lancaster. I stopped on my way down to your place. I'm sorry, man. Until I heard you talkin' to her on the phone . . ."

"Lancaster? How far is that from here?"

"It's just on the other side of Marion."

"Let's go get it," said Sam. "If we've still got one of the tapes, that changes everything."

They climbed into the Porsche and backed out of the drive. Sam headed up the gravel road until he hit a county blacktop and turned left. He went a couple of miles before he realized he was heading the wrong direction.

He made a U-turn and headed the other way. A few miles north, he turned left on State Route 35. They passed through Marion, took a right on State Route 18 and drove into Lancaster. On the right, a lump of decaying stucco had a sign on it: BUS DEPOT. He killed the engine and turned to Johnny Gee.

"Give me the key."

Johnny Gee fished in his pocket and handed him the key to the bus locker.

"Wait here. I'll be right back."

Sam pushed open the door. Everything in the bus depot was yellow with age: yellowed walls, yellowed floors, yellowed vaulted ceiling, yellowed stucco support beams and yellowed fake granite columns, yellowed glass partition between the two ticket booths, yellowed marble counters. The years had not been kind to bus travel, and they seemed to have dealt the Lancaster depot a particularly vengeful blow.

Even the resident collection of depot denizens seemed further down on their luck than usual. Most of the old wooden benches in the waiting room had been taken. Homeless men were stretched out full length on piles of their worldly possessions. The sound of fitful wet snoring filled the room. An odor of cheap wine hung over the benches like a low fog. Sam walked up to the row of lockers along the wall and found number 213. He inserted the key and turned it. The locker popped open a crack. He looked in and saw a small canvas overnight bag. As he was about to retrieve it, a nightstick pushed the locker closed.

"You mind telling me what you've got in there, pal?"

He turned around and came face to face with a Lancaster cop on night patrol. The cop was about forty, but a drinking problem had him looking closer to fifty. Sam could smell the cheap gin mixed with Sen-Sen on his breath.

"It's my overnight bag, officer. I left it here earlier. I'm here to pick it up."

"Where you headed?"

"Home, officer. I'm picking up my bag, and I'm going home."

"You got a bus ticket?"

"No, sir, I don't."

"Then how you traveling home, mister?" asked the officer, moving closer. The gin/Sen-Sen was almost overpowering.

"I'm driving, sir." He stepped to the rear. His back hit the locker.

"We been having a lot of trouble 'round here with drugs coming into this town," said the officer. "They been moving them drugs in here pretty regular. More'n once, we found drugs right in these here lockers. Did you know that, friend?"

"No, sir, I didn't." He looked past the officer, out the glass doors of the depot. He could see the Porsche idling across the street with Johnny Gee in the front seat. If this cop took one look out that door and saw what he saw . . . they'd be locked up first, and answer questions later.

He tried to smile nonchalantly. He hoped the smile didn't come off as arrogant.

The officer tapped the locker door with his nightstick.

"Mind if I look in that locker of yours?" he asked, tapping the door.

"No, sir, I don't." He stepped aside.

The officer flipped the door open with his nightstick and peered inside. The overnight bag sat by itself at the front of the locker. The officer pushed it to one side with his night-stick and looked behind the bag. Nothing.

"You wouldn't have no drugs in there, would you, mister?" asked the officer.

"No, sir, I wouldn't."

"Mind if I have a look in that bag of yours?"

Sam hesitated. He didn't know precisely what was in the bag beside the surveillance tape. And if the cop seized the tape . . . he didn't even want to think about it. He took a chance.

"No, sir, I don't mind."

"Open it up," the officer commanded.

He took the bag out of the locker and unzipped it.

"What's under them clothes, mister?"

He took one of Johnny Gee's pairs of pants, a shirt, and some underwear from the bag. The officer looked inside.

"Got some videos there, I see," said the officer.

"One. Yes, sir, I do."

"There wouldn't be no bags 'a drugs hidin' in that video box, would there now?"

Sam fished the videotape box from the bag, pulled the cassette from its cover, and showed it to the officer.

The officer nodded.

"You can zip it up," he said.

Sam put everything back in the bag and closed it.

"You wouldn't have no ID on you, would you?" asked the officer with a stupid grin.

Sam pulled out his wallet and flipped it open, showing his military ID. A set of Airborne wings and a Ranger tab were pinned inside the wallet across from the ID.

"You're an army officer?" asked the officer.

"That's right, sir."

"Well, gee, I'm real sorry . . . uh . . . Major," said the officer. "But we do have some drug runners through here, and you never know, you know?"

"Yeah, I know."

"I served me a stretch in the army, myself," said the officer, backing up slowly. "Plei Khu. Sixty-nine."

"Vietnam, huh?"

"Viet-fuckin'-Nam," said the officer, seemingly at a loss for words.

"I'm stationed down at Fort Campbell," said Sam. "And I'd better get going or I'll be AWOL."

"Don't let me keep you," said the officer. He touched the brim of his cap with his nightstick in a mock salute. "Airborne Ranger, all the way," he said, grinning drunkenly.

"Right. Airborne," Sam echoed flatly, picking up the bag. He walked past the officer, pushed open the glass door, and walked across the street to the car. He opened the door and slid behind the wheel.

"What the fuck was that all about?" asked Johnny Gee. "I seen that cop headin' for you . . . I seen the whole thing."

"You don't even want to know."

"He seen the tape?"

"He saw everything. He was looking for drugs. He was also lit like a Roman candle."

Sam started the Porsche and pulled into the traffic. He took the first right out of town.

"That cop coulda blown the whole thing," said Johnny Gee.

"He sure could have, but he didn't."

"Where we goin' now?"

"Back to the lake. Betsy's calling tomorrow morning, and now we've got something we can show her. The fact that we've got one of the tapes makes a big difference. You were selfish to keep this thing, but it's probably the smartest thing you've ever done."

"I figured, you know, you always got to keep yourself close to an exit," said Johnny Gee.

HE BENT THE Porsche through an easy curve, pressed the accelerator to the floor and watched the speedometer climb past ninety. They were leaving the farm country around Lancaster. Long straight passages of two-lane blacktop with winter wheat fields alongside towns spaced about fifteen miles apart. You could see them coming up ahead, even at night, a clump of lonely elms and oaks and a couple of grain elevators on the horizon against the sky. Sam slowed for the last farm town before they hit the rolling hills and woods around the lake. They coasted through the blinking yellow light at thirty. On the other side of town, he eased the Porsche back up to speed.

"What you thinkin' about, Major?" asked Johnny Gee.

"I'm trying to figure out what having this tape in our possession does for us."

"I thought you said this was gonna make things easier."

"That's what I thought at first. Now I'm not so sure."

"What's the problem?"

"We're in the same spot we were in before. Technically, we're in possession of something that doesn't belong to us. If it was stolen, then we're in possession of stolen property. And either way, having seen the tape, we probably have knowledge of a felony. This is what we were trying to solve when we gave the tapes to Spicer, so he could send them to the authorities."

"Yeah, and you see where that got us. And where that got Spicer."

"I know. We've got to break out of this loop we're in. We've got to figure a way to land the whole business in Harlan Greene's lap, where it belongs."

"You got any new ideas?"

"That's what worries me. Not a one."

"Maybe your girl Betsy will come up with somethin' to-morrow mornin'."

"Maybe." Sam turned off the county blacktop onto the gravel road leading to the lake. In a few moments, they could see the outline of the cottage through the trees. Sam parked the Porsche in the grove of pines on the far side of the cottage, and unlocked the front door. It was pitch dark inside. He flipped the light switch, and a floorlamp next to the sofa came on.

"I wish we had a TV and VCR out here. I sure would like to take another look at this tape," he said.

"Hey, Major. You better come in here." Johnny Gee was standing in the door leading to the bedrooms.

Sam strode quickly from the kitchen to the first bedroom. The bed had been turned over and the mattress knifed open. All of his grandfather's old fishing and hunting clothes in the closet had been gone through and tossed on the floor. They walked across the hall to the guest room. The mattress was shredded, leaning against the headboard, and Johnny Gee's clothes were scattered across the bedsprings.

"Looks like we've had visitors," said Johnny Gee.

The .45. The .45. Where is it? Sam panicked.

He ran down the hall through the front room and out the door to the car. He unlocked the driver's door, felt under the seat until his hand landed on the pistol, and then silently blessed the day the army switched over from the Colt .45 to the 9 mm Beretta, giving all active duty officers the opportunity to purchase their sidearms surplus from the government for twenty-five dollars. He tucked the .45 in his waistband and returned to the cottage.

Switching on the light in the kitchen, he saw that the cabinets had been emptied and the garbage searched. One of the panes in the pantry window had been broken and the lock jimmied.

"Here's where they got in. Come on, Johnny. We're out of here."

"Where we goin', man?" asked Johnny Gee, hustling to the door. Sam turned off the lights and locked the front door.

"To my mother's. If they know we're here, they sure as hell know where she is, and I don't like it, Johnny. I don't like it at all. She doesn't have anything to do with this, and the way things are going, she's liable to get hurt." He took a deep breath as he climbed into the Porsche.

"Or killed."

Johnny Gee got into the seat next to him, and they hit the

gravel road in second gear at forty. Sam kept up the pace
through the woods, out of the Shawnee National Forest. The
first time he slowed the Porsche below ninety was when he
saw Harrisburg up ahead. As they neared the town, traffic
picked up. It was pretty heavy traffic so late at night, he
thought. What night was it? Of course! Wednesday, and this
was midweek date traffic, movie traffic, dinner at the Sizzler
traffic, driving around traffic, a relentless stream of headlights and taillights and jacked-up Camaros and tall-boy
pickups and screeching tires and stoplight chatter and ham-
burgers and six-packs and Levis and bleached-blond flips
and high heels and lipstick and high volume cassette player
automotive rock 'n' roll. It was Wednesday night in southern
Illinois, and Sam recognized every pounding corpuscle of it.

He hung a left at the second light. State Route 17 North
took them out of town. The traffic thinned out. Hay bales
littered the fields beyond the road. Fence posts flew by as the
Porsche picked up speed. They crested a hill at 85, heading
down the far side onto a long stretch of two-lane at better
than 110 miles an hour.

"Man, you're making this thing fly," said Johnny Gee.

"This car was built for roads and speeds just like this,"
said Sam. "We'll be home in less than an hour."

"How far is it?"

"Ninety-five miles from the light back there."

The speedometer said 120 as the Porsche leaned gently
into a long sweeper around a stand of trees. Outside, a hard
wind whispered at the edge of the window.

Mrs. Butterfield's bedroom light went on as the Porsche
pulled into the drive. Sam parked the car in the barn, closed
the creaking door, and caught his mother in his arms as she
ran out to greet them in her robe.

"Is there something wrong, Sam?" she asked.

"I'm so glad you're okay, Ma," he whispered in her ear.

They spent the next hour bringing her up to date, then went to bed.

The phone rang while Sam was checking the oil and tire pressure on the Porsche. His mother came to the door and called to him. It was just past ten.

"I called the cottage, and you weren't there, so I called your mother," said Betsy.

"I've got something to tell you," he said, breathless from the gallop across the barnyard.

"And I've got something for you," she replied.

"You first," he said.

"There is absolutely no information in state government about any surveillance videotapes, missing or otherwise. I spoke to my friend at the IBI. I spoke to another friend in the governor's office, one of his top political assistants. I didn't bring up the tapes, exactly, but I got him to talking about Harlan Greene, and Sam, there's nothing going on. No trouble. No problems. The governor's been downstate twice in the last couple of months. They're getting ready to buy another big tract of land next to the Shawnee National Forest to add to the Oxen Springs State Park down there. It's a very good deal for the state, Sam, and Harlan has been the key to putting the package together. I've been on the phone since eight-thirty, Sam, and at this point, I just can't come up with anything that even vaguely resembles what you've been talking about."

"Betsy, thanks for everything you've done. Really."

"Sam? Sam? That's it? That's all you're going to say?"

"I don't know what else I can say, Betsy. You've done what you could. Nobody knows anything. It's my problem, not yours. Maybe I should just take it from here."

"Sam, you sound . . . I don't know how you sound."

"Betsy, the cottage . . . the cottage was broken into last night while we were gone. That's why I'm here at my mother's. I'm worried, Betsy. I'm afraid someone else is going to get hurt, and I don't want it to be my mom. Hell, I don't want it to be me."

"I don't know what to tell you, Sam."

"Well, I've got something for you, like I said. We have one of the surveillance tapes."

"What? You didn't tell me that last night."

"I didn't know it. One of the tapes got left behind. It didn't get sent off by Spicer. The tape turned up last night. So if you had, or have, any doubts about what I'm talking about, you can dispel them mighty quickly by coming over here and taking a look at this tape."

"Sam, I've got a job here. I can't just pick up and leave anytime I want."

"Then come after work. Where are you? Carbondale?"

"Yes."

"Betsy, you're not forty-five minutes away. I'll come over and get you, if you'd like."

"That won't be necessary. I get off at five-thirty. I'll be there by seven o'clock."

Sam thought quickly.

"Don't tell anyone what you're doing, Betsy. I mean your friend at the IBI, or anyone else. Let's wait until you have a look at this thing. Then we can discuss what we ought to do."

"Okay, Sam. I'll be there at seven."

She hung up. Sam turned around. Johnny Gee was sitting at the kitchen table sipping a beer and smoking a Picayune.

"Hey, it's ten in the morning. We're at my mom's house now. Finish the beer and put out the cigarette. Have some respect."

"That's all right, Sam. I understand." Mrs. Butterfield walked through the door from the dining room, a dust mop in hand. "When I get nervous, I clean. Look at me. This house is immaculate. I wet mopped every room in the house, and now I'm going over them again with a dust mop. Ridiculous. Absurd."

Sam laughed nervously. Johnny Gee stepped out on the back porch and lit another Picayune.

"This place is just like you read about in books," he said, taking a deep drag. "Barns and fields and stuff. This is great."

It was just before seven when Sam heard Betsy's car on the drive. He opened the front door and stood on the porch as she stepped from her car, an old Volkswagen Rabbit convertible with a faded top and more than a few dents on the front fenders. She was wearing a dark gray business suit, high heels, and a bright yellow blouse open at the throat. She was still a brunette, her hair swept in easy curls behind her ears at collar length. Sam walked down the porch steps as she finished straightening her jacket. She picked up a briefcase and turned to find him standing next to the car's front bumper.

"Sam . . . I . . . I . . ."

"It's been over ten years. It's good to see you, Betsy. You look great."

She smiled faintly and ran a hand through her hair, leaving it tousled on top, frothy in the dim light.

"You haven't changed a bit, Sam. I bet you haven't gained a pound."

"Reveille runs," laughed Sam. He reached for her briefcase, and Betsy surrendered it willingly. "You look wonderful. Successful and grown up and wonderful."

Betsy laughed. "I wanted to change before I came, but I had a meeting right up until the last minute. I feel grubby and used. But that's government for you."

"Why don't you freshen up in the bath at the top of the stairs, and I'll meet you in the kitchen."

Mrs. Butterfield was standing on the porch stairs wiping her hands on her apron.

"Betsy, it's so good to see you again. How many times have we talked on the phone? Twenty? Thirty? I kept trying to picture how you looked, then I remembered Sam still has a picture of you two at the ROTC hop in his room, so I went upstairs and found it on his dresser. You look just the way I remember you. Both of you."

"Come on, Ma. Betsy doesn't want a personal appearance analysis."

"You all get ready for dinner," said his mother. "I've got chicken frying and mashed potatoes and gravy and butter beans and a cucumber salad when you're ready."

"Betsy, this is Johnny Gee," said Sam, introducing her to the skinny figure who had come to the door.

"It's nice to meet you, Johnny," said Betsy.

"Same here," said Johnny Gee, shifting a toothpick from one side of his mouth to the other with his tongue.

When Betsy came downstairs, everyone was in the kitchen. She hung her jacket over the back of a chair and they sat down to eat. She and Mrs. Butterfield caught up on political gossip, and when they had finished eating, Johnny Gee cleared the table, and Mrs. Butterfield made coffee. Sam suggested they move into the living room.

It was simply decorated with a couch, a wing-backed armchair, and a love seat. A twenty-five inch television sat against one wall, an antique quilt hung on the other. The two windows at the front of the house had balloon shade curtains in a floral pattern. A braided rag rug covered the floor.

"Where's your bag, Johnny?" asked Sam.

"Right here," said Johnny Gee. He dumped out the contents of his overnight bag and picked up the tape and handed it to Sam.

"I keep thinking there's something we missed when we first looked at the tapes," Sam said. "That there's a weak link in here somewhere staring us right in the face, something so obvious we keep missing it because it's obvious."

He turned on the television and VCR, inserted the Sheraton tape and hit play. The screen flickered and the video came on, showing the hotel room in black and white.

He hit the fast forward button. The action sped up crazily until he hit play again. The tall man called Frankie walks in, does a sound check with an unseen man whose voice can be heard on the tape. The unseen man says:

"Step out in the middle of the room and say something, so we can get a sound level, Stillman."

"I think I know who Stillman is," said Mrs. Butterfield. "Your father had some trouble with him."

They watched the tape for a few more minutes. The man called Frankie Stillman is drinking a beer, waiting for the others to arrive.

"Stop the tape," said Mrs. Butterfield. "I've got him now."

Sam stopped the tape and punched mute on the remote control so the television sound was turned off.

"Your father had a run-in with him quite a few years back, I don't know how long ago it was." She turned to Sam, who was pouring coffee in Johnny Gee's cup. "You remember, when we had all that trouble getting our grain to market."

Sam nodded. "And this guy was involved?"

"Frankie Stillman. He was with a Teamster's local that was raising holy hell down here, threatening people, slashing tires on people's cars and trucks, smashing in windshields with baseball bats. The way it happened, the Teamsters raised their rates to haul our grain, and they raised them so high, so fast, they were way ahead of the market price on the grain itself, and we couldn't make much of a profit. So some of us, and your father was the first one to do it, started leasing trucks and hauling the grain to market ourselves. That was when the trouble started. Stillman showed up with some thugs, and they started terrorizing anybody who even thought about trucking their grain with any outfit that wasn't affiliated with the Teamsters, didn't have a Teamster contract. The whole thing happened when they shut down the railroad spur to the grain elevator we used. That was a political deal, a fix. One day the spur was open, and the trains were running in cars to pick up grain. The next day the spur is shut down, and we're forced to truck our crops to Continental Grain."

"And you're sure he was the one who was behind it?"

"Oh, I don't think Stillman was behind shutting down the spur. But he was working for somebody who was. He was just a thug sent down to enforce the Teamster business on us. But that's him, all right. He's older, but it's him."

"What do you mean, shutting down the spur was a political deal?" asked Sam.

"It's all political, son. Every time something happens in this state, it's political. With the spur open, the railroad's making money hauling our grain, we're making money selling it. When the spur closed, the railroad's not making any money hauling our grain, and if we want to sell it, we get it trucked from our elevator down to Continental's, and the trucking company is the one making money, and of course, the Teamsters, the union, and the drivers. It's like poker. One day this one's got the cards, he's got the good hand, the next day that one's got the good hand. The only thing being, the dealer's crooked, and they're playing with a marked deck. The little fellow, the farmer, the small grain elevator operator, we're just standing in the room watching them shuffle the cards and move the money around the table. That's what I mean by political."

"Jesus," breathed Johnny Gee. "I always knew stuff was crooked and fixed and everything, but I never heard it spelled out like that."

Betsy laughed softly. "Oh, yes, oh, yes," she said under her breath. "As a general rule, you can count on things being worse than they seem. Especially when it comes to politics in southern Illinois."

"You've probably dealt with situations like this at the governor's offices, haven't you, Betsy?" asked Mrs. Butterfield.

"We had to settle for a very bad deal not long ago. Midwest Pacific wanted to close twenty depots around the state, and we got them to keep fifteen open by removing the requirement that they service certain spurs here and there.

They had us coming and going. We were damned if we didn't and damned if we didn't. The farmers were mad at us for letting their spurs be closed down, but if we hadn't made the deal, we'd have lost freight service over half the state. It was terrible. A terrible situation."

Sam stared at the television screen. With the VCR off, a movie was on, black and white. A fishing boat was putting out to sea and Stewart Granger was its captain. He watched the soundless action for a moment, then he spoke.

"So whoever Frankie Stillman is working for is the person these tapes belong to."

"It sure looks that way," said his mother.

"So they might not belong to Harlan Greene at all."

"I would say the chances are that they don't belong to Harlan Greene. I think they belong to someone who wants Harlan out of the action," said Betsy.

"What about Stillman?"

"Oh, Sam," said his mother. "He's a jack of all trades, working for the highest bidder: the Teamsters here, someone else there. I heard he was involved with liquor licensing at one point, several years after the Teamster trouble."

"Liquor licensing?"

Betsy stood up and paced the floor, a study in frustration. "You've got to have a license to bring liquor into the state. For example, say you have the license to bring Johnny Walker Scotch into Illinois. Every bottle of Johnny Walker Scotch whiskey sold in Illinois yields you fifty cents, as your licensing fee. Johnny Walker is a popular Scotch, so that's a lot of fifty cents adding up over the course of a year. Somebody else has Dewar's, somebody else Cutty Sark. Suppose someone comes along, and he wants all the Scotch licenses. These are state licenses, governmental licenses. Getting and holding a license is a political matter. So you work to under-cut the Dewar's guy, the Cutty Sark guy, the Johnny Walker guy. You give more money than they do to the winning gubernatorial candidate. You make sure your contributions get noticed. This is politics. When a new governor comes in, you increase your Scotch licenses by one, or perhaps two. Stillman was probably in the business of 'arranging' liquor import licenses. A dozen of those guys come out of the woodwork every time a new governor gets in."

"He's had his grubby little mitts in all kinds of stuff, huh?" asked Johnny Gee.

"Yes, indeed," said Mrs. Butterfield.

"So who's Frankie Stillman working for right now?" asked Sam rhetorically. "Somebody who hates Harlan Greene, which isn't a hard thing to do. Half the political types in the state of Illinois would like to nail his hide to the wall of their dens."

"You're getting the hang of it now," said Betsy.

"I've picked up a thing or two over the years," said Sam. "Even the army has its brand of politics."

"You want to see more?" asked Johnny Gee.

"Run the rest of the tape, Johnny," said Sam. "Let them watch the big man, Harlan Greene himself, work his magic."

They ran the Sheraton tape. When Harlan Greene and his assistant walked in, Betsy stopped pacing, riveted to the screen.

"That's Harvey Pugh!" she yelled. "That little worm. He's been attached to Harlan like a pilot fish for so many years, they're practically the same person. They finish each other's sentences . . ."

"Yeah. Keep watching. He starts talking for Harlan in a minute."

The tape ran through, and Betsy sank into the armchair in the corner.

"Those sons of bitches. They weren't talking about the land purchase for the state park, that's for sure. They've got something going on the side. I should have known . . ."

"What do you mean, Betsy?" asked Sam.

"The thing that surprised the governor on this state park deal was the fact that Harlan wasn't asking for anything. He put the deal together gratis. Usually, he's got his hand out from day one. But this time, all he asked for was a couple of campaign appearances by the governor next spring during the primary for his candidates down here. I didn't think anything of it, and I guess the governor didn't either. When he hears about this, he's going to have a seizure."

"How is he going to hear about it?" asked Sam.

"I'll *tell* him, first thing in the morning," said Betsy.

"Wait a minute," said Mrs. Butterfield. "You all had better have a look at something before you go making plans to talk to the governor."

MRS. BUTTERFIELD GOT up from the sofa and started rummaging through a stack of newspapers in the corner.

"I clipped it a couple of weeks ago." She flipped through the stack of papers carefully. Finally she pulled a single page of newsprint from the pile.

"Here it is," she said. "You remember, Sam, the way your father used to clip official notices from the paper? I guess I inherited the habit when he died. I've been clipping official notices from the paper for years. You'd be amazed what you find in all the boring legalese."

"What do you mean, Ma?"

"Well, they've got to file official notices in the paper for all kinds of things. For example, if you're applying for a zoning variance, you've got to print a notice of your filing for three successive days, including the details of the variance you're filing for. If you're applying for certain kinds of construction permits, you've got to run notices of your application. Many are environmental certifications which involve details regarding projected sewage discharge and the plans to deal with any sewage produced by the project. In certain instances, you have to print a notice if you're applying for a liquor license. Your father used to watch the notices carefully. Very carefully."

"Why?"

"Jobs," said his mother. "Remember how your father used to pick up extra money working as a plumber? Well, every time they build something, it's got to be plumbed. Factories have to be plumbed. Restaurants and bars have to be plumbed. Condos, apartment buildings, office buildings. Lots of plumbing jobs in those notices. Watching them, he used to find out about jobs before the want ads ran in the classified. He lined up quite a bit of extra work that way."

"So what did you find out?"

Mrs. Butterfield studied the page of official notices she held in her hand.

"There's a very interesting notice right here," she said, tapping the page. "They're getting ready to build some kind of huge facility down there in Rock County, right near where you say the state just purchased that land for the park. I know the Shawnee Forest is one of the prettiest, most unspoiled, places in the state. But right next to the National Forest are thousands of acres of reclaimed strip mines."

"That's right!" said Betsy. "That's part of the deal. We're getting half forested land and half land that has been strip mined and reclaimed. It's part of the governor's environmental package. You know, they passed the mining reclamation act years ago, and now the governor's trying to show that it really hasn't cost the state a cent, if land that was once strip mined can be turned into a state park."

"It looks like they've got more in mind for some of that land than recreation," said Sam. "On one of the other tapes we saw, Harlan Greene, that man Pugh, and a bunch of other men were standing in a big field down in Rock County. It was lined-out with surveyor's stakes and tape, and they were consulting some kind of blueprints. If they're going to build something there, it's going to be huge."

"And our man Harlan was right there in the middle of things, was he?" asked Betsy.

"I'll say he was."

"You said 'they' are gettin' ready to build this thing down in Rock County," said Johnny Gee. "Who's they?"

Mrs. Butterfield consulted the clip from the paper.

"A company called American Evacusystems."

"Evacusystems!" said Betsy with a start. "They're a big waste disposal company from Cleveland! Of course. It all makes sense now. They opened a plant on the lake north of Chicago about ten years ago, and the local people have been fighting them ever since. There have been all kinds of charges that they're polluting the lake and the groundwater and everything else. But so far, they've been able to hold off the critics with lawsuits and other delaying tactics."

"Lawsuits?" asked Sam. "The company is suing people?"

"And the other way around. Evacusystems is famous for suing people for libel when they go public to oppose them. They tie up their critics in a suit, then settle out of court with the provision that the person will never speak publicly about Evacusystems again."

"And that's legal?"

"Completely, so long as the defendant signs the settlement."

"Jeez. A real friendly outfit."

"Lovely people," said Betsy. "The governor has kept his distance from them, but it's difficult. They are big contributors to the party, and they're very close to Kennedy . . ."

"The attorney general?" asked Sam.

"In the flesh. The governor expects Kennedy will run against him in the primary, although Kennedy hasn't said anything publicly."

"There is very little love lost between those two," said Sam's mother.

"So what do you think Harlan is doing for this company, Evacusystems?" asked Sam.

Betsy started to pace again.

"If I ask you for one of those cigarettes, Johnny, don't give it to me, you hear? I quit two years ago, and this kind of thing is just what it would take to get me started again."

Johnny Gee laughed. "I'll guard 'em with my life."

"All kinds of legislation has to be passed in order for a company to do anything in the waste disposal field. There's a ton of regulatory requirements, a hundred different variances, probably a bunch of tax credits, too. The lure of a waste disposal facility, as in any other kind of industry, is jobs. Hundreds of jobs at the waste facility, thousands when you begin counting employment by trucking companies, truck drivers, subcontractors, maintenance and repair people, not to mention ancillary employment at credit unions, new bank branches, fast food outlets, gas stations, shopping centers—a big plant like that is a job magnet. I'd say that part of the state is looking at five to six thousand new jobs in, near, or related to that plant. Rock County is dead center of the very poorest part of the state. Five thousand, six thousand jobs in that market is like putting honey under a bear's nose. You can write your own ticket when you come in with those kinds of political sweets."

"What's Harlan's take?" Sam leaned forward on his chair, entranced.

"Probably stock in the company. I wouldn't be surprised if he doesn't realize more than a million in stock for his efforts. Wouldn't surprise me in the least. People have made more for doing less in Illinois. Much more for far less." Betsy stopped pacing and sat down next to Mrs. Butterfield.

"And the videotapes?" asked Sam. "What do you figure is the reason for all the surveillance?"

"There has to be more than one waste management company that would be interested in opening such a facility," said Betsy. "Look at the location alone. They can pull business in there from three other states: Kentucky, Indiana, Missouri. That's a four-state draw, including Illinois, and Illinois has got enough industrial waste by itself. I'm sure if you looked into it deeply enough, which would probably be impossible to do, I think you'd find plans already made for expansion two years, four years, six years down the road. Probably find the enabling legislation sitting there, already written, ready to be introduced when the time comes. This is a very, very big deal, Sam. And somebody wants Harlan's hide real bad on this one. What the surveillance tapes amount to is political blackmail. Those tapes are worth millions if they're put into the right hands. Tens of millions. Maybe hundreds."

"That's why they killed Spicer. They figured if he'd seen the videotapes, he was as dangerous as if he still had them."

"You think he sent them on to the attorney general, then, Sam?" asked Mrs. Butterfield.

"There's no doubt in my mind. If Spicer said he was going to do something, he did it. And this guy Kennedy, if he's as close to Harlan as Betsy says, he just put them on a shelf."

"And went looking for the one that was missin'," said Johnny Gee.

Sam turned to the skinny man.

"They knew there were five. Spicer sent them four. They had to figure either you or I had the last one."

"So what do we do now that we got all this stuff figured out?" asked Johnny Gee.

"I think you ought to let me take the videotape to my friend in the IBI, and see what he's got to say," said Betsy.

"You can do that right away?" asked Sam.

"He works out of their downstate office in Carbondale. I can show it to him first thing in the morning."

"You ain't gonna tell him where you got it, now, are you?" Johnny Gee looked nervously at Betsy.

"I can protect you, Johnny, don't worry. Besides, he's a good friend. He won't do anything with the tape without my approval."

"Anything like taking it to his superiors, you mean," said Sam. "There's no telling what might happen to that tape if it disappears into the upper reaches of that particular law enforcement bureaucracy."

"He won't do anything with it before I check with you, Sam. I promise. I'll sit there while he watches it. I'll take it with me when I leave. And I'll call you as soon as we've discussed it."

"That's good enough for me, Betsy," Sam said. He stood

up and removed the videotape from the VCR, handing it to Betsy.

"And now I've got to get out of here and drive myself home before I drop off to sleep right here," Betsy said.

Out on the porch they paused to look at the softly rolling farmland before them in the moonlight.

"I want you to know how much I appreciate your coming tonight, and everything else you're doing for us. Are you sure there's no chance you'll get in any kind of trouble, taking this thing to the IBI guy?"

"Not a chance. When you've been through a campaign with somebody, a bond forms that's rather difficult to break."

"You're, ah, seeing this guy, as well?"

"Don't be silly. We're just close friends. Why?"

Sam looked down at his feet, then across the barnyard. His eyes wandered back to hers.

"I don't know . . . it's just that seeing you again after all these years . . . I didn't expect . . ."

She touched his lips with a forefinger.

"Shh," she whispered. She removed the finger and kissed him gently on the lips and skipped down the porch steps.

"I know what you mean, Sam," she called over her shoulder. "Don't go anywhere. I'll call you before noon."

The Volkswagen Rabbit backed around and disappeared down the drive and over the hill. Sam turned around to find Johnny Gee watching through the front door.

"She got her stuff definitely well put together," said Johnny Gee. "You could do worse. . . ."

"Let's get a beer," said Sam.

*   *   *

The phone rang at ten-thirty. Sam picked up on the first ring.

"Sam, it's Betsy."

"What happened? What have you got?"

"Not much, I'm afraid," she began, hesitating.

"What do you mean?"

"I showed the tape to my friend Charlie at the IBI. He agrees that the mere existence of such a tape is very damaging to Harlan Greene, and everyone else present in that hotel room at the Sheraton. But he says nothing on the tape is sufficient to tie Harlan Greene to any kind of illegal activity."

"He's got to be kidding. They're sitting right there talking about buying votes, fixing legislative committees—"

"You know that, and I know that, and Charlie knows that, but in strictly legal terms, no one ever mentions a payoff, or buying a vote . . . it's all very circumspect. They're very careful with what they say, and all Harlan himself says, besides asking for a Coke, is 'That's right,' 'That's right,' over and over again and no money changes hands on this tape."

"That's because his boy Pugh was doing all the talking for him."

"I know, Sam. I pointed that out to Charlie. Still, he said there's not enough on this one videotape to bring any charges against Harlan or anyone else."

"Did he ask you where you got the tape?"

"No. I told him I was not making a formal report of the commission of a crime, that I just wanted his opinion. He understood. And nothing he saw will go any place outside the walls of his office. I told him how sensitive the thing was, and he understood completely."

"Jesus. I guess I was expecting you to come up with some

kind of answer to this whole thing. I guess I was expecting too much."

"I'm sorry, Sam, but you can see what he means. The surveillance tape is damaging, but damaging in a political way, not a criminal way. It could be used against Harlan effectively in a political campaign, but . . ."

"We can't wait around until Harlan has to run for county leader again," said Sam.

"I know. I know. But there's one other thing Charlie said."

"What's that?"

"He said it was obvious that Harlan had a pretty strong reason to gain possession of such a tape, to insure that it not fall into the wrong hands. And then he kind of opened the door."

"What do you mean?"

"He said that this tape, in conjunction with something proving that Harlan Greene was making an attempt to buy or otherwise secure possession of it, would present potential criminal liabilities for Harlan. Those were his words. Potential criminal liabilities. And he said anything Harlan might say concerning the events on the surveillance tape would be very, very damaging to his interests."

"So he's telling us that if Harlan Greene were to further incriminate himself . . . if for example, he were to get more specific than he is on the tape, then something could be pinned on him?"

"Essentially, yes."

"Let me think this thing over and get back to you, Betsy. Okay?"

"What do you want me to do with the videotape?"

"I'll drive over and get it from you later this afternoon."

"You know where my office is? It's right outside Carbondale on the road down to De Soto. We're in an old one-room schoolhouse, about five miles outside town on the right. You can't miss us."

"I'll be there in an hour," said Sam. "And, Betsy, thanks a lot. I know you did everything you could. I'll figure out something, believe me."

"I'll see you soon," she said.

Sam turned around and grabbed Johnny Gee by the arm.

"Come here," he commanded. "I want you to call your friend Sheila. She knows Harlan Greene? Well, I want her to set up a meeting with our boy Harlan."

"For when?"

"For tomorrow night."

"Where?"

Sam thought for a moment. "Tell her I've got a place, but we're not going to tell them where until tomorrow. And tell her if Harlan has any questions, just ask him if he remembers the Sheraton Hotel. That ought to pique his interest."

"What if she says no?"

"You know her better than I do. Figure out a way to get her to say yes."

"What are you gonna do, man?"

"I'm going over to Carbondale to pick up the tape. Then I'm driving back down to Fort Campbell. I should be back tonight or early tomorrow morning. Ma?"

Mrs. Butterfield was outside. He walked across the barnyard to the chicken coop and found her gathering eggs. Through the slats of the coop, he could see the black modified in the shed next door, dusty again, low and menacing in the half-light.

He told his mother where he was going and when he'd be

back. Then he climbed in the Porsche and sped down the drive, headed south.

It was three-forty-five when Sam pulled up to the Fort Campbell post headquarters building. He parked in a visitor's slot and hurried inside. On the second floor, near the end of the corridor on the left, was Hillary's public information office.

A female Spec-4 mumbled, "Hello, Major," as he walked by. He found Hillary behind her desk.

"Sam!" she said, startled. "What are you doing—"

He didn't let her finish the sentence.

"I know you don't agree with what I've decided to do about that situation back home in Illinois, Hillary. But we've known each other for a long time now. You know me well enough. I'm here to ask you for a favor, Hillary. It's not exactly SOP, but if you help me out, I can maybe get things resolved back in Illinois and be back here for work on Monday."

"What—what are you asking, Sam?" She stood up and walked around the desk.

"I know you use videotape cameras and all kinds of video equipment here to film parades and maneuvers and awards ceremonies . . . well, I want you to loan me one of your professional cameras and recorders."

"What—"

"And I need one of those special low-light image-enhancing lenses, you know what I mean, like a Starlight Scope lens. I've seen your crews use them at night in the field. I really need this stuff, Hillary. I can promise you I'll have it back for you first thing Monday morning."

"Sam, that lens is classified. Even if I wanted to, I couldn't—"

"Look, Hillary. I know I'm asking you to do something that's not on the books. I'm asking you to take a chance on me. I promise you I won't let you down."

"Sam, you don't understand. I made major on the five percent list. I've worked hard to get where I am. If I do what you ask and there's some kind of political scandal up there . . . I could lose it all, Sam. Twelve years down the drain. I really don't know how you can walk in here and—"

"That's all I needed to know, Hillary. Thanks anyway."

He turned to leave.

"Sam, wait." She caught him at the door, and he turned. "I'm not sure you completely understand where I'm coming from on this."

"You don't have to explain anything to me. You don't owe me this favor. If anything, I owe *you* the favor of yanking me out of the funk I've been in since my divorce. I know what I've asked you for isn't regulation, and if you look at it hard, it doesn't make a dime's worth of sense."

"But, Sam, I *want* to explain myself." She led him to a green leather sofa against the wall. "If we loved each other, Sam . . . if we were together going to invest the rest of our lives in each other, I wouldn't hesitate. I'd sink or swim with you. But we both know we're not right for one another. Not now, anyway. We're both too raw. Our careers are really all we've got. I've got to protect mine, and you've got to protect yours, too, Sam."

"I know, Hillary. The only thing is, I've made a decision to suspend the defensive perimeter I threw up around myself after my divorce. But I understand if you can't go along with me. I was asking you something I probably shouldn't have."

"Sam . . . I . . . I wish you the best. I really do."

He stood up.

"I know, Hils. And thanks."

He walked out of the office, down the stairs, and climbed into the Porsche.

Twenty minutes later, he was at his battalion headquarters. When he walked into the colonel's office, he saluted despite the fact that he was wearing jeans, boots, and a blue poplin jacket.

He explained the situation, and his need for the video camera and Starlight Scope lens to Colonel Duchamp.

The colonel heard him out, then he withdrew a cigar from a brass box on his desk. He took his time lighting it.

"You sound like a fuckin' sergeant, Sam."

"What do you mean, sir?"

"I mean, you sound like one of those scam artists I've installed up there in the motor pool. If Uncle Sam had his proper way with them, they'd be in Leavenworth by the end of the week. But what are they doing? They're keeping every damn vehicle I've got in top running order, as ordered. Do I want to know what they've got to go through to accomplish this? No, I do not."

"What does that have to do with me, sir?"

"The only difference between you and them is the fact that you've come directly to me and asked me *permission* to pull off the impossible but necessary. Sam, the impossible but necessary has to be pulled off every hour of every day in this man's army. It's the nature of the beast. They don't give us enough money, enough men, enough materiel to accomplish the mission they also load onto our shoulders. So what are we left with? We're left with the likes of mess sergeants who know how to secure extra chickens when the men are hungry. We're left with supply sergeants who know where the surplus sleeping bags are buried when we lose a couple. We're left with motor sergeants who can *manufacture* tools and parts if necessary, when command maintenance inspection time comes around. And we're left with majors, like you if we're lucky, who have the pluck and the initiative, when given an impossible task, to secure the necessary implements for its completion."

"Sir, I . . . I . . ."

"I've thought about what I said to you out on the obstacle course, Sam. It was crap. Everything is political, Sam. How much money we're paid. What budget we're given. What mission we're assigned. The color of our goddamned uniforms, *that's* political. You're a fool—no, check that. *I'm* a fool to have tried to tell you any different. And I'm a fool to have warned you away from something you've got to do. You want to videotape those sons of bitches in the dark in the middle of the night up there in Illinois, Major? Sit right where you are."

The colonel picked up the phone and ordered the supply officer, into the office. He told him to requisition the necessary camera, lens, and other equipment and take his personal vehicle and pick it up immediately at post supply. Within an hour, Sam loaded the camera, tripod, recorder, and the case containing the image-enhancing lens into the back of the Porsche and headed north. It was six o'clock. He'd be home by ten.

JOHNNY GEE, MRS. Butterfield, and Betsy were sitting on the front porch in the dark when Sam drove up the hill to the farmhouse. He parked the car and cut the lights. He sat for a moment leaning his head against the steering wheel before he got out.

The car door opened and he looked up to find Betsy.

"You look exhausted, Sam. Come on inside. We saved you some dinner."

His mother was already at the stove by the time he hit the front door. Johnny Gee handed him a cold beer.

"What happened, Sam? Did you get what you needed?" asked Betsy, once he was seated at the kitchen table.

"First, I need to know what Johnny found out."

"Man, Sheila gave me some trouble, but she made the call."

"Yeah?"

"I think we got a meetin' with Harlan Greene, but there's still a little problem."

"What's that?"

"He wants Sheila there. He said, she's makin' the connection, she gotta be there. Only thing is, she won't do it."

"How did you leave it?"

"She gave me Harlan's number at home. She said we can call him, or she'll call him and relay instructions, but no way is she goin' to any meetin' with Harlan Greene and the likes of us. The other thing is, he'll only meet one on one with you, and like I said, Sheila's gotta be there."

"That's okay. We'll figure something out."

"What about you, Sam?" asked his mother.

"I got everything we need. All we've got to do is set up the meeting, and we'll get the IBI what they want. There's only one other detail to get straight. Johnny, I need you to call Moon and see if he can get down here by tomorrow afternoon. If you need to give him directions, Betsy will help you out."

"I'll call him right now," said Johnny Gee. He and Betsy left the kitchen for the living room.

"Hey, Ma. You remember the old quarry, over on the other side of Delafield? In the woods? It's still deserted, isn't it?"

"Sure, Sam. Why?"

"That's where we're going to set up the meeting with Harlan Greene. I'm going up there to scout it."

"*After* you eat, Major Butterfield," said his mother, shoving a full plate of stroganoff in front of him. He dug in voraciously. Just then, Johnny Gee and Betsy appeared in the kitchen door. Johnny Gee signaled "all's well."

"Moon will be here tomorrow at four," he said.

"How is he getting here?" asked Sam.

"Drivin' his Mercedes, of course," said Johnny Gee with a wide grin.

"Good. We're going to need him."

"You got everything, Sam?" asked Betsy, sitting next to him at the table.

"I got it all. One of the video techs gave me a demonstration in a darkened room before I left. You won't believe what this stuff will do. When they cut the lights, you can't see your hand in front of your face. You turn on the camera, and the monitor shows the room as if it's daylight. We're going to set it up when I'm finished. You know that old quarry, up past Delafield?"

"I think we went there one afternoon years ago and shot tin cans with your .22. Is that the place?"

"That's it. We're going to set the meeting there and film every moment of it. That ought to give your IBI boys something to work on."

"If you get Harlan Greene there, it will."

"We've got the last tape," said Sam, finishing his supper. "He doesn't have much of a choice. I'm going to tell him if he wants it, that's where it's going to be."

"I hope you're not underestimating him, Sam. He's been at the game a long, long, time."

"Betsy, you've learned a lot over the past ten years you've spent in political campaigns. I've learned a lot in the army. One thing I learned along the way is that you can never underestimate the ability of the powerful to delude themselves about how much power they actually have. I'm banking on Harlan Greene being just that sort of man. Everything I've learned about him tells me he is. Besides, that's all I've got to go on. There ain't no more, Betsy. This is my best shot."

A few minutes later, with Sam and Betsy in the front seats and Johnny Gee wedged into the back, they headed down a series of gravel roads west of the farm. Almost by instinct, Sam found the road that led up the hill to the quarry. He followed the contours of the hill, then took a left on a road that was rutted and narrow and hadn't been graded in years. At the top of the hill the road forked, and they went left through the woods, around a ridge. Then the woods opened up, and they drove through a narrow gap between a pile of gravel and a brush-covered dirt mound. They were in the quarry. They got out of the car and stood in the shadow of its cliffs.

It was a big quarry, maybe two hundred yards wide and a half-mile long. Its sides rose three hundred feet above the trees. Over on the right there were several metal temporary buildings that were long out of use, their sides corroded and roofs collapsed. There wasn't anything else. Just a big open stadiumlike arena with a rocky floor and granite sides. It was stark and gray and oddly beautiful in the soft moonlight, like the inside of a cathedral that was missing its roof.

"This is some spot," said Johnny Gee. "What made you think of it?"

"Had to be someplace out in the open, and it had to be somewhere he's never been. We want him off guard and confused about where he is and what's going on." Sam pointed to the walls of the quarry. "This place will be black as pitch at one in the morning tomorrow. There's a moon right now, but by one it'll be below the lip of the quarry."

"There's only one road in here," said Johnny Gee. "What if he comes with somebody else, and they block the fuckin' exit? What if they leave a couple of cars at the bottom of the hill?"

"I've already thought about that," said Sam. "I don't think they'll try to block us up here in the quarry. They don't know there's only one entrance and exit."

"What about the tape? Are we gonna have it with us?"

"We'll have it all right."

"Don't you think that's taking a chance, Sam?" asked Betsy.

"Sure we'll be taking a chance. But if this thing doesn't work, having that surveillance tape in our possession won't do us any good. You already said the IBI guy told you the tape is no good without corroborating evidence. This is the only chance we've got to hang it on Harlan Greene. If this doesn't work, he gets away free and clear, and Spicer died for nothing."

"This whole thing is about your friend Spicer, isn't it?" asked Betsy.

"They killed him because he helped me out, Betsy."

"Okay, Sam, I understand. What next?"

"I'm going to take the car and retrace these dirt roads and make sure there's no other way in here," Sam said. "Maybe there's some way we can buy ourselves a little extra insurance. Come on, Betsy. You want to go with me?"

"Sure."

"And you're gonna leave me here by myself?" asked Johnny Gee, lighting a cigarette, cupping his hands against the wind. "No way."

They climbed in the Porsche and headed out of the quarry. Sam drove through the woods around the ridge to the intersection where the rutted dirt road ran down the hill. He continued straight, following a narrow, graded trail. The trail followed a ridge line, dipped to ford a creek, then ran in a zigzag pattern uphill for a mile. At the top of the hill there was another intersection. The right fork looked like it headed back downhill to the road they came in on.

Sam turned left. The trail went downhill for a half mile, passing through a meadow. Then it reentered the woods and became a well-graded firebreak. He followed the firebreak for two miles. It dead-ended at a T-intersection with a blacktop county road. He turned right. The blacktop wandered out of the woods through some marginal farmland and into a small town they had passed through earlier. He turned left at the town's blinking red light, and ten minutes later arrived at the turn for the quarry. He continued straight on the blacktop, turned left up the rutted road, left again at the top and drove straight into the quarry. They'd come full circle.

"Did you think about the entrance? It's pretty narrow, man," said Johnny Gee as they passed into the quarry.

"Yeah, I had a look from both sides. I can make it over that little hill covered with bushes. See it?"

"I don't see him comin' in here with an army," said Johnny Gee.

"Maybe," said Sam. "But we can't take the chance they'll play fair. This is the way I've got it figured. I'm going to be standing in the middle of the quarry waiting for him. Betsy, you'll be over here on the far side of this shed, so you can see the whole quarry and the entrance. Johnny, you'll be in the car between these two sheds, with the camera set up next to you." He pointed out a narrow alley between two of the metal buildings.

"As dark as it will be, they'll never see the car back here. If they come in with several cars, Betsy, you run behind the shed and get in the car with Johnny. I'll make it to the car, and we'll at least stand a chance of beating it out of here."

"Pretty impressive," Johnny Gee said.

"What do you mean by that crack?"

"I'm not makin' a crack. I'm sayin' your plan's got some juice. They musta taught you some good shit in the army."

"It's not military tactics. It's just logic. You take a situation, and you figure out everything that can go wrong, and you try to subtract out the negatives. You subtract out as many as you can, and only then are you making the best of the situation for yourself. It's, ah, just instinct."

"I don't know about your instincts, Sam, but I think you've got it covered," said Betsy. She reached over and kissed him on the cheek.

"We'll get here early and check things out. The meeting will be at one, but we'll be here at midnight. If they send somebody early, we're out of here. If not, we go through with it."

"Sounds good to me," said Johnny Gee.

"Yeah? Well, I'm glad you all approve. Let's go."

SAM FELT A tap on his shoulder and jerked around. He checked his watch. Three-fifteen. He was napping in his boyhood bedroom upstairs.

"Moon's here," said Johnny Gee. "Wait 'till you see what he brung with him."

Sam sat up in bed and glanced out the window. A gray Mercedes sedan was parked next to the Porsche. He rubbed his eyes and stood up and followed Johnny Gee downstairs. He paused in the kitchen door. Moon was standing across the room, facing the door, arms folded across his chest, glowering intently at a man seated across the kitchen table from him. He looked up as Sam entered the room.

"Major, how you makin' out?" Moon asked.

"You've met everyone, Moon? Betsy? My mother?"

"Sure thing, man. Somebody here you ain't met." Moon pointed at the man across the table. "Stand up when my man comes in the room, Frankie." The man stood up. "Turn around." The man turned around. He was a tall man wearing a beige polyester jumpsuit with contrasting stitching. Sam looked at him uncomprehendingly, and then it came to him.

It was Frankie Stillman.

"Johnny told me yesterday you all seen my friend Frankie on that videotape you got," said Moon, motioning Stillman to sit down.

He did.

"Me and Frankie go back a ways, don't we, Frankie?"

Stillman nodded desultorily.

"Frankie and some of his goons done busted up a thing I was involved in a few years back, didn't you, Frankie?"

Stillman nodded.

"What was that, Moon?" asked Sam.

"I was involved in a community thing up in Chicago back in the mid-seventies, tryin' to get a couple 'a construction unions to open up their membership to blacks. The unions didn't think that was such a good idea, so we picketed their work sites downtown. The unions called Frankie and his boys in, and between them and the cops, they broke up our pickets. Then one night, what happens? A bomb goes off at the storefront headquarters we had down on Western Avenue, and one of my friends, cat by name of Rufus Johnson, he's killed in the bombin', and they never caught them who was responsible, did they, Frankie?"

Stillman shook his head.

"And me? I got busted couple 'a days later when they find

a couple 'a bags of smack I never seen before hidden in the trunk of my car. They ended up droppin' the charges against me, but that stopped us picketin' the job sites, and it took a federal court to get their unions to loosen up. Am I right, Frankie?"

Stillman nodded.

"So I figured to myself when Johnny told me yesterday about Frankie bein' the star of his own little picture show, and all the trouble you been havin', I figured I'd look Frankie up after all these years, and see what he knows about this shit. And you know what, Major? I visit him at his house, and we sit down and have us a bottle of wine and talk things over, discussin' old times together, and Frankie, he decides it would be a real good idea to drive on down here with me and tell you what he knows. Didn't you, Frankie?"

Stillman looked up from studying his fingernails and shrugged his shoulders.

"What you want to be knowin', Major?" asked Moon.

Sam looked around. His mother was at the stove, making a pot of coffee. Betsy and Johnny Gee were standing by the bay window. He sat down at the table across from Frankie Stillman and motioned for Moon to sit next to him.

"Mr. Stillman, let's start with who the surveillance tapes actually belong to," said Sam.

Stillman studied the fingernails of one hand and leveled his gaze at Sam.

"I don't think you know what you're getting into," he said.

"Oh, I think I do," Sam replied.

"Frankie . . ." Moon shook a forefinger at the tall man.

"They belong to Midwest Waste Products," he said.

"And who made the decision to carry out this surveillance?"

"Midwest knew that Evacusystems was working a big deal to build a facility down in Rock County, and they knew Harlan Greene was running interference for them. They decided they would throw a wrench in Evacusystems plans. They'd lost two battles over waste sites to Evacusystems over the past ten years, one over in Ohio and one in Pennsylvania."

"And?"

"They didn't want to lose another one. They figured either they'd ruin Evacusystems chances, or they'd come up with the site themselves. Either way, they couldn't fail. All they had to do was box in Harlan, and they had it, because Harlan, he just wants the money. He don't care one way or the other. He sets up the legislature, they vote his way, the facility goes in, he don't care what name is on it."

"How did you get involved?"

"There are some unions I've done some work for, and they've got some pension funds in Midwest Waste stock. They had a heavy financial interest in Midwest getting the facility. I've worked with Harlan over the years on this and that. I got asked to lend a hand, you might say."

"Who did the actual surveillance?"

"Some firm out of New York. Pros. Industrial spying types. They're for hire."

"And then?"

"Then that fucking Howie Radian figured out what was going on, and he had one of his brother's local cops bust the surveillance van when it was on its way from Springfield headed down south, and they grabbed all the tapes that had been made up until that point, and that queered the whole deal."

"And he was trying to sell them to Harlan Greene."

"Stupid bastard."

"What happened to your friend Howie Radian, Johnny?"

Johnny Gee shrugged. "I haven't heard from him in, I don't know how long."

"And what happened to the waste facility?" asked Sam.

"The initial votes went through, then Harlan bottled up the enabling vote in committee until he could get his hands on all the tapes. He wanted the insurance. He didn't want the votes going through, and Midwest stepping in somehow and queering the deal at the last minute. He wouldn't put through the final vote until he got the last tape."

"Which we've got."

"Which you've got."

"What happened to Midwest Waste Products?"

"The surveillance company got cold feet after they got busted and went back to New York. That ended that. They've been trying to come up with the tape you've got."

"In what way?"

"I heard you got broke into the other night . . ."

"Yes."

"That wasn't Harlan Greene's boys. It was Midwest."

"And what do you know about Spicer's death."

"Nothing. Midwest didn't have nothing to do with that."

"So that was Harlan Greene?"

"You draw your own conclusions. All I know is, Midwest didn't have anything to do with any killings."

"Well," Sam said. "This puts a whole new complexion on things, doesn't it?"

"What do you mean, Sam?" asked Betsy.

"Now we know the following: we know who carried out the surveillance, we know who the major players are, we know the deal for the waste facility down in Rock County is on hold, and we know, if we can believe Mr. Stillman, that Harlan Greene was behind Spicer's death." Sam stood up and walked to the bay window, standing next to Betsy. He stared out the window for a moment, thinking.

"What you want me to do with this piece of shit, boss?" asked Moon, pointing at Stillman.

"What do you think, Moon?"

"I think we better refrigerate my man Frankie, boss. Let him cool his sweet se'f fo' a while, leastways till we're finished with our bidness. I notice you got a barn over there."

"Yes."

"We could put him in the barn and restrain him enough to kind of discourage him goin' anywhere till we done with our bidness, if you get what I mean."

"Do you want to take care of that, Moon?"

"Me and Johnny be glad to," Moon said. He motioned Stillman to stand up, and pulled a pair of handcuffs from his back pocket. "C'mon, Frankie, me and Johnny gonna find you a nice post to cozy up to for the evenin'." Moon handcuffed Stillman behind his back and led him across the barnyard with Johnny Gee following.

"You're worried, aren't you Sam?" Mrs. Butterfield asked, resting her hands on his shoulders.

"I'm worried, Ma."

"Is everything going to be all right?"

"I think so."

"Are you sure what you're doing is right?"

"It's the only thing right enough for me." He stood up.

"Come on, Betsy. It's time to call Harlan Greene and get this show on the road."

"We've got to get up there," Sam said. He was sitting in the front seat of the Porsche, leaning his forehead against the steering wheel. Betsy was sitting next to him. The lights were off. The engine idled quietly in the dark.

Standing next to the Porsche, smoking a cigarette, Johnny Gee said, "I know, man."

"I feel ridiculous," Betsy said. She was wearing a leather skirt and an old fox stole of Mrs. Butterfield's. Over her own hair was a black wig on which she had painted a gray streak with white tempera paint. Under the fox stole, a black silk camisole glistened in the dark. On her feet were the highest heels she had in her closet.

"I swear, I don't know how the hookers do it," she said. "Sheila for a day. Jesus."

"You look stunning," said Sam. "Hey. In the dark up there, you'll look just like her. Close enough for government work, isn't that what you say, Johnny?"

Johnny Gee nodded.

"You ride with Moon, Johnny." He motioned over his shoulder. Moon was sitting in the modified, the engine fired up, growling, the body trembling, rattling to the engine's idle.

"Where am I gonna sit, man?"

"Sit on the floor next to the fire extinguisher. I don't care."

"Yeah? You won't have to ride them bumps on a damn steel floor," said Johnny Gee.

"Let's go," said Sam.

He turned the key and started the Porsche and switched on the headlights. His mother leaned in the window and kissed his forehead.

"Keep an eye on Stillman, Ma. Moon's got him cuffed hand and foot to that stall on the right, but if you go in there, take the shotgun anyway. It's loaded, with the safety on."

"I know, Sam. I'll be careful. I just want you all to do the same."

"We'll be back in a couple of hours. I promise."

The four-cylinder Porsche engine had a nice, tight exhaust note. He goosed it. The engine wound up and calmed down to a purr. He put it in first and gave it some gas. The Porsche leapt into the darkness. They drove to the quarry in silence. He watched the road unroll at the edge of the headlights.

The road was different at night, its grassy shoulders crowded the Porsche's fenders, corners ran up on you, narrower, curved more radically than before. When he turned up the rutted dirt road, the headlights poked into the woods on either side of the car, illuminating strange shapes that didn't look like the tree trunks and branches he knew they were. He drove into the center of the quarry. When he cut the lights and engine, it was even blacker and quieter than he'd thought it would be. He couldn't even see the quarry walls. Up high was a lighter shade of black, almost a charcoal gray. He knew the moon lit the night sky just over the lip of the quarry.

"It's spooky," said Betsy. Her voice bounced off the quarry walls in the silence, echoing into the distance. . . . ooky . . . ooky . . . ooky.

"Weird," intoned Betsy. Ird . . . ird . . . ird. "Listen to that." . . . at . . . at . . . at.

"I'm going to back up the Porsche on the far side of that shed so it faces the center of the quarry," Sam said. He put the car in reverse and carefully backed it next to the shed. Then he cut the engine and lights and got out.

He and Betsy joined Johnny Gee and Moon. His eyes now accustomed to the darkness, he looked back toward the sheds. The car was tucked into the dark alley so far back that he couldn't see it. He walked around, looking from other angles. Still couldn't see it.

"Okay," he said. "You guys pull the modified in there between the sheds. When you get back there, switch on the camera and recorder like I showed you, and see if you've got me on the monitor."

Moon backed the modified into the space between the metal sheds. The video camera was mounted on a tripod in the driver's compartment, shooting straight out the windshield, which in the manner of all modified race cars, was open, without glass. Behind the camera, Johnny Gee crouched next to the recorder and monitor. He switched on the equipment. In a moment, he appeared next to Sam.

"Walk back there and have a look yourself," he said. "Clear as a bell, man. Like it was daylight out here."

Sam and Betsy walked over to the modified and looked in the driver's window. On the video monitor, Moon's face was in close-up. They could even see the pattern of his jacket.

"Amazing," said Betsy. "Just amazing."

Sam walked back to the center of the quarry where Moon stood. He carried a wooden box. He put it on the ground, lifted the top, and switched on a tape recorder that was inside. "Testing. Testing. Testing," he said into the darkness. A tiny wireless mike under his shirt collar picked up his words. "Okay, Moon, now you say something."

Moon stood a few feet away from Sam and spoke in a low voice. "Ten, nine, eight, seven, eight, nine, ten."

Sam leaned down and punched reverse on the recorder, then punched play.

"Testing. Testing. Testing." His voice sounded tinny but it was clear. "Ten, nine, eight, seven, eight, nine, ten." Moon's voice was thin, but audible.

"You got this shit down," said Moon.

Sam picked up the box and carried it twenty feet back and put it down behind a pile of rocks.

"Get in the car. See if you can see the box."

Moon walked over to the car and got in. In a moment, he called out:

"No, I can't see it. It's too dark."

Sam checked his watch. It was twelve-thirty. He walked to the car.

"Engine off. Headlights off. I want total silence, so if anyone comes in on foot, we can hear them. You've got everything straight, don't you?"

"Yeah. I know my part," said Johnny Gee.

"If anything's queer, and I mean if it's *one iota* different from what we discussed, start the car."

"Sure, man. We got you." Johnny Gee reached for a cigarette.

"Not now." Sam grabbed Johnny Gee's hand. "You can see the glow of a cigarette for a mile in this darkness."

Johnny Gee put the cigarettes away.

Sam checked his watch. It was a quarter to one.

"We're going over to the shed now," he whispered. "I won't go out there until I see Harlan Greene all by himself in the middle of the quarry, holding the car keys."

"Okay, man," said Moon, his voice steady.

"When you hear his car engine, turn this switch here, and press this button," said Sam, indicating the recorder, and the on switch for the camera. "The FM receiver for the mike is already on. It's voice-activated. You'll pick up my voice on the monitor. The video equipment will do the rest."

"What's the box for, then?" asked Betsy.

"It's a backup system," said Sam. "If everything else fails, at least we'll get a complete audio record."

Behind the shed, Sam checked his watch. It was three minutes after one. He reached down to the box at the small of his back and turned on his radio microphone. He spoke softly into the dark:

"Moon. Johnny Gee. Can you hear me? Throw a rock against the side of the shed if you can."

A rock hit the roof of the shed and rolled to the ground.

"Betsy, you know what to do?" he asked.

"When we hear the car, we walk out there and I wave my arm."

"That's it. That's all there is."

Darkness. Silence.

They listened. Nothing. Then, a low rumble and the sound of tires on gravel. Sam prayed silently that Moon was turning on the video system. He touched Betsy's shoulder and kissed her lightly on the cheek. She pressed his hand and they headed for the center of the quarry. She walked precariously as her heels struck an occasional rock.

He watched the entrance to the quarry. He thought he saw something . . . a flicker . . . yes. There it was. A flicker of light. Car headlights, bouncing up and down over a rough road. Brighter, brighter, then focused into two level beams. The beams moved forward and stopped. A car stood at the entrance to the quarry, a single car, idling, headlights on.

So far pretty good, he whispered to himself.

The car's headlights went out, and the engine stopped.

Keep it up, he whispered.

The driver's door opened. The driver got out and closed the door.

That's one. He looked around the corner of the shed.

The passenger door opened, and a second man got out. He closed the car door. He raised his arm and shook it. Sam heard the jingle-jangle of keys.

"That's it, Harlan," he whispered. "Now do it."

The second man walked toward the center of the quarry. When he had gone about fifty feet, Sam called to Betsy:

"Okay, Sheila, you can go now. You brought us together. There's no need for you to stay."

"The whore stays," said Harlan Greene.

"Okay. Okay. She stays right here." Sam left Betsy's side and walked over to the center of the quarry. He hoped the guys had the equipment working.

Harlan Greene was holding the car keys in front of him.

"I'm Major Sam Butterfield," said Sam.

Sam halted about five feet from the man, close enough to see that he was short as well as quite fat.

"You're the man I've been looking for," said Sam.

"You're looking for me? That's a good one."

"Harlan Greene."

"Wonderful. You can pronounce my name. Now let's get down to it. You've got something I want, and I want it very badly."

"What happened to the other four tapes?"

"They're in a safe place. They're not your concern, anyway. Unless I've got you completely wrong, you're not in this for the money, am I right, Major?"

"That's right."

"And you're not exactly in this by choice."

"I am now."

"Let's have the tape, and we're finished."

"Why is this tape so important, Mr. Greene? What is it you bought all those votes for? A waste dump?"

"It's not a dump, son. It's the largest toxic waste facility in a four-state area. And the votes? Hell, they were going to vote one way or another anyway. May as well vote my way, huh? It's done every day, son. You've been in the damn army too long to understand. Your old man understood. It's politics. It's just politics, son. Plain and simple Illinois politics."

"It wasn't Illinois politics that had Spicer killed. Why, Mr. Greene? Why did you have to kill him?"

"He got in the way. No, I'm wrong. *You* got in the way that night you stepped in and interrupted my men going about their business at the diner. Spicer . . . you brought him into it."

"Spicer wasn't in your way. He didn't do anything to you. He didn't know anything. You didn't have to kill him."

Sam looked hard at the fat man. He stood only five-five or five-six and was dressed in a blue suit. An overcoat was draped casually over his shoulders. He had one hand in his pants pocket, and the other held the car keys. Sam could barely make out the man's facial features, but he could see the shadow of at least one chin draped over the top of the fat man's tie.

"You got a lot of nerve telling me my business, son," said the fat man. "You got a lot of nerve period. What made you think you could hang on to that videotape? What makes you think you can tell people what to do? You got the same disease your dad had, the same one your mother's got. You put your nose in people's business where it doesn't belong."

"You're the one with business where it doesn't belong, Mr. Greene. You're going to put a toxic waste facility right next to the new state park? Do you really think you're going to pull that off?"

"It's already done, son. The votes are bought and paid for. It's a sweet deal. That is what people like you fail to understand about politics, son. In politics, when the game is played right, everybody gets a little piece. The environmentalists, they get their park. The feds, they get a new piece of national forest. And old Harlan Greene and his folks, well, they get their site for their waste facility. All the folks in Rock County, they get their jobs. Everybody's happy. Everybody but you."

"That's right, Mr. Greene."

"I'm supposed to be frightened, son? Intimidated? You and some cheap-ass ex-con punk out of left field start sounding off, and I'm supposed to shiver in my boots? You're dumber than I figured you for, Butterfield. Even your old man was smarter than you're acting."

The fat man pulled a pack of cigarettes from his pocket, tapped one out and lit up. He took a long drag on the cigarette, tilted his head back, and blew smoke into the night sky. He took another drag, held the cigarette in front of him, and flicked the ash off the tip with his index finger. The cigarette tip glowed orange-red in the darkness.

For an instant, Sam thought the cigarette might be some kind of signal, but it wasn't. The fat man was too confident, too self-assured. For the first time since he'd driven up, Sam felt relaxed. Harlan Greene had arrived alone, with his driver, just like he said he would.

"What are we going to do about this situation, son?" the fat man asked.

"I don't know," said Sam, stalling for time. He didn't know what was going to happen next. He wasn't sure he had filmed enough to nail Harlan Greene, and because of this, he couldn't take the next step. Suddenly, he felt very alone. He glanced over at Betsy. She was still standing about fifty feet away. He knew that somewhere over there in the darkness, Johnny Gee and Moon were waiting for him. In Ranger school, they used to talk about the loneliness of command, and he had felt it before, but he never thought it could feel this bottomless, a black emptiness, a ringing in his ears. . . . He knew he still had the tape, and he figured the fat man wouldn't do anything rash until he got it back, but who knew? He had killed before. . . .

"You've got something I want. Something that belongs to me. I think you ought to do the smart thing and give it back," said the fat man.

"Why should I do that, Mr. Greene? Those surveillance tapes belong in the hands of the authorities. I don't know what happened to the other four, but that's where this one is going." The words came out of his mouth before he could think about them.

"What are we doing here, son? You bring me all the way down here, and you're telling me this? Who do you think you're dealing with? You think this thing is a game, and the rules say, you make a move and I make a move, and some time goes by and you make a move and I make a move, and when it's over we add up the points to see who wins? You think it's like that, son? You inherited your father's innocent bullshit? You figure you play by the rules and you win?"

"I know it's not a game, Mr. Greene, but there are rules, and I abide by the rules and so will you."

The fat man laughed, nearly choking. He spat on the ground and looked at Sam. Even in the darkness, Sam could see the fat man had laughed so hard his eyes were tearing up.

"You are priceless, son. You really are. Now let's cut the crap. Tell me where the videotape is, and this thing will be done with."

"I think you're right, Mr. Greene. Let's cut the crap. I've got the surveillance tape. As long as I've got the tape, all you've got is a plan for some kind of huge project down in Rock County and a bunch of empty threats. Now, you make one move to harm my family, my friends, or my associates, and we'll see who understands the way the game is played."

The fat man took a last drag on his cigarette, flicked it on the ground, and stepped on it.

"I've got one more thing to say to you," Sam said.

"Bring her to me," said Harlan Greene.

A light came on inside the car, and he could see a figure being pulled from the back seat. The figure stood next to the car, hands tied, head wrapped in a piece of cloth. He wondered . . . it couldn't be. He lifted his hand, a warning to Johnny Gee and Moon to stay where they were, not to follow procedure.

"Bring her over here, Jason," said Harlan Greene, lighting another cigarette. The driver pulled the figure by the hands. The figure stumbled forward in the gravel, fell, was pulled up and stumbled forward again.

"Come here, son," said the fat man. "You've got something I want? I've got something you want."

He pulled the cloth from the figure's head.

It was Mrs. Butterfield. Another piece of cloth was tied around her eyes, and she was gagged with a sponge.

Sam took a step forward.

"Not so fast, son," said the fat man. "Don't touch."

He was standing about five feet from her. The driver stood beside her, a revolver in his right hand pointed at her rib cage.

"I want to talk to her," Sam said softly.

"Talk all you want, son. She ain't going nowhere. You ain't going nowhere."

"Alone," said Sam.

"Whatever you say," the fat man said derisively. He signaled the driver and the two men stepped away.

Sam approached his mother and put his arm around her. "Can I take this thing out?" he asked, pointing to the sponge.

"Don't touch the blindfold," said the fat man.

Sam pulled the sponge from her mouth and dropped it on the ground. His mother was cursing faintly through clenched teeth.

"What happened?" he whispered.

She coughed. "They came and got me not ten minutes after you left the house. They must have been waiting down the road."

"I'm sorry, Ma."

"Don't worry, Sam. In one way or another, I've been waiting for this moment all my life. Your father hated this man, and I hate him, and now we're finally doing something about him. *All* of us. Your father is here. I can feel him."

Harlan Greene and the driver walked back to the center of the quarry. The driver took Mrs. Butterfield by the arm.

"This is what we're going to do, son," said the fat man.

The driver put the gag back in her mouth and led her a few feet away.

"We're going to play by my rules now. You got that?"

"Yes."

"Now I've got something you want, and you've got something I want. We're going to make a trade. Is the tape here?"

"Yes."

"Where is it?"

Sam lifted his jacket and pulled the videotape from his belt.

"Hand it over."

"Let her go first," Sam said, nodding toward his mother.

Sam held the tape in front of him and walked toward the fat man. When he was almost to him, he started to open the tape box.

"Here, Mr. Greene. Here's the tape." He reached into the tape box, pulled out a .32 caliber pistol, and pressed the muzzle against the fat man's neck.

"Take the blindfold off her," he called to the driver. He poked the muzzle deeper into Harlan Greene's neck.

Harlan Greene nodded frantically. "Do as he says!" he yelled.

The driver tore the blindfold off.

"Get behind me," Sam commanded his mother.

She moved behind him.

"Betsy?" called Sam over his shoulder.

"Yes."

"Listen to me. Walk up here and stand next to me."

Betsy walked over.

"Mr. Greene, tell your driver to throw his gun on the ground."

"Do it," said Harlan Greene. The driver tossed his pistol on the ground.

"Tell him to kick it over," Sam said.

"Kick it. Do as he says."

The driver kicked the gun and it skittered to a halt behind Harlan Greene.

"Pick up the gun, Betsy," said Sam.

Betsy walked around Harlan Greene and picked up the gun.

"Now the keys to the handcuffs. Hand them to her," said Sam.

The driver handed the keys to Betsy.

"We're going in this direction," he said. With the .32 stuck under Greene's chin, Sam lifted his left hand and motioned to Moon and Johnny Gee. Between the sheds, the modified started, headlights came on, and the car rumbled to a halt next to them.

"Get in the back, Ma," he said. "Through the window." Johnny Gee reached for Mrs. Butterfield, and helped her through the window. She sat behind Moon, bent forward under the modified's roll cage.

"Look in there, fat man," Sam whispered.

Harlan Greene gently lowered his chin into the barrel of the .32 until he could see inside the modified. The video monitor glowed brightly in the sheet metal driver's compartment. As clearly as if it were day, the monitor showed his driver standing in the middle of the quarry, in close-up.

"We've got the whole thing on tape, every word you said. What you said about killing Spicer? We've got that. Your kidnapping of my mother and bringing her here at gunpoint? We've got that. Now stand up."

Harlan Greene straightened up, the .32 still planted deeply in his chins.

"Take her home, Moon," said Sam.

The modified leapt in a shower of gravel. Moon screeched it to a halt next to Harlan Greene's car. Johnny Gee climbed out the window and stuck a knife in two of the car's tires. With a loud *hissss* the tires went flat. Johnny Gee climbed back through the modified's window, and the car disappeared through the entrance of the quarry.

"Come with me, Harlan."

They passed along the side of the shed to where the Porsche was parked, and Sam opened the passenger door. Betsy crammed herself into the jump seat in the back. Sam backed into the Porsche, easing the fat man behind him with the .32.

"Stand still." He poked the .32 into the fat man's belly, and backed into the driver's seat, swinging his legs over the gear shift.

"Get in."

"I can't."

"Get the fuck in."

The fat man turned sideways and sat on the passenger seat, swinging his legs in afterward. Sam pressed the .32 against his neck and turned to Betsy.

"You okay back there?"

"I'm fine," said Betsy.

Sam hit the gas and the Porsche leapt. It careened around two corners and was heading for a third when he hit the breaks.

The Porsche screeched to a halt.

Sam reached for the handle, opened the door, and shoved Harlan Greene onto the shoulder of the road.

"You're a lucky man, Mr. Greene," he called after the fat man.

Harlan Greene looked up from the weeds uncomprehendingly.

"My father always told me, never hit a man when he's down. You're down. I'm not going to hit you."

The Porsche spewed gravel, and they were gone.

Sam watched the rightside mirror for cars following them. Nothing back there but the gloom of the night forest.

"YOUR MOTHER JUST told me you have someone back at Fort Campbell," said Betsy. She and Sam were standing in the farmhouse kitchen.

Johnny Gee and Moon had taken a couple of beers and were walking around inside the barn, marveling at the farm equipment stored there—a couple of old Ford tractors, the shell of an early harvester, a couple of plows, and a hay bailer. "Looks like Star Wars, man, look at this. You could fight a damn war with this stuff."

Sam and Betsy could hear Johnny Gee and Moon across the barnyard. They laughed.

Mrs. Butterfield was upstairs soaking in the tub. Betsy's friend Charlie from IBI was on his way from Carbondale.

Moon had dropped Frankie Stillman at the bus depot with a twenty-dollar bill and a gentle push out the door of the Mercedes. Harlan Greene and his driver, presumably, were walking along one of the gravel roads leading from the quarry, looking for a pay phone. And the .32 caliber pistol was back in the kitchen drawer where Mrs. Butterfield always kept it.

"I was seeing someone for a time," said Sam, reaching for Betsy's hand. "It didn't work out." She turned slightly and touched him. He drew her close.

"It's not very far away, Fort Campbell," she said.

"And I've got a really nice car," he said.

"A really fast car."

"Two really fast cars."

"That's right. Two. I forgot that damn hot rod of yours."

"It's not a hot rod. It's a modified."

"You're not thinking of racing that wreck again, are you? You're not a kid anymore, Sam."

"Neither is the modified."

She laughed.

"You know, for six months my mother has been working on me to call you."

"She's been working on me, too. She finds some reason every week to call me. And every time we talk, she mentions you. I've got to tell you, though, on the phone she never mentioned your friend down at Fort Campbell."

"That's my mother for you. Ever the one to maintain proper discretion."

"What about her, Sam? Were you serious?"

"No, not really."

"You don't sound very sure of yourself."

"It was one of those things. We knew each other years ago

at Fort Benning, then we ran into each other at Campbell and tried to recapture something that wasn't really there in the first place. It didn't work. We saw a lot of each other there for a while, then we drifted apart. Two middle-aged divorced people groping for a past that never existed. I didn't know what to tell her."

"What did you tell her?"

"She told *me,* that's the funny thing. I thought she was falling in love with me, but she straightened me out on that."

"Did you love her?"

"No. But I'll tell you something. I loved you. God, how I loved you. It almost destroyed me when we broke up."

"I know. But we were so young. What did we know?"

"Not much. I wanted the army. You wanted to stay here in Illinois. Neither of us could see past the end of our own noses."

Betsy rested her head on his shoulder. "It seems like a long time ago, doesn't it, Sam?"

"It *was* a long time ago. But I never forgot you. I never forgot the times we had together."

"Neither did I."

"Is that why you agreed to help me so quickly? I mean, I just picked up the phone and called you, and you were here. You surprised me, Betsy. I thought you might tell me to get lost."

"Sam, when I talked to you on the phone that day, it was like you were coming home. After all these years, finally you were involved right here at home, in something I knew about. I remembered how you *hated* politics, how you could never understand your father's love of the political game. And then, suddenly, there you were, right in the middle of everything you hated, everything you left home to get away from. And you were behaving exactly like your father would have behaved. You were standing up to them. You weren't afraid. Your father would be so proud of you, Sam. I know he would. He hated Harlan Greene and everything he stood for, and he spent his life fighting men like him."

"Yeah, I know he did."

"You really are your father's son, you know that, Sam?"

"I guess so. But I still hate politics."

"That may be. But you seem to have inherited the ability to play the game pretty well."

"Politics can be a place to hide, Betsy. That's what I always thought about my father. He hid behind southern Illinois politics."

"Maybe he did. What's so wrong with that? He did a lot of good for this place in his time."

"You're right about that."

"The army can be a place to hide, too, Sam."

"You know, it's taken me years to admit that. It's like getting a haircut, the army is. They can shave your head, but under the burr haircut, you're still you. The army is more political than I've liked to admit. Defense budgets, even where the posts are located. It's just like Harlan Greene's waste facility. It's all jobs and money. It's all politics."

"I never thought I'd hear you say that."

"I never thought we'd be standing in this kitchen with our arms around each other again."

"What do you mean?"

"I guess I thought, after what happened between us when we broke up, that we were just too different to ever expect that getting together again would work. I mean, both of us were so headstrong. We wanted what we wanted, and we both got what we wanted, but it meant we were finished. I thought you've always resented that."

"Resented what?"

"That I would never bend, that I thought you were a hometown girl, and that was it."

"I did resent your attitude, at one time. But people, change, Sam. I've changed. So have you. We're older. We'll be forty before the end of the century. Now isn't the time to cling to old pains and resentments and angers."

"Well, Fort Campbell isn't that far . . . maybe we could . . ."

"Do you want to give us another chance, Sam?"

"I do. I really do, Betsy. I've got to tell you, ever since I came back here last year on my way to Campbell, I couldn't stop thinking about you."

"Your mother wouldn't let me stop thinking about you."

He turned her in his arms and held her tightly and kissed her for a long time.

"I've got to get back down to Fort Campbell tomorrow. I have to return the video equipment. Do you want to drive down with me and spend the weekend?"

"That sounds interesting. I'll have to think about it."

He kissed her again, longer, lifting her off her feet.

"I'm thinking, I'm thinking . . ."

He covered her mouth with his, tasting her, breathing of her, swirling, swirling, dizzy . . .

She pulled back and took a breath.

"I've thought about it," she said.

"So?" he said.

"So I just have one question. What are you going to do with me between now and the time we leave?"

"I'm going to take you to bed."

"In your mother's house?"

"In my mother's house."

"The two of us?"

"The two of us."

"Can I have the right hand side of the bed?"

"You can have any side you want, as long as you don't steal the covers."

"But I do steal the covers," she said.

"That's okay, too," he said. "Come on. We've got a long drive ahead of us, and tonight we've got some catching up to do, and not much time to do it."

"You've got all the time you want, Sam Butterfield. As long as you spend it with me."

"That's a deal?"

"That's a deal."

Out the window, they could see Johnny Gee swinging from the hayloft pulley on the front of the barn. Moon was pushing him with one hand and drinking his beer with the other. Sam raised the window and yelled across the barnyard:

"You guys better get some sleep. We've got to deal with that guy from the IBI first thing in the morning."

Johnny Gee dropped from the pulley and walked slowly across the barnyard, followed by Moon. They reached the bay window and Johnny Gee said, "Not us, man. We're out of here by daybreak."

"What do you mean?" Sam asked.

"I don't think it's the best thing for our health, to be talkin' to the IBI. We're ex-cons, the both of us. How much are we gonna count?"

"Wait a minute . . ."

"He's right, Sam," Betsy said, touching his arm. "The two

of us and those videotapes are all the evidence anybody will need against Harlan Greene."

"I guess you're right," Sam said. He turned to the two men standing outside the window. "I can still get you at Moon's pool hall, can't I? You know, in case I need to invite you to something."

"Sure, man," Moon said.

"You got any more beer, man?" called Johnny Gee.

"In the fridge."

"We'll be okay, man," said Moon. "Don't worry 'bout us."

Sam lowered the kitchen window and turned to Betsy.

"Come on," he said, taking her hand, heading for the stairs.

"In the army, don't they say 'follow me'?" she teased.

"Yeah, but in southern Illinois we say, come on. So come on."

"I'm right behind you, Major," she said.